VAMPIRES IN DEVIL TOWN

WAYNE HIXON 

GRINDHOUSE PRESS

Published by Grindhouse Press
POB 292644
Dayton, OH 45429
www.grindhousepress.com

Vampires in Devil Town
Grindhouse Press #002
ISBN-13: 978-0-9826281-3-3
ISBN-10: 0982628137
Copyright © 2010 by Wayne Hixon. All rights reserved.

This book is a work of fiction.

Cover art and design copyright © 2010 by Brandon Duncan
www.corporatedemon.com

No part of this book may be reproduced, stored in a retrieval system, or transmitted by any means without the written permission of the author or publisher.

Vampires in
Devil Town

And all my friends were vampires

Didn't know they were vampires

Turns out I was a vampire myself

In the devil town

 -Daniel Johnston, "Devil Town"

One

Rachel Stokes' bed warmed her against the cool October air blowing in through the half-open window to her left. The air brought with it the smell of dead leaves and the grim promise of frost. Perfect sleeping weather, she thought. But why wasn't she asleep?

The house was quiet. Her parents had gone to bed hours ago. The whole neighborhood had to be asleep. The only sounds coming through her window were the occasional drearily slow hissing of a passing car and the distant chirp of crickets. Maybe she just had a lot on her mind. This was the last week she would spend in this house. Jacob had proposed to her last month and they both felt like they should live together for at least a year before marrying. Although, at this point, marriage seemed inevitable. She and Jacob were perfectly compatible and they had been through just about everything two people could go through save for those sometimes tedious and boring household endeavors all couples are subjected to. It was a big jump, a huge change in her lifestyle, and she didn't really know if she was ready for it.

She was only nineteen years old and there was still, probably always *would be*, a part of her that wondered if she was just too young. But she would have plenty of time to think about that after moving out. That's what the year was for.

Right now she just wanted to lie in her bed, a bed she increasingly thought of as her "childhood bed," and feel the cool wind blow in through the window and listen to the comforting sounds of quieted nightlife around her.

Above the cars and the crickets, she heard another sound. A sound so hideously out of sync with everything else it startled her, causing her to jump. Some kind of petulant whine just below her window. The first thing she thought about was the sound of a baby crying. She criticized herself for thinking of that. It was so unoriginal. So clichéd. Why did everything seem to come back to those primal childhood horror stories? The ghost of a dead baby crying in the attic. A monster just beyond the closet door. A serial killer hiding in the backseat of the car.

She knew there were worse things than that out there. She knew there were things out there with no earthly explanation whatsoever and it was those things that bothered her the most.

The Devils.

She had tried so hard not to think of them the past two years. She had tried so hard to simply focus on how happy Jacob made her and forget all about the circumstances that had brought them together. But it didn't take much to bring all the horrifying memories back, angrily swarming around her brain, trying to prick her sanity with razor sharp stingers.

After everything, she had managed to keep it together. She wasn't about to let something like that sound from outside bring all those things back, make all those things real again. She wasn't going to think about the ways she had changed.

Once more, the sound screamed up from outside.

What the hell *was* that?

Then it hit her.

It was a cat in heat. That was the only thing she could think of capable of making a sound that hideous. It sounded pained and broken. Maybe there was a cat outside the window but maybe it wasn't just in heat.

Maybe it was hurt.

Maybe someone hurt it.

Stop.

Again, the sound screeched up.

She threw the covers away from her. Her brief moment of panic had warmed her anyway, made her feel like her insides were burning, immunizing her to the chill of the room.

Hopping out of bed, she pulled her tight gray muscle shirt down her white belly, adjusting the black boxer shorts she always wore to sleep in. She didn't know what she wanted to do. Well, she knew what she *wanted* to do. She wanted to close the window on the damn mewling cat and try to get enough peace and quiet to go to sleep. But she didn't think she would be able to sleep if she knew there was something sick or hurting right outside her bedroom window and she didn't do anything to help it. Damn conscience.

Walking over to the window, the true coldness of the air found her. It was probably too cold to be sleeping with the window open anyway. She placed her hands on the cool wood of the sill and looked through the screen. The streetlights afforded just enough light to grant her a meager view of the side yard, shaded by a huge oak tree. Squinting her eyes, she looked out into the darkness, now half-hoping the cat would make another sound so she would have a better idea where to look.

As though not wanting to disappoint, the animal screeched out again.

If she knew *exactly* what a cat in heat sounded like, she could convince herself that's what it was and be done with it. It occurred to her she didn't really know if she had ever even heard a cat in heat before. She had read descriptions of it in books. She had heard conversational references to it. Wasn't this the wrong time of year for animals to be in heat? She thought that was in the spring or something. Wasn't that the rutting season?

The sound came from somewhere off to her left, toward the street.

She didn't figure it would hurt to go check it out. She wasn't a veterinarian. She didn't really know or even care that much for animals so she wasn't expecting to give this thing some kind of kitty physical but if it was hurt badly she figured she would notice. And if it was in heat... well, then she figured she could just shut the window and drift off into sleep with a clean conscience.

She took a deep breath, thinking it was really just entirely too late for this shit. She turned and headed toward her bedroom door. Her room was at the end of the hallway on the upstairs floor. Turning to her right out of the door, her bare feet padded along the plush camel-colored carpet. The hallway light was on, as it was every night, turned to its dimmest setting. Reaching the bottom of the steps, she wondered why she was so freaked out by this. It was as simple as going out to get the morning paper, right? Only it was dark and...

And Rachel knew that, in Lynchville, things moved in the dark that didn't move at any other time. Bad things. Evil things. Some of them clichéd, sure, but *she* knew they were real.

No, she told herself. Those things are gone. You and Jacob got rid of those things. Those things cannot come back to hurt you.

Her feet squeaked along the highly polished wood floor of the formal living room. She turned right, toward the front door. Standing in front of the thick wood and beveled glass, she reached out with her left hand and switched on the porch light. Her parents always turned out the porch light when they went to bed and this made Rachel wonder why they bothered turning the light on at all. If you were going to turn it on, wouldn't you want it to be while you were sleeping, so neighbors could see if any unsavory characters were creeping up to the front door?

She knew she was thinking things to keep her mind off going outside but, whatever worked, right? She unlocked the dead bolt, the second dead bolt, and then the lock on the knob itself.

Swinging the door open, the sound greeted her again. Jesus, it had a way of spiking right through her ears.

She really hoped there wasn't a broken and injured cat out on the lawn somewhere. She almost *hoped* she couldn't find it.

Stepping out onto the porch, she looked around at all the neighboring houses lining Maple Street. Somehow, knowing those houses were there, with people inside of them, gave her a great sense of comfort. Leaving the door open behind her, she descended the steps until she reached the front walk leading to the sidewalk. She turned toward the west side of the house, roughly where she thought she heard the sound coming from. She wondered if she should call it.

No, it wouldn't do any good to make any more noise than the cat was already making.

The grass was damp and cold on her feet. She walked until she nearly reached the tree and heard the sound again. It definitely came from her left, toward the road. Slowly, now thinking of rabid cats jumping from the darkness to claw out eyes, she walked toward the street. She walked the few steps, her eyes scouring every direction, until she reached the sidewalk.

She did not see any signs of a cat, injured or in heat.

Hmmm, she thought. She wasn't just imagining the sound. It had been too concrete to be her imagination.

Maybe you're going crazy.

Losing your mind.

But now she heard another sound. This time it was the sound of a car, speeding down Maple. Her heart froze up. Cars did not travel that fast down her street. She moved back into the shadows of the oak tree, away from the road.

A black van sped past and she caught just the briefest glimpse of the driver. Her heart skipped a beat. She didn't even think about looking at the license plate.

She was certain the driver had been staring at her, even as he sped down the road. She got a good look at him too. A teenage boy. He hadn't looked right. He was too pale, a shock of black hair surrounding his head. He looked like one of *them*. And why was he staring at her? How would he know she was standing off in the shadows?

Jesus, she thought. You *are* going crazy. Wild paranoid crazy.

She thought she was starting to sound like her racist grandfather. People not looking right. Us and Them. She almost chuckled at her next thought.

Sure. The driver of that van was probably just out looking for his little cat who had wandered away from his house in the lusty throes of heat.

Sure. Whatever. She was going to bed.

The longer she stood out here, the crazier her thoughts were going to become.

She wanted to go up to her room and shut the window on all the sick and horny cats of the world, all the screeching speeding vans filled with creepy teenagers, all the legends and rumors seeping in from the night and screaming around in her head.

No. She shut the last thought out before it could crawl in and infest and destroy every good, happy thought she was capable of having. Sometimes, she still felt too naked. Sometimes, things still felt too close. Sometimes... like standing out in the front yard in the middle of the night, wearing only her pajamas and letting the dew from the grass numb her bare feet.

She turned to walk toward the house. When she reached the first step to the porch she heard a rustling to her left. She jumped and her heart went wild. She fought the urge to dart to the door. The mums in the garden were trembling. Maybe she had found her cat. Something human-size couldn't possibly hide in there. She took a deep breath, steadied her heart rate. She crouched down in front of the plants.

It came lurching out, broken and mangled. Rachel covered her mouth with her hands, a plaintive noise coming from her throat. Someone had hit the cat with a car and just driven on. If it had been anything like that van she'd seen earlier, they might have been completely unaware they had hit anything. Either way, it was inexcusable.

The cat again made its painful mewling sound. Its tortoise shell fur was caked with blood. Rachel glanced up at the door to the house to make sure no one stood there. She glanced behind her to make sure no one was on the road. *Wild paranoid crazy.* She placed her nervous hands on the back of the cat, its bloody fur thick beneath her palms and between her fingers. She ran her hands along its knobby spine, feeling those spots where it was rent out of place. There, her hands lingered. Slowly, it felt more normal. It was like a tuning fork running through her body. One minute, while touching the animal, she felt a sloppy and disturbed connection with it and then it was humming along so finely it was nearly unnoticeable. She continued this way—hands lingering over splits in its skin, shredded tendons in its legs, loosely hanging jawbone, broken tail—until the cat began rubbing itself against her shins, purring happily. She could heal it on the inside but she couldn't get it clean. When she rose to finally head back inside, she left the cat lying on the lawn, contentedly licking itself between the legs.

She walked back into the house, stopping off in the kitchen for a glass of water. She took a healthy chug of the water. It felt good on her dry throat. She was also now aware of the ringing in her ears and the headache. She thought about going to the medicine cabinet for an Advil but was so tired she would just go to sleep and, hopefully, the headache would be gone upon waking. She emptied the glass into the sink and, figuring it was clean enough, placed it back in the cupboard. Flipping off the light in the kitchen, she headed up to her room.

Before she could cross the room and pull the window down she heard the sound again.

Fuck it, she thought. I'm not going to play this game.

She pulled the window down and heard the noise again.

This time it didn't come from outside.

This time it sounded like it came from her closet and she didn't think of a desperate and broken cat, scraping along in the yard. No, for some reason, she thought of an old man, an old man bent over in her closet and weeping. It was a stupid thought and one she found oddly devoid of any danger whatsoever.

Well, she thought, I'll just put *that* image out of my head right now.

She turned militantly to her right, toward the closet, reached out her hand and turned the knob, yanking the door open.

And for a brief, heart-stopping second, she saw the man, hunkered over on her pile of shoes and staring up at her, tears beading his red-rimmed eyes.

She nearly laughed when she saw it was only darkness. Darkness and the human form clothes can take when hanging up.

She took a deep breath and closed the closet doors.

A hand closed around the back of her neck.

Another closed around her mouth.

She wanted to scream but she had to fight just to breathe. The hands were incredibly strong and everywhere at once. She wished she had turned her bedroom light on. It felt too dark. Too confusing. For the first time that evening, she thought she might be asleep. She *hoped* she was still asleep and this was just one of the nightmares, trying to rise up and drag her down.

She kicked her legs up, trying to find a grip on the wall to push back with. Planting her feet on the wall, she shoved backward but whoever held her merely spun her around, driving her down. The side of her face hit the bedpost and she thought she felt something come loose within her mouth. Now, besides the hand covering it, her mouth filled with blood.

A gurgling scream came from somewhere in her throat. The intruder yanked her upright once more, turning her toward the closet.

The door was open and Rachel still had enough of her mind to know this was not how she had left it. She remembered shutting the closet door, hearing it click, and there wasn't any way a single intruder could hold her arms, her throat, and her mouth and still manage to turn the knob of the door.

She forced her body to go limp, trying to propel it to the floor, but the person continued to pull her toward the closet.

What she saw in the closet didn't seem right at all, not that anything else did.

All the contents of the closet were slid over to the right side and the wall was open on the left side, a mouth of blackness replacing the white of the wall.

What was this? Rachel wondered. And then her mind screamed at her body. It screamed not to let this person take her in there. Because if she was taken in there she didn't think there was any way she would be able to get out.

All of her muscles rigid, the person carried her into the closet, stuffing her into the opening.

The intruder had to let go of her arms in order to shove her into the opening. Rachel reached her arms out, already halfway in the opening or the hole or whatever the hell it was, desperately trying to find something to grab onto.

She couldn't. Her fingertips reached out, trying to find traction on the wood or the drywall, whatever made up the walls of this house. Instead, they touched something that felt like slimy rock, a smooth stone covered in slippery river muck.

And then she was falling. Falling and wanting to pass out. If she blacked out, went unconscious, she wouldn't have to feel the impact.

The blackness never came.

She kept her arms in front of her, ready to brace herself for the fall, subconsciously wanting to keep the majority of the damage away from her face. She hit the bottom and wondered if the sound she heard was her skin smacking the surface or her arms breaking. It wasn't until this moment she realized how badly she was hurt. She knew this because her brain told her body to stand up, her arms to move, her eyes to open, yet her body wouldn't do any of those things.

A broken heap in the darkness, she waited for what would come next and thought to herself that the past was never that far away. Not really.

Two

Earlier that evening, Jacob Riley returned to his apartment from the gas station two blocks away on the corner of Main and Cherry Street. His apartment was on the second floor, located in the middle of a series of old row houses lining Main. It was just before dusk, a clear and beautiful fall day coming to a close. He walked slowly down the cracked sidewalk, enjoying the sights and sounds of his beloved Lynchville. Children rode their bikes down the street. A gaggle of teenagers stood around the pay phone in front of the library across the street from his apartment, talking on their cell phones. Old men and women sat on their porches. Some of them busied themselves by bringing in flowers and houseplants before the first major frost. Grasses were being mown. This was as lively as the town usually got.

As he thought just about every day, Jacob wondered why he was still here. Did he really have some kind of sick love for the town itself? There were parts of it he enjoyed, sure, and the people were always friendly, but he knew that was not the reason he and Rachel had decided to stay. Something lingered in the back of his head. It was a tickle of something he got from time to time. Especially since what he had come to think of as "The Incident." That something, that tickle, was a sense of unfinished business. He didn't feel like they could leave Lynchville until their time had come. Part of him wanted this to happen, whatever it was going to be, just to get it over with. Another part of him wanted it to wait for years so he and Rachel could grow old in the town they had grown up in. There was a wonderfully silly and romantic sheen to this notion that he relished.

Just a block away from his apartment now, he stopped at the crosswalk and packed the cigarettes he had bought at the gas station against the heel of his hand, peeling the cellophane off, opening the box and yanking out the foil, stuffing the trash in the pocket of his jeans. He pulled out a cigarette and lit it, dragging the smoke deep into his lungs.

Someone was on the sidewalk in front of his apartment and, at first, he thought it might be Rachel, even though he knew she wasn't coming over tonight. They had decided, since she was moving in with him, she should spend as much time with her parents as possible. Of course, this was also supposed to give them a little time apart to decide if they each really wanted to be with the other person. Besides, it would seem more special when she moved in if she wasn't already living there. Until this past week, they had spent nearly every waking moment together.

He continued walking down the sidewalk. He walked slowly, savoring his cigarette and the last shreds of warmth.

After a few more steps, he saw the person in front of his apartment was obviously not Rachel and, after realizing who it was, he felt ashamed about ever even thinking it was.

It was his landlady, Mrs. Benson. She had suffered a stroke a little over a year ago and had been completely insane ever since. Her husband had been dead for years and she lived in one of the ground floor apartments with her son, Jeremy, who now performed most of the landlord-type functions.

She stood on the sidewalk and turned slowly in circles, her arms raised toward the sky.

Jacob had become accustomed to her craziness. He knew she was completely harmless. He just hoped she didn't wander out into the road and get hit by a car.

He drew closer to her, moving toward the brick of the apartments so he didn't get clobbered by one of her waving arms. Her head was thrown back, matted white hair hanging in a clump, and her eyes were closed. She hummed something under her breath. Jacob thought it was some kind of hymn he remembered from his parents' born again phase but he couldn't quite put a name to it.

He stood in front of the door and called to the woman, trying to bring her back from whatever Eden she danced in.

"Mrs. Benson?"

She didn't acknowledge him.

"Mrs. Benson? You okay?"

Still, no recognition.

He decided to abandon his Good Samaritan mission and go up to his apartment. Just as he turned his back on her, her hand clamped down on his shoulder and she whispered into his ear.

"She's lost in a storm. Lost in a storm. Ain't gonna be no findin her once the storm takes her."

Mrs. Benson removed her hand from his shoulder and Jacob turned to ask her who was lost in a storm but she had already returned to her muttering reverie.

He opened the door and entered the dim foyer of the apartment. Mrs. Benson's door was to his right, at the bottom of the stairs. He knocked on the door, hoping Jeremy was home. The door opened after a few moments of listening to the hushed TV through it. Jeremy stood in the doorway, the smell of pot drifting out with the boy, around his collective girth. He stepped all the way out into the vestibule, as though he were hiding something, pulling the door to a narrow crack behind him, and looked at Jacob with his bloodshot eyes. Jacob saw disinterest and a few brief scenes of his mother caring for Jeremy when he was little. He felt pain and loss and quickly looked away.

"Your mom's outside on the sidewalk. I think she's dancing or something. You might want to go get her before she gets hurt on the street."

The boy stared vacantly at Jacob for a second with his heavy-lidded eyes, slowly processing what he had just heard. Then he said, "Uh, yeah, thanks... I'll go get her."

"Need any help?" Jacob volunteered.

"No. She's been doing this a lot lately. I have to jerry rig the door so she can't get out. I must have forgot."

"Good luck," Jacob said, flashing a smile and heading up the old wooden steps to his apartment.

He had lived in this apartment nearly two years. He liked it. It was small and old but he didn't need a lot of space and he found most of his likings leaned toward things that were older rather than newer. The apartment was furnished modestly with things pilfered from a thrift store in town that purported to be an antiques shop. Luckily for him, the prices were more thrift store than antique shop. The door opened into the living room. The wall to his left was outfitted with old floor to ceiling windows. Outside the windows was an old wrought iron balcony. He liked to go out to the balcony and sit, watching the town go about its business. The balcony reminded him of pictures of New Orleans. A corn plant sat off in one corner of the balcony. He kept telling himself he was going to bring it in but it was just one of those things that didn't take priority.

A ratty couch sat in the middle of the living room. He couldn't see the point in owning both a couch and a bed so he made sure they were combined. The only times he ever pulled it out into a bed were the nights Rachel stayed over. Her parents frowned upon that sort of thing so those nights were few and far between. Against the wall opposite the door an old 19-inch television rested on a garishly yellow-painted metal TV stand. The stereo was below this, a record player resting on top of it, speakers sitting on the floor to either side. He listened to music more than he watched TV.

The wood floor was the color of coffee with a lot of creamer in it and he thought the lightness of it brightened the whole room. The kitchen was separated from the living room by a bar. The kitchen was very small and narrow. The only thing it really housed was a refrigerator. He had never seen the point in having a kitchen table when he ate everything in the living room. There was also a small bedroom to the right of the kitchen. He stored his books and music in there. Ever since leaving the farm where his parents had lived, moving out on his own, he bought many books and obsessively read them. Most of them came from the Den of Iniquity downtown, owned by the curious Mr. Stoop.

Jacob stood in the middle of his apartment, feeling somewhat helpless. He had grown so accustomed to Rachel's presence he felt lost when she was not there, like he didn't know what to do with himself. Actually, there were many times he was not around her. She had a job and took college classes online. He guessed it was more the idea that she was not coming over tonight that bothered him. The fact that he had a, to him, *copious* amount of alone time to fill.

As had become his custom, he thought he would fill this alone time with music and beer. Anything to stave off the panic attack that was nearly inevitable. The panic attack that would leave him lying on the couch in a cold sweat, thinking all the worst thoughts that could possibly run through his head and knowing, just knowing, bad things were going to happen.

He went to the refrigerator and pulled out a Guinness. He took the magnetic bottle opener from the refrigerator and pulled the cap off. He reached into the sink and found a glass. Sniffing it, he deemed it useable. He poured the beer into the glass and instinctively reached for the cordless phone resting on the counter.

He wanted to call her. But he knew he shouldn't. The whole reason for her not coming over was so she could spend time with her parents and they could spend time apart. If he called her then she might as well just come over.

Instead, he dialed the only other number he knew by heart—his psychiatrist, Dr. Samuel Bettermore.

Usually, when he called after hours, he got some sort of voice mail prompt telling him to leave a message and the good doctor would get back to him as soon as possible. To his surprise, Dr. Bettermore, who insisted Jacob call him Sam, picked up.

"Dr. Bettermore."

"Sam. This is Jacob Riley."

"Of course it is. How are you doing, Jacob?"

"Oh, you know, okay..."

"Really? Is that why you're calling after hours?"

Jacob had the impression Dr. Bettermore had been on his way out of the office. He could practically see him standing by his desk, pushing papers into his briefcase.

"I didn't think you'd pick up."

"Is it an emergency?"

"I don't know. I just feel... I don't know what I feel."

"That's what we're trying to find out, Jacob. You have to work through those feelings."

"But I don't know if I can."

"What do you mean?"

Jacob moved over to the couch, taking a sip of his beer and pulling another cigarette from the pack.

"I just have so many feelings, Sam. I don't know if I can sort through them."

"Are you taking your medication?"

"Of course." This was a lie. The doctor had prescribed a very powerful anti-depressant but he refused to take them because it got in the way of the drinking.

"You're sure you're taking your medication? It helps you think a little more clearly. You can sort things out."

"I'm glad you're talking to me, Sam."

"You sound lonely, Jacob. Are you lonely?"

"I've been lonely all my life."

"What do you mean by that?"

"I don't know."

"Let's get back to your feelings. You said you were having too many feelings... Let's start at the top. Have you found a job?"

"No. That's not a feeling-type question."

"I know Jacob but, in a way, it is. If you get a job, you can be around other adults. You can *interact* with other adults. That way I think you would realize you're a little more like everyone else than you know."

"I'm not like everyone else though. You know that."

"Of course, Jacob. Nobody is just like everyone else. What about Rachel? Is she why you're feeling bad?"

"A little bit. She's not here. I don't know if she's going to come back... you know, to live? And that worries me."

"Okay. And what else?"

"I'm scared."

"Scared of what?"

"Everything."

"That's irrational."

"I *know* that's irrational. That's why I'm seeing a psychiatrist."

"There is nothing to be afraid of, Jacob."

"Do you mean that?"

"Yes, I mean that. You have no more to fear than any other person."

"That's still a lot."

"That's part of being human."

He crushed his cigarette out in the ashtray beside the couch.

"So what are you going to do this evening, Jacob?"

"I don't know. Probably watch some TV."

"Have you heard from James?"

"No. Why?"

"Nothing. I think it would help if you try your hardest to reestablish that family connection."

"Maybe. I think James is finished with Lynchville."

"You should at least give it a try. Jacob, try not to worry so much, okay? The world is a beautiful place. It is not all gloom and doom. Have some fun. Stop brooding all the time. *That* is what keeps people away from you."

"Okay. Sure. Thanks, Doc. I'll see you on Tuesday."

"And, just to let you know, I'm going to be out of the office tomorrow. I'm trying to get away for a little three-day weekend. But, if you need anything... anything at all, leave a message and I'll get back with you. I *do* check them. Okay?"

"Okay."

"Take care, Jacob."

"You too, Doc."

Jacob clicked the OFF button on the phone and sat it on the floor.

After hanging up the phone, Jacob got up from the couch, went into the kitchen, and poured himself another beer. He put a Ramones album on the stereo and went about vigorously cleaning the apartment, trying to burn off some of his nervous energy and focus on something that wasn't Rachel. When did he get so possessive? He didn't really know but figured he had never cared about anyone in quite the same way he cared about Rachel. She was the only person in his relatively short life that had been able to offer herself completely to him. He had greedily consumed each and every offering.

In the process of cleaning, he polished off three more beers. He finally ventured out to the balcony and brought in the corn plant, centering it in the row of windows he had left open, letting the autumn breeze blow in, cleansing the apartment of the old wood smell that seemed to rise from the floor during the summer. When the music finally stopped, he was oblivious to it. He was in the bedroom alphabetizing the books he had read that week (there were twelve of them) and the CDs and albums he had listened to (there were nearly fifty of these).

The beer, as usual, had made him more sleepy than drunk and, even though it was only around eight o'clock, he decided to lie down, not really knowing if he would sleep the entire evening or not. It seemed like he spent a lot more time *trying* to sleep than he actually spent sleeping. He could lie on the couch for hours before falling asleep for a half an hour or an hour only to wake up and lie there for three more hours, trying desperately to go back to sleep.

Though physically debilitating at times, this process seemed to keep the nightmares away.

He dreamed about things happening to Rachel.

He dreamed about things happening to James, out there on the road somewhere, searching for some secret and terrifying underworld.

He dreamed about things happening to himself and wondered why the dreams ending in his own death were somehow more comforting than those ending in the deaths of his loved ones.

He flopped down on the couch and, pointing the remote control at the stereo, cued up Miles Davis' *Bitches Brew*. This was one of his favorite albums to fall asleep to. It was long and some of those sleepy trumpet notes just seemed to hang on for an eternity, coaxing him into a cool and comforting place. There were not any words to distract him, no words to feed him grains of thought destined to turn into something sinister.

With the chilly breeze blowing in through the window, he fell asleep as Miles ran the voodoo down.

Jacob woke up screaming.

Jacob woke up in hell.

At least, it felt like hell.

Cacophonous noise surrounded him. The room seemed entirely too bright. He was too hot. He could feel the sweat on his skin, disorienting him—he shouldn't be sweating. Unable to open his eyes against the bright light, he slid from the couch, trying to organize what was happening in his head.

The first thing was that he felt incredibly nauseous.

Already on the floor, he doubled over, hunching his back as he heaved up the contents of his faraway dinner and four Guinnesses. He vomited until he couldn't vomit any more and this seemed to bring a little bit of clarity to his situation.

A storm raged outside, rare for this time of year, even though it had been unseasonably warm. But the violent flashes of lightning couldn't account for all the blinding light in the room. He looked over toward the wall of windows. The corn plant had blown over. The open windows swung lightly in their wooden frames, rain and cold air spewing into the room. He knew he should close the windows but he didn't have any interest to crawl over there and do that just yet.

Thunder rumbled and smacked its charged lips up in the heavens. But that wasn't the only sound. There was a much more constant sound rumbling the floorboards beneath his knees.

He turned away from the windows so he faced the television.

Yes. This was where the rumbling sound came from. It seemed impossible for a sound that loud and that resonant to come from this ancient TV with its tiny speaker.

Blinding light emanated from the TV and he knew this was not right at all.

The television had been off when he fell asleep. There wasn't a remote control that went to it so he knew he couldn't have rolled over on it during his slumber. But it didn't make any sense for the TV to just come on all on its own unless... *unless it was all happening again.*

That was the only explanation for all of this, wasn't it?

His walking nightmares. His *hallucinations*, as Doc Sam called them. Those violent things that threatened to rip his brain apart. Those things that had never happened before the Incident.

That's what was happening now.

He had to tell himself that.

None of this was real.

He scooted closer to the television, dragging his jeans through his puke, wanting only to get close enough to reach out a hand and turn it off. To turn off the nightmare. Turn off the hallucination. The television's screen was filled with a glowing orange image like someone had taken a camera into hell. He reached his hand toward the TV, ready to press the button, when he saw a shape emerge from this blinding orange image.

He retracted his hand, kneeling in front of the TV like it was some kind of altar.

The screen became much less bright and much clearer, although the image remained grainy.

The camera shot was of a small gray room. A bluish light filled this room even though he could not see any signs of actual lighting. He figured they must have kept the light behind the camera. If that was the case then it meant what he was about to watch was planned.

There was a man in the gray room. The man looked terribly frightened. Jacob thought he could make out a urine stain on the front of the man's pants. He looked vaguely familiar at first and it took Jacob only a couple more seconds to realize just who it was. It was Mr. Leavingworth, the pharmacist. A nice man, Jacob had always thought. He knew something bad was about to happen to him and he wondered why he had been the one chosen to view this.

Two men entered the room from behind the camera. At least, Jacob assumed they were men. Call him sexist, but he always thought men were more the torturing type. They both wore large black cloaks and at the same time he wondered about the cliché of this, he also found it a highly utilitarian disguise. Not only could he not make out their faces, he wouldn't be able to describe their builds or even really how tall they were.

One of the men lashed Mr. Leavingworth across the face. He fell to the ground, clutching the red weal of blood rising there, kicking his legs against the floor. Once down, both of the men gathered around him and brought their whips down several more times.

Mr. Leavingworth screamed. It was a horrible sound, coming out of that deep rumbling like a bright stitch of pain.

The men bent down toward Mr. Leavingworth, each of them grabbing an arm and pulling him up. Mr. Leavingworth tried to go limp but the men dragged him back toward the camera.

It was at this point Jacob wondered if it was a camera capturing this at all. What if it was just something that was happening out there in the dark underground and was psychically transferred to his TV? What if it really *was* just another one of his hallucinations, projected *onto* the TV rather than coming *from* the TV? The camera pulled away from Mr. Leavingworth, showing his bloodied face and terrified eyes open wide. Then the camera did a kind of floating off thing, swinging around the gray room and then coming to rest somewhere else entirely.

Now it was a panoramic side view of a completely different interior and from much farther away. Whatever room this was in had to be cavernous.

Mr. Leavingworth stood on a stone platform, supported by the men. It had to be at least twenty feet from the floor, which wasn't even in the image. The men strapped some kind of harness onto Mr. Leavingworth. He kicked and screamed but this did not have any effect on the men. The harness was made out of a metal chain and a single strand of this chain led from the harness up to the ceiling.

The men steadied Mr. Leavingworth on the platform before shoving him off.

He went swinging out, trapeze-like, headfirst, toward a huge open fire on the right-hand side of the screen, the camera or all-seeing eye or whatever following his arc.

The flames nipped at his hair, igniting it until it was quickly melted to his scalp. His screams intensified as he was pulled back toward the darkness by the heavy chain before beginning his second arc toward the fire.

This time he went a little deeper in, the flames hissing as they evaporated the tears from his eyes, sucking the moisture from his mouth.

Jacob wanted to turn away. He wanted to turn the television off but he couldn't. He was powerless against whatever it was he watched.

Mr. Leavingworth's screams rose until they were something continuous, unabated.

A grown man screaming... It chilled Jacob. He didn't know if he'd ever heard a grown man scream before.

He watched the flames scorch off the man's clothes. He watched as the man became blacker and blacker each time he swung into the flames. He watched as patches of his skin melted, opening up, vital fluids sizzling onto the fire. And, he didn't know how long it took but, eventually, the man was no more. The only thing left in the image was the charred black harness and a few random hunks of skin sizzling on the hot metal. The source of its momentum gone, it hovered, nearly motionless in the middle of the television screen.

He reached out his hand to turn it off but it went off on its own before his finger could press the button.

He swore he could feel warmth coming from the screen.

Slowly, shakily, he dragged himself across the room and sat on the couch, staring out the open windows at the dying storm on the other side of the screens. He drew his puke-spattered knees up to his chest, oblivious to the smell, oblivious to anything except the fear, its hands wrapped around his soul, paralyzing his body and dragging his thoughts back to the past when the nightmare was no mere hallucination but alive and vibrant and throbbing right there in front of him.

Three

Fucking in a graveyard had never really been Charlotte Black's idea of a perfect evening but, apparently, that was exactly what Zack Corbin had in mind tonight.

It had been well after midnight when Charlotte awoke to a cold hand roughly shaking her shoulder. She opened her eyes, disoriented, trying to adjust to the darkness. The hand moved down her cheek, coming to rest on her neck.

"Wake up, sleepyhead." The voice was instantly recognizable.

"Zack?"

"Yeah."

"What are you doing here?"

"I couldn't sleep. I wanted to go for a walk."

"How did you get in here?"

"That's a secret."

"What time is it?"

"I don't know."

She craned her neck to look around him, sitting on the edge of the bed, at the glowing red digits of the alarm clock on her night-stand.

"Jesus, Zack, it's almost two o'clock."

"I know. I couldn't sleep."

"But *I* was sleeping..."

She sat up on her elbows and he bent down over her, covering her full lips with his, his tongue entering her mouth and playing with hers. He held her like this for a while, his rough tongue encir-cling hers, and she knew she was going to go anywhere he wanted her to.

"Do you still want to sleep?"

"Not so much. But... you want to go for a *walk*?"

"Yeah."

"Did my parents hear you?"

"Nobody heard me."

"Where do you want to walk to?"

"I was thinking we could go walk around in the cemetery."

"But that's like a mile away."

Zack pulled the cover from her body. She slept in an old t-shirt and a pair of black underwear. He ran a finger up the inside of her thigh, creamy white in the moonlight, stopping at the elastic hem of her panties.

"In the cemetery, no one can hear you scream."

"You're a pervert."

"No. I'm passionate. There's a big difference."

"You're luring an underage girl out of her bed after midnight to take her to a graveyard and fuck her. That's a pervert."

"Okay, I'll give you criminal, but I still don't think there's anything perverted about it."

She ran a hand through his short black hair and leaned her head up toward him, kissing him deeply once again. If she wasn't careful, they'd never make it to the cemetery.

"Do you mind if I put on some clothes?"

"I guess I can wait."

"Is it cold outside?"

"Not that bad, really."

Charlotte scooted out of bed and went to the closet, conscious of Zack's eyes on her scantily clad bottom. She pulled out a pair of old blue jeans and a baggy black sweater. Zack, lying back on his elbows, continued to watch as she pulled on her clothes. She fluffed out her shoulder length black hair and asked him if she looked okay.

"I don't think many people are going to see you," he said. "I think you look great. You always look great. Clothes aren't really that important anyway."

She pulled on a pair of old blue Converse and held her hand out to him, pulling him up off the bed.

"Do you ever sleep?" she asked him.

"Only during the day."

"You're weird."

"That's why you like me."

"Fucking vampires."

"Hey, watch what you say."

She walked him over to her bedroom door and turned toward him.

"Now," she said, "here's the part where we have to be very very quiet. We have to use our catlike skills."

"Understood," he said. "I got in, didn't I?"

"I'll give you that."

Slowly, she opened her bedroom door. She was making a bigger deal out of this than she really had to. She lived in a huge house on Walnut Street. Her parents' bedroom was on the second floor and hers was on the ground floor. She had chosen this room knowing it would be a lot easier to come and go as she pleased. All she really had to do was cross the living room and leave through the back door and she was certain she would probably be able to stomp through the house and still not be noticed. Holding Zack's hand, she led him to the back door. He was right. He was very good at being quiet. She wouldn't have even known he was behind her if he hadn't been holding her hand. She unlocked the glass back door and slowly slid it open. She shut it until just before it latched. This would ensure her reentry would be equally as soundless and she didn't really think her parents would be burgled or maimed within the next couple of hours.

"We're free," she said.

"Free at last." He pulled her toward him and kissed her deeply.

"You know," she said. "We don't *have* to go all the way to the cemetery. There's a perfectly secluded patch of woods right back there." She nodded behind her back yard, where the Lynchville Nature Reserve began.

"I know. But I want to go to the graveyard. It's not going to be this warm much longer."

"It's not exactly warm now."

"But it isn't winter yet."

"Okay. You win."

"This is definite graveyard weather."

Together, they walked through the back yard and across the side yard until they were on the sidewalk. They would have to keep to the side streets. If a cop were to see them out walking this late, they would most definitely have to answer some questions. If the police found out she was under eighteen she would either get an escort home or a call to her parents. Technically, the curfew for minors in Lynchville was ten. This relaxed a little on Friday and Saturday.

And it didn't seem to really apply so much to those over sixteen. Charlotte was seventeen. But it was Thursday. She didn't know how old Zack was but she didn't know if an officer would take so kindly to him escorting a high school girl around town at two o'clock in the morning. That kind of behavior just had prurient written all over it.

"So why do you want to go traipsing around a creepy old graveyard, anyway?" she asked.

"I don't know. I just want to."

"Do you do *everything* you want to?"

"Mostly, yeah."

"That's good, I guess. Are you ever going to take me to your house?"

"Someday."

"Do you still live with your parents?"

"Something like that."

"Yes or no. What, do you live with like an older sibling or grandparents or something?"

"No. Just some friends."

"*Older* friends."

"Yeah, I guess. I don't know. I don't really think about age so much."

"So how old are you?"

"I told you I don't think about age very much."

"You didn't answer my question."

"And I'm not going to."

"That's frustrating. It's a simple question."

"Did I ask how old you were?"

"No. I'm seventeen."

"Good for you."

"You don't have to be a dick about it."

"You can always turn around and go home."

"I just might."

"Can we just forget about it? You'll find out everything you need to know about me eventually."

"What if I want to know *now*?" She tried to sound petulant and spoiled, doing her best Veruca Salt impersonation.

"Nah. Ruins the mystery."

They continued to walk along in the darkness. Sometimes, she didn't know why she was with Zack. Of course, when she thought about it, she wasn't really *with* him. None of her friends knew about him. They didn't really go out or anything. He just showed up periodically, dragging her someplace and fucking her until she thought she was going to die. She had met him just a few weeks ago on a sleepless night when her parents had been out of town and she had thrown a party at her house. Everyone else had gone home or passed out and she had been sitting on the porch when she saw him walking down the sidewalk. She was just drunk enough to wander across the yard and talk to him, assaulting him with an endless barrage of questions she didn't even really hear the answers to. From the second she had drawn close to him, she was completely lost to him. There was something about his eyes. They were somewhere between brown and hazel but when the light hit them a certain way they looked almost golden. And with his pale skin, skinny body and black hair, he looked like one of the rock stars she swooned over. They didn't really have much in the way of conversations but she felt like that was something that would probably come to them over time and if he wanted to get rid of her when the sex got stale or vice versa, then she figured she would be okay with that too. The lack of conversation also meant a lack of emotional connection. Plus, she was young and had plans of getting out of Lynchville and going off to college somewhere and didn't even know if she really wanted a stupid, sometimes transient thing like love to hold her back from doing that.

"So where *is* your house?"

"Jesus, back to the questions... I'll take you there someday."

"When?"

"I don't know. Soon. How's that?"

"Afraid your friends won't like me?"

"No. I'm sure they would like you just fine."

"Then why not?"

"Because I like this."

"What? Walking?"

"No. I like the game of it. I like having to sneak off. I like the thrill of thinking we could be caught at any time. I like not knowing much about you and you not knowing much about me."

She couldn't argue with that.

"You're causing me to lose a lot of sleep, you know?"

"I'm sorry. Don't come then. Go back home. Christ."

This silenced her. Two times in one night. She thought it was mean of him to say something like that. He didn't have to say it more than once for it to hurt. Maybe he knew she didn't really have any choice but to come with him. He was like some kind of drug she always wanted more of. While that may change, especially if he kept being an ass, it was unavoidable for now.

They were just outside of town now, on the same road as the cemetery, aptly called Cemetery Drive.

The cemetery was on a large hill. The hill displayed an impressive array of tombstones, some of them monolithic, in a grand fashion. They stretched up the hill and ran down the far side of the hill, out of view, ending at the edge of the woods. For a town so small, Lynchville had a huge cemetery. She could never figure out if this was because a lot of people died in Lynchville or if the town was just old or if the people that left chose to be brought back and buried there. Any of those things could account for the graveyard's bounty. Although it was probably because it was the only cemetery in Lynchville.

Or maybe it was because of the Devils, she thought.

This was a legend that never failed to enthrall her. She had never heard of them anywhere outside of Lynchville and she had never quite been able to figure out what they were supposed to be. In some stories, they came across as werewolves. In other stories they came across as vampires or zombies. Nevertheless, it all came back to the dreams. Rumor had it the people of Lynchville always had been and always would be nightmared to death. People died in their sleep here. They died of natural causes. A lot more people than usual, if the rumors were correct. Charlotte had studied the obituaries for a while but she couldn't see that any more people died in Lynchville than in any other small town. Of course, if you listened to the rumors, then you knew the newspaper only printed about half the death toll. The people who really believed in this thought it was all some kind of big conspiracy.

Charlotte was not one of the believers. She thought the Devils were probably just some lame excuse to take the heat off an inept police department and lack of federal interest in rural, small town America. Disappearances, strange deaths—Oh, must be the Devils. It was ridiculous.

Standing at the gates of the cemetery, Zack pulled them back, greeted with the squeaking of wrought iron, and slid in between them. Charlotte followed.

"Shouldn't those have been locked?"

"Not a problem." He tossed the padlock up in the air and caught it again, sticking it in his pants pocket. "Wouldn't want anyone locking us in here."

She could only stare at him. He was like a magician. She knew they were both very close to doing what each of them wanted and she felt the usual blood coursing through her body, speeding up her heart, choking up the back of her throat.

They walked up the central asphalt lane of the cemetery, climbing up the slope.

Zack moved behind her and put his hands on her hips, lifting up her sweater so he could feel the warmth of her sides.

"I'm going to tear you apart," he whispered into her ear.

"Yeah?"

"Absolutely. As soon as we get over this hill. So no one can see what I'm going to do to you."

"I hope it's good." This was why she liked Zack.

"No. It's bad. It's very very bad."

"I..." she began before he cut her off.

"Stop talking now. And I don't want you to make a sound while I'm fucking you," he whispered into her ear. "If you make a sound then it's over. We must not disturb the dead."

Charlotte's nipples hardened against the inside of her shirt. She hadn't bothered putting on a bra and she desperately wanted to feel

Zack's hands on her, on *them*, squeezing, pulling, *twisting*... It had never been said aloud, but she liked it when he hurt her.

Once over the rise, Zack's hands guided her to the left. Then he forced her down onto a plot with a moderately sized tombstone. She hadn't really thought they would be fucking on an actual grave but with the little knowledge she had gained from Zack she now realized he probably wouldn't have had it any other way. The name on the tombstone was "Gordon Turner." She briefly wondered why that name sounded familiar to her but her thoughts were cut off when Zack whispered harshly in her ear. "Not one mutter until we are out of this graveyard. Understand?"

She nodded her head, her eyes burning into him, eager and nervous for what was about to happen.

He unbuttoned her jeans and yanked them down her legs. He kissed the inside of her thigh, working his mouth up to where her leg joined her groin. There he bit down. She wanted to shout at him to stop—it was so shocking and painful—but she knew he was serious about what he said and she didn't think she could live with the knowledge that her protestation had cost her everything. She bit down on her lip and his teeth worked their way into her skin. She closed her legs around his ears, dug her fingertips into the back of his head. She could swear she heard the soft pop of her skin as his teeth found admittance. Once opened, he drank of her. She arched her back into the moist, cool grass, her muscles straining against his mouth. Tears streamed from her eyes. But, at the same time, she found this as pleasurable as if his mouth were clasped over her sex. She orgasmed before he had her underwear pulled from her hips.

He rose to his knees, blood-stained around his mouth. With his left hand, he shoved her shirt up over her breasts and went to work on the nipples—flicking them, twisting them, pulling them until she thought they would tear. With his right hand he unbuttoned his black pants and pushed them down. He stroked himself, moving his left hand down to brutally pinch her clitoris between thumb and forefinger.

When she thought she couldn't take it any more, he took his hand away. For just a few moments, there was no contact at all and she felt her body reaching for his.

Then he was in her, all the way in, all at once, and she wondered how someone with such cold hands could be so warm inside her. Raking his shirt out of the way, she closed her mouth around his shoulder and, remembering how he bit her, let her teeth bite into him. She heard him grunt and, at the same time, felt him grow impossibly large within her, thrusting even more brutally until he spasmed, pulling his cock out and rubbing it against the lips of her cunt.

Clutching himself tightly in his right hand, he scrambled out from between her legs and came to rest on his knees, feeding his cock into her mouth. She didn't want it there but she couldn't say anything now. He filled her mouth, his left hand keeping her from backing away. She tasted herself, gagged as the tip of his penis pushed against the back of her throat before exploding in warm ropes of come.

He pulled it out. She coughed, thinking it wasn't nearly as bad as she thought it would be.

He looked into her eyes and, in that second, everything was washed away from her. All the pain, all the pleasure dissipated, leaving her with an eerie sense of complete and total calm. Complete and total satisfaction.

He stood up and pulled up his pants. She stayed on the ground, collecting her underwear, damp with her own come. She pulled them on before reaching for her jeans she just knew were grass stained. She stood up and pulled them on, watching him as he stared out toward the woods at the foot of the cemetery's hill. She shook, unable to control her muscles.

A thin fog had developed. There was something strange about the fog. There were parts where it seemed to be thicker than others and these parts, maybe it was just her imagination, resembled human forms. She looked all around and noticed these were everywhere. She thought she could even see them rising from the graves. Not zombies, but some blue essence. She didn't think she would ever be able to explain it and would probably have forgotten all about it in the morning. Maybe Zack's come was a hallucinogen.

Before zipping and buttoning her pants, she reached her hand inside to rub the bite on her thigh. It stung greatly but it didn't seem to be bleeding. The welts felt hot on her hands and for the first time she wondered not *who* Zack was, but *what* he was.

He started down the walk to the cemetery gates and she followed him.

When he had first bitten her, she had grand plans of reaming him as soon as they were outside of the cemetery. She was going to tell him he needed to give her a little warning if he was going to pull shit like that. He had trumped that with his finale, however. And once they were back on the streets of Lynchville, she realized she didn't really care about any of it anyway. In fact, as they walked silently back to her house, she was almost certain she wanted him to do it again.

They didn't say a word until they were in front of her house.

She threw her arms around him and kissed him deeply, thinking of what she could say that would bring him back.

"That was great," she said, feeling lame.

"Yes. It was. You were great. You tasted good."

"I got a little taste of myself."

"Mmmm, that."

"When will I see you again?"

"When I'm standing in front of you."

"Jesus, that's so cryptic."

"I can't make promises I might not be able to keep."

"What is *that* supposed to mean?"

"It means you'll see me again if I'm able to come to you."

"I'm still not sure I understand. Are you in some kind of trouble?"

"We're all in some kind of trouble, if you stop to think about it."

"Maybe I don't think about it that much."

"I want to see you again. Is that what you want to hear? I very very much want to see you again."

"That's something, I guess."

She gave him another hug, pressing his bones into her bones, before turning to go back into the house. She felt his eyes watching her as she walked across the side yard. She even thought she felt his eyes watching her as she lay in her bed, drifting off in the narcotic smell of his sweat and the taste of his come on the back of her tongue.

Four

Zack wandered down out of the hills into the clearing of the hollow. It was too small to be called a valley. It was a place of secrets. A dark place. Hills rose on all sides, nearly obliterating the sky. Even with the moon hanging swollen and full overhead this was a place too dark for shadows.

Coming into the clearing, the same fear gripped him that gripped him every night.

What if he didn't see the house?

Zack knew, in order to see the house, the owners of the house had to *want* you to see it. That was the first step. The house was a place of great power. Or, maybe, the people living in the house contained the power. Part of this power was the giving and taking of the house. Ever since seeing those people from his bedroom, months ago in a California suburb, Zack had desperately strove to be in their favor. Ilya and Ernst. Zack had yet to find out their last names, if they even had last names. It had taken him quite some time to figure out their first names. They had seduced him in much the same way he was seducing Charlotte. After seeing them for the first time, he wanted to be with them. They made him feel powerful. They promised him some of their power. They said he was chosen.

Zack stood at the edge of the clearing, marveling at the way the hollow seemed to absorb the moonlight, and waited for the house to appear. Standing on a gravel road running along a ridge traversing the hollow, Zack strained his eyes into the darkness. Since meeting Ilya and Ernst, he had become something of a nocturnal creature. His eyes had adjusted well to the dark. Still, he could not see the house.

Longing for the sight of the house, desperation scrabbled around in his head. He knew this was part of it. It was all just part of their game. Part of his training. The panic. The anxiety. So far, the house had not failed to appear to him.

All of a sudden it was there, standing in front of him in its sad and dark glory.

It did not slowly appear as Zack had at first assumed it would, as it usually did. Most times he watched it carve itself out of the mist and darkness hanging in the air, like a ghost putting on substance for a haunting. This time was different. One second he stood there staring at nothing and then when he got tired of staring he blinked his eyes and when he opened them again the house was there with all the blinking suddenness of a light bulb. Waiting for him. Begging him to come in.

He walked down the hill from the ridge, across the clearing, deeper into the hollow, his insides tingling with some dark revelation.

Since coming to Lynchville, he had familiarized himself with many of the legends surrounding the town. Some of them were simply mundane—haunting, disappearances, insanity—common rumors surrounding any small town. Others were terrifying. Some of them were merely disgusting. He didn't know how many of them were true and he didn't know how many of them were attributable to Ernst and Ilya and, in truth, he didn't really care. There was a time when he would have cared. There was a time when what he was doing would have appalled him, but that time had passed. It passed the second he had looked out the window and saw Ilya standing curiously beneath an oak tree in his front yard. There had been a light radiating from her eyes. A milky bluish white that reached through the darkness of the night and wrapped itself around his very being. There was magic in those eyes and he would spend the rest of his life searching for that magic, if necessary.

That was the last night he had spent in his house, the last night he had seen his parents or any of his friends. The last night he had felt anything resembling a childhood.

Over the past several months, Ernst and Ilya had trained him. Trained him to be like them. And all the while, they had regaled him with tales of power. Power was something he had never had. Power was only something his lawyer father and advertising exec mother wielded over him. Power was something he craved. And now there were these people, strange though they had seemed to him at first, who promised him unlimited power. Freedom from death. Freedom from money. Freedom from society. Freedom *was* power. And all he had to do was die first.

This was what his training built toward. Death. Followed by life. It didn't make any sense but he had seen it work. It wasn't like a Christian afterlife, something built solely on faith. This other death, this other afterlife, was something he had seen firsthand. It was something he could believe in. He had seen both Ilya and Ernst drink from the jugular of countless people. He had seen those people walk after death. So he believed and belief, like freedom, was also power.

Like tonight in the graveyard. He knew Charlotte did not understand what they had seen—the shapes in the fog—but he did. They had seen the Devils. These were not the powerful Devils, people like Ilya and Ernst, but they were people who lived a life after death, free to roam the dark countryside. The shapes in the graveyard were what anyone living outside Lynchville would call ghosts.

Here, they were not ghosts, they were the Devils, harmless Devils, unwilling to take human life. Just like Ilya and Ernst were not vampires or serial killers. Here, they were also the Devils. Perhaps Zack was beginning to understand why they had wanted to come here. Why they had brought their house here.

The house was an old Victorian farmhouse. The whole structure sagged into the earth, decomposing into its original elements. Whatever paint covered it at one time was long gone and now the wood was gray and warped and smelled faintly of decay, better years buried deep within its pulp.

Its porch had completely collapsed on the right side, the porch's roof threatening to go next. Four large windows lined the second floor of the house. Once upon a time, he supposed, these windows used to be ornate. Now they were without glass, little more than holes in the side of the house. The two windows on the end were larger than the two in the middle and made him think of eyes. Two large windows stood empty on the first floor, a door in the middle. The door used to be fairly elaborate also. Now the carvings had been worn away and the door looked like it could be kicked in easier than it could be opened.

Drawing closer to the house, he could feel its power, like a vacuum, sucking him in. Carefully treading the warped steps of the porch, he pulled the front door open onto a sparsely furnished living room. The only thing in the room was a Tiffany blue couch pushed back against the far wall. It was an odd, vibrant color, clashing with the decay of the house's interior.

Ernst and Ilya sat on the couch, waiting for him.

"Zack," Ernst said.

He stood up, unfolding his tall, thin figure. He wore a suit that looked like it had once belonged to an undertaker, formfitting, filthy and moth eaten. His skin was very pale and his knotty black hair hung down to his shoulders. His golden eyes gleamed at Zack.

"Have you brought anything for us today?"

"No."

"Of course," he said, almost sadly. "Ilya and I are hungry, Zack."

"I know you are. I *will* bring something, I promise."

"Why do you wait so long?"

"Because I want it to be something you enjoy. I brought you a taste."

Zack approached the daunting height of Ernst. The man reached toward his face and, with the chipped fingernail of his index finger, flaked away a piece of dried blood from the corner of Zack's mouth. Then he leaned down and placed his mouth over Zack's, his tongue rubbing against Zack's teeth, scraping away whatever essence remained of Charlotte's blood.

"Mmmm," he said, a disturbing smile curving the corners of his mouth. "That *is* good. Ilya, come and taste this."

The woman stood up from the couch. She smoothed her long

black skirt, brushed her blond, almost-white hair from her shoulders and approached Zack. She was as short as Ernst was tall. She stood in front of Zack and plaintively extended her head toward him. He bent down and let her kiss him. With Ilya, he kissed back, putting his tongue in her mouth, tasting the murky bitterness of death. She never protested, so absorbed in sucking this flavor from Zack.

"Mmmmm. That *is* nice. When will you bring her to us?"

"Soon."

"'Soon' will not do," Ernst said. "We are starving. All of our captives are going just to feed the Fire. We watch as their blood is boiled away inside their bodies. And I don't know how long that idiot is going to last before he gets caught. He can't be expected to feed both us and the Fire. That would get him caught for sure."

"Yes, I know."

"So when are you going to bring us this girl?" Ernst said. "It is a girl, isn't it?"

"Yes. I will bring her to you when you are ready to make me one of you."

"I'm afraid it is not that easy."

"So you've been lying to me."

"No. Not at all. We can turn you into a Devil. That is not hard. I could kill you right now and, just by dying at my hand, you would become a Devil. But only time can make you what Ilya and I are.

Time and training."

"I know I have to start somewhere."

"So why don't you start with this girl? Bring her to us and we can all share and you can feel death and when you wake up she will be the first thing you taste. You will feel, in death, her blood come alive on your tongue and dance in your mouth. Is that what you want?"

"Very much so. That is the only thing I want."

"Then you shall have it. Tomorrow. We cannot go another night without sustenance. If you can't do it then we will have to find someone who can. The Idiot is working on his own project or I'd have him bring us some meat and leave the fire to suffer."

Zack nodded his head. "It will be done."

"We have to leave you now," Ernst said.

"Until tomorrow," Ilya said, her lips curling up in the same creepy smile as Ernst's.

They walked to one of the back rooms of the house and Zack knew they were going below. While he had been allowed below the house, he had never been farther than the first room. He had never been allowed into the Low Church, where the Dark Fire burned. He had been tempted to go down several times when he knew Ernst and Ilya would either be asleep or away but he knew they would still be able to see him, to see what he was doing. Sometimes he could feel them in his head, behind his eyes, processing the information he took in. He knew they already knew Charlotte's name, what she looked like, what she felt like and, after tonight, they now knew what she tasted like.

He went back out onto the porch, sitting on the top step and watching the faint blue shimmers of the harmless Devils flicker in the woods.

He had plans of his own but he couldn't think about them at length, afraid Ilya or Ernst would know what he was thinking. If they knew about his plans then he would be dead and, knowing life after death was exactly what he wanted, they would prevent him from ever achieving that.

Five

Rachel thought her eyes were open but she couldn't be sure. If they were then, wherever she was, it was seriously dark. She lay in the cold muck, listening to the splashing sounds around her head that now felt oddly swollen and tried to figure out how many people surrounded her. It didn't really matter how many of them there were. The more important thing was what they planned on doing to her. Something inside of her wanted this to be some dark nightmare but she knew that wasn't the case. Whatever was happening to her was real and she had to treat it as such. She could not allow herself any of the passivity her nightmares had afforded her.

Footsteps sloshed around her.

"How do you want to do this?" a woman's voice asked. Or maybe it was a girl's. She didn't sound very old.

"I don't know," another voice said. This one belonged to a man. A young man. Possibly a teenager. "Why don't you grab hold of her ankles. I'll get her under the arms."

Were there only two of them? If so, this came as a comfort to Rachel, although she didn't know if she stood any chance of escaping at all. She hadn't moved since hearing them come down, playing dead or at least seriously injured. And she wasn't sure she would be able to move appropriately when the time came.

A pair of hands grabbed her beneath her arms. Another pair grabbed her ankles. Together, they lifted her up with relative ease. She tried very hard to make herself as heavy and burdensome as possible. Dead weight.

"You think she's dead?" the girl asked.

"No. I can hear her breathing. Besides, it wasn't that big a fall. Cunt's heavier'n she looks."

She wondered where they were taking her. She hoped it was someplace out in the open. Somewhere that allowed her to run if she was able to break free of them.

The two people carrying her didn't say very much. She was lost to the darkness, the gentle sway of her transport, and the soft sloshing of the water as the two cut through it. She tried to block it all out, which wasn't incredibly hard to do. Things were already growing fuzzy. She fought to keep her eyes open but was not entirely sure if that was working. She hurt badly and she could feel her body trying to numb itself to the pain. She fought to stay conscious but everything conspired to drag her under. And once she waded out into the black waters of unconsciousness it was impossible to fight her way back.

When she came to, Rachel opened her eyes. She was laid out on her back, very cold, in a lot of pain, and noticed the absence of hands around her arms and ankles. Overhead she saw stars twinkling benignly on their black canvas.

She smelled cigarette smoke and heard the voices of the girl and boy. There was something about the way they talked that told Rachel they had to be teenagers. Probably just high school kids. Only a year out of high school herself, she wondered if she knew them.

"Aren't you worried she's gonna get away?" the girl asked.

"Nah, she's *out*. If she tries to run I'll bury my knife in her. I'll fuckin tear her up."

"You'd better be careful."

"I won't kill her. I'll just... wing her or something."

"What are we gonna do with her?"

"What do you want to do with her?"

"Me? I just want to drop her off and get the hell away. Those people give me the creeps."

"Don't forget that they're the reason we're doin this. Too late to take her there tonight anyway. We got all tomorrow to play with her before we drop her off."

Rachel cringed at that.

"It just doesn't make a lot of sense."

"Makes perfect sense."

"I guess it makes sense if you believe them."

"You don't believe em?"

"I don't know. I just think maybe they're sick, you know? A couple of sickos."

"No. I *don't* know." The boy sounded kind of angry. "If you think they's so sick why you goin along with this whole thing? I think it's cause, deep down, you know they's tellin the truth."

"Truth," the girl scoffed. "I don't know what's true anymore."

"Think about it, Rain. We get this girl to them and we're set. Everything we've ever wanted could come true. We can go any-where we want to. We don't have to get jobs or any of that bullshit. We become one of them and we're like all those vampires you like to read about."

"Those are just dreams. That kind of stuff can't really exist. I wouldn't *want* that stuff to be real."

"Is that what you're afraid of? Having your dreams turn into re-ality? Because that's really fuckin stupid. That's what most people would kill for."

The girl snorted. "Isn't that what we're doing? Killing for it?"

Rachel cringed again. Although a lot of what they said was nonsense to her, she definitely didn't like the gist of their conversation. *At least they want to "play" with me before killing me.* She shuddered.

"We ain't killin anyone for it. All we're doin is takin this girl to that house and then the rest is done. This's the big payoff."

"And you think it's going to be that easy?"

"I don't have any reasons to believe anythin else."

"I just don't know."

"You'll be happier when it's all finished. Trust me. There's absolutely nothin to worry about. People like them don't go to jail. They don't get punished. Once this is over, we'll be free from everything. Forever."

"Jesus. You sound like a fucking cult member."

Rachel heard the sound of skin on skin. A brisk crack. The girl barked out in pain.

"You ain't backin out on me now. It's too late to pull this kinda shit. Now ain't the time to be a little bitch."

Crack! He smacked her again. This time Rachel thought she heard the girl hit the ground. Rachel wanted to turn her head and see what was going on but she didn't want to draw any attention to herself. If this was how this kid played with his girlfriend, she squirmed at the thought of what he would do to her.

"I'm sorry," the girl whimpered.

"That's a good little bitch," the boy said. "Bein a snivelin little brat don't help none."

"I know," the girl said, crying.

"Stop cryin. You should be able to take a smack now. You don't cry like that when I smack your ass."

"I know."

"But you like that, don't ya... little bitch?"

The girl was silent.

"Say you like it or I'll bend you over and thrash you right now."

"I like it," the girl said. Was there a trace of sarcasm there? "I love it when you hit me."

"What I thought," the boy said.

Rachel imagined the boy reaching over and placing a consoling arm around the girl. Or maybe he was wrestling her out of her pants. She heard the shuffle of clothing and figured now was a good time. She jumped up onto her feet, hot electric fire shooting through her stiff muscles and achy bones. Her head felt like it was encased in cement. She took off running in what she figured was the opposite direction of the voices. She didn't have any idea where she was. It was a clearing that looked a lot like the clearing where everything had happened two years ago. She wished she could summon that power now. Wished she could dive into that prick's head and play with his thoughts but she was too beaten, too weak, too panicked.

Six

Rachel ran as hard as she could, her body threatening to lock up.

The couple ran just as hard behind her, their feet cutting through the grass.

Rachel knew there weren't many houses out here but she decided to scream anyway. Maybe, just maybe, there was some wandering insomniac who would hear her.

Then she felt something smack into her back as the boy tackled her, driving her down onto the ground. She tried to twist herself away from him but he scooted farther on top of her, crushing her with his weight. He put his knees on her thighs and leaned his hands on her upper arms. The girl stood over them.

A deeper pang of fear ripped its way through Rachel when she saw the gleaming knife the girl held. Rachel tried to make eye contact with the girl. Her cheek was red from where the boy had smacked her and Rachel thought, maybe, the tears gleaming on her cheeks were tears of guilt.

But the girl didn't look at all guilty. Hate filled her eyes. Hate and maybe just a little bit of dread as she focused on Rachel's neck. Probably not afraid to strike if her man was threatened.

The boy craned his head over his shoulder, looking up at the girl.

"Why don't you run that blade across the bottom of her foot," he said. "Show her we ain't fuckin around."

Ever so obedient, the girl kneeled in the grass. A shiver ran through Rachel as she felt the blade touch the bottom of her right foot.

"No. Don't," Rachel said.

The boy stared down at her, wide-eyed and angry, ignoring her plea.

"Now, this might keep you from runnin. It won't do no good to run anyway. You know that. If you get away today, we'll find you tomorrow. Or the day after that. Or maybe the *year* after that. And that'll be much worse. Why don't you just lay back and take what's comin to ya."

"Why are you doing this?" Rachel asked, trying to reach whatever strand of sanity the boy had.

"Because we're sick people who like doing sick things," the boy said, as if this made all the sense in the world. "Does that make you feel better? And the more you try and get away, the sicker the sick things get. Unnerstand?"

Rachel didn't acknowledge the threat. Wasn't about to give the fuck the satisfaction.

He leveled a headbutt against her forehead, causing her vision to turn red. The bone-on-bone collision jarred all the teeth in her head.

The girl ran the blade across her foot and Rachel cried out, feeling the flaps of skin separate and hang open. Flowing blood tickled her heel.

"Oh... *fuck*," she muttered through clenched teeth, wanting to raise her foot and hold it in her hands.

"You're going to want to watch it with the talkin," the boy said. "Now you know what we do when we don't want you to get away, do you really want to see what we do to you to shut you up?"

Visions of tongue removal shot through Rachel's mind. She shook her head.

"Good. Very good. Because if you think you're gettin away, you're not. And I, for one, would hate to see you lose yer tongue. It just ain't the same if it ain't in the mouth. All good little bitches need a fat little tongue."

He craned his neck back to the girl, once again hovering over them, now staring at the bloody blade with something like horrified shock.

"Rain, bring the van around. Let's get er in there."

The girl walked slowly off into the misty darkness. Rachel lay there, feeling dew-dampened beneath the weight of the boy. He leaned down close to her, covering her in his smells—his cigarette and whiskey breath, his dank leather jacket, old blood, the stink of death and desperation.

"I can see why they want you," he said.

"*Who* wants me?" Rachel said, still trying to make some kind of sense out of this. She liked this less and less. It was too much like last time. Those guys had spoken of people wanting her also.

But those guys were dead.

"*Who wants me?*" she repeated, louder this time.

"Me, for one," he said.

He removed a hand from her arm and slid it across her breast, squeezing the chill-hardened nipple through her cotton shirt.

"Very nice," he said.

"You're disgusting."

He bashed his hand across her face. The pain was there but it was merely a pebble plinking into an ocean of hurt.

"I know that," he said. "Oh boy don't I know that."

He put his hand under her shirt and ran it up to her bare heated breast. Unfortunately, she hadn't had a chance to put on a bra before they snatched her.

Rachel realized the girl had taken the knife, assuming there was only one knife between the two of them.

The boy's one-handed pawing freed up her left arm. She made a fist with her small hand and rammed it into the boy's ear.

"Fuck!" he shouted, unmoved.

He quickly retracted his hand from her shirt and put it back on her arm, sure to dig his fingers in especially hard this time. They wrapped around her bone, dug into the tendon and muscle.

He put his face down close to hers, cloaking her in that stink. The blood from her smashed nose prevented her from smelling most of it.

"Don't ever try nothin like that again. When Rain gets back, yer gonna pay for that."

Keeping himself mashed into her, he laid his body on top of her. She could feel the hardness in his pants. He licked her face, his disgusting tongue running over her nose and eyelids, lapping up her blood and tears. She spat in his face and he rammed his head into hers again, driving it into the dirt and grass. Jesus, she wished she would just black out or something.

"Maybe I'll tell Rain to go for a little a walk," he said. "Would you like that? You want to be alone with me for a few minutes? Bet your pussy's wet just thinkin bout it."

He ground his erection against her crotch.

"Go fuck yourself," she said into his ear.

"Oh, I'll fuck you all right," he returned and Rachel wanted to laugh with the dumbness of the comeback.

The van was near. Rachel saw the headlights bobbing as it ran over the nearly flat meadow. The van pulled up next to Rachel and the boy and stopped. The boy stood up and grabbed a handful of her hair, twisting it around his fist, pulling the skin on her already throbbing head taut.

The van was black with a crude white painting of a skull on the side. Who *were* these people? she wondered.

The boy slid open the side door of the van, climbed in ass first and dragged Rachel after him.

"Help me tie this bitch up," he barked to Rain.

The girl put the van in park, stood up from the captain's chair and, stooped over, came into the back of the van. She found a coil of white rope that looked like clothesline and tried to hand it to the boy.

"I'll hold her," he said. "You tie her up good. Hold your hands out," he said to Rachel, giving a sharp yank to her hair.

Rachel obediently held out her hands in front of her. What was the point in struggling? She would have to bide her time. The girl began wrapping the rope around them tightly. She even wove it in between Rachel's fingers. Rachel knew these people had done this before and that made it somehow more terrifying. They had done this before and, if they had done this before and were able to do it again, that meant they had gotten away with it.

The girl pulled Rachel's hands down until they were in her crotch. The boy pressed Rachel, face first, to the floor of the van. The girl (*Rain*, Rachel thought) brought the rope between her legs, pulling her feet up to her ass. Rachel was being hogtied. The girl wrapped the rope around Rachel's ankles and then, as a final touch, coiled it around her neck so that if she tried to move she was going to choke herself to death.

"There," Rain said, once finished, as though she had finally straightened a picture perfectly upon a wall.

"Good work, babe," the boy said.

"Thanks, Bones," she said.

They exchanged a quick kiss and retreated to the front of the van.

Bones took the driver's seat, as Rachel figured he would and, rather than sitting in the passenger's seat, Rain sat down on the floor between the two front seats, turned to where she was facing Bones but could still keep an eye on Rachel. Rachel wondered how young this girl was. She had jaggedly cut pink hair that came down to just below her ears. Her skin was nearly baby-soft looking, but there was a hardness in her eyes that upset her overall youthful appearance. It was the look of a killer or a methamphetamine user. Or *both*, Rachel thought. The van began moving and Rachel rocked slightly to her side, the rope constricting as she did so. She coughed. They were quite serious about her not getting away.

"Now, don't choke to death before we get there. Don't throw up in my van neither."

Rachel looked at Rain. The girl just kept staring at her. Surely, there had to be something in this girl she could identify with. Rachel figured if she just kept staring at her, it would force the girl to look into her eyes and maybe, just maybe, if the girl did that then she would be able to see what her and her boyfriend were doing was absolutely atrocious.

Fat chance, Rachel thought. She had come this far. What was the reason to stop now?

Bones lit a cigarette and the van filled with the acrid scent.

"How do you like this van?" he asked, almost jovially, as though it were some grand prize. He didn't really wait for a response. "You see," he said, "the great thing about this van is that it looks so suspicious. No one would ever suspect it of harboring a kidnap victim or anything like that because it would just be too... too *obvious*, you know? Hell, I've carried bodies around in this thing for days. I've had cops pull me over but not one of em's ever searched it. Because they'd feel stupid. Like they were profiling or somethin like that. Plus it gets pretty good gas mileage."

"I love you, Bones," Rain said, reaching out for a hit of the cigarette. "He put a lot of thought into this van," she said, looking at Rachel.

"Yeah," Rachel said sarcastically. "While you were gone, your boyfriend felt me up."

Rachel said this while the girl made eye contact with her. She saw a hurt look flood into those almost translucent blue eyes and knew she had seized upon something.

"Bones wouldn't do that."

"Well, he did. Why don't you ask him why his ear's all red?"

"Did you mess with her, Bone Man?"

"Baby, I just had to keep her in line. Bitch's got a mouth on her. Shit, if I weren't drivin this van, I'd fuck her up."

But now the girl was mad. "What did you do to her?"

"I didn't do nothin!" Bones shouted.

"He put his hand in my shirt," Rachel said. "Humped me. He was hard as a rock."

"Did you do that, Bones? This girl get you hot."

"She's fuckin nuts, baby. You're the only one I want to touch."

"Is that why you wanted to get her? So you could drag her out somewhere and fuck her? Are you tired of me?"

"If I wanted to fuck her, I'd stop this van and fuck her while you watched. Or I'd fuckin kill you first. I could do that, you know. You keep given me shit, I just might. Keep your dead bitch eyes open while I plug her up the ass. How'd you like that, bitch?"

Rachel decided to exaggerate somewhat, just to drive as much of a wedge as possible between her captors.

"He said he wished you had tits like mine."

"You say that?" Rain asked. "Her tits are a little bigger. You like that?"

"Baby, she's lyin. Can't you see that? You that fuckin stupid?"

"He said he wanted to get me alone."

Bones had reached some kind of breaking point. He pulled the van onto the shoulder of the road, slamming on the brakes, the van sliding a little on the gravel. He stood up from the seat, still crouched over and, reaching over Rain, took several vicious swings at Rachel's face. Each time his fist connected, the rope pulled on her neck, abrading it.

"Shut the fuck up!" he shouted.

Rachel wanted to slump, wanted to collapse with exhaustion and pain, but the ropes kept her upright. Maybe she brought this attack upon herself. No. That was exactly what victims thought. She wouldn't let herself become a victim.

Bones whipped himself back into the driver's seat, jerking like a barnyard rooster, and pulled the van back onto the road.

"Let me out," Rain said. "I don't want to be near you right now."

"Like hell," Bones said. "She's a liar, Rain. Just a stupid liar. I don't want anyone but you."

"What about that one time?"

"I don't know what I was thinkin. You was on yer period. You know I don't like it when yer bleedin."

"Yeah, but it happened. I coulda just sucked you off or somethin but you had to go and do... *that*."

"I'm not bitchin with you. I'll slice you up and down before I get in an argument with yer bitch mouth."

The van hummed along the road. Bones fired up another cigarette, his hand trembling, his head jerking forward on his neck.

"So you don't want to fuck her?"

"No way. She's a skank."

And you're a real fucking prize, Rachel thought.

"Then you don't care if I mess up her face?"

Rachel cringed at that. Maybe she had only succeeded in making this girl jealous. A jealous girl, Rachel knew from experience, was nothing to take lightly.

"Go right ahead. I'd like to see her messed up. Just don't make her bleed *too* much."

Rachel heard the slow unsheathing of the knife and all her muscles drew tight within her bondage. She didn't know which would be worse—being dead or going through life as a hideously scarred freak.

Rain ran her finger along the blade and looked almost furtively at Rachel.

Seven

Rain crouched down in front of Rachel, trying to steady the knife in front of her as the van raced through the night. Rachel continued to probe the girl's eyes, unable to discern any singular emotion in them.

"Time for some music!" Bones shouted from the driver's seat, obviously thrilled at the prospect of more bloodletting from the back.

Suddenly, the van exploded in music. It was Nancy Sinatra and Lee Hazelwood singing "Some Velvet Morning." Not really something Rachel would have expected Bones to be a big fan of.

Rain leaned in toward Rachel, placing her cheek against her ear. The girl had a hint of the same whiskey and cigarette stench Bones had, but there was something beneath it. Something sweeter. Something a little more innocent.

"I'm going to cut your ropes," she whispered. "Just whimper a lot so he thinks I'm cutting you." Her voice was more the compassionate girl Rachel hoped she was rather than the vicious slob she feared.

Rachel didn't say anything. She didn't know what to say. For the first time in this whole horrifying evening, she saw a glimmer of hope. A tingle ran through her. Was Rain just putting her on? Building up her hopes to make the cutting more painful? This *was* the same girl who'd slashed her foot only moments before.

"What is this shit!" Bones shouted from the front.

Rachel's heart skipped a beat. At first she thought he had heard what Rain whispered to her. Then she realized he was talking about the music. He frantically slapped at the dial, searching for something louder, undoubtedly. He stopped when he got to some kind of testosterone-driven crap metal.

"That's more like it," he muttered. "These guys fuckin rock."

Rachel wasn't familiar with whoever he was talking about and she didn't really care. Rain leaned over her and severed the rope running from her neck to between her legs. Rachel let out a loud moan. She hoped it sounded miserable but it could just as easily have been a moan of pleasure. The rope had been stretched tight against her groin, rubbing that sensitive area nearly raw.

She wondered if Bones would be able to see this treason taking place in the rearview mirror but when she looked up she noticed the van did not have a rearview mirror. Of course not, she thought. A vehicle this fine couldn't have a rearview mirror. It would have been like an insult or something. It probably didn't have power steering either.

"Slice that bitch up good!" Bones shouted over the driving music, hopping up and down in his seat.

"I'm cuttin her up," Rain said, running the knife along the coils of rope binding Rachel's wrists. She pressed her lips against Rachel's ear again, whispering, "When I get you free, you have to promise to take me with you. You can't leave me behind to deal with him."

"I promise," Rachel whispered back, punctuating it with a loud wail.

"I can't wait to see that bitch!" Bones shouted.

The van roared on. Rachel's spirits continued to climb beneath the quivering of Rain's knife. Bones took a turn very fast and Rain slipped with the knife, dragging it over Rachel's forearm. She barked out in pain and Rain met her gaze with a look that said she was sorry.

"Are we almost there?" Rain asked.

"Just a few more minutes, baby. Just a few more minutes then I can join in."

"Good. I'm runnin out of places to cut. I might have to take her tits off if you don't hurry up."

"You know," Bones said. "*I* was thinkin about cuttin her tits off. But I thought they might want em. You know, to play with and shit."

"We think so much alike."

"Then I don't have to tell you what I'm gonna do to *you* when we drop this cunt off."

"I think I already know, baby. I thought we was gonna wait til tomorrow to drop her off?"

Rain loosened the rope from around Rachel's body and just the ability to breathe and, if she wanted, *move* made her feel better.

"I figure it won't hurt to swing by. See if they's there. Maybe we can leave her with that Zack freak."

Rachel caught the look of concern cross Rain's face. If Bones was taking them to someone's house, that meant more people to get away from.

Hope that doesn't make her lose her nerve, Rachel thought.

"What if they ain't there?" Rain shouted toward the front.

Rachel stayed low, on the floor, feeling the van make the transition from asphalt to gravel.

"It better fuckin be there," Bones said. "If I gotta haul this bitch around til tomorrow night, ain't no guarantee what she's gonna look like."

If? Now Rachel was thoroughly confused. It sounded like they were talking about the Sad House.

"I'm sure they'll be there," Rain reassured him. "They know you're comin, don't they?"

"That don't mean shit to them. We might still not be able to find it."

The van went down a steep hill and skidded to a stop.

Rachel pulled herself up to her knees. Rain turned her back on Rachel as the van stopped, obscuring her from Bones' view.

"I wanna see what you done to this bitch," Bones said, swiveling his body around to face the back.

"It's pretty bad," Rain said and Rachel was almost certain she saw the girl smile. It was a beautiful thing. The kind of smile that probably reached right into boys.

Rachel met Bones' eyes as he turned around and saw just a brief second of surprise before Rain plunged toward him, attempting to jab the knife into his left eye. It went wide, slicing his ear. It hit about midway down, cutting into the lobe.

Rain shrieked and tried to bring herself away from Bones but he already had her in his grasp. Rachel knew now would be the time. Now had to be the time to spring up and out of the sliding side door, disappearing into the night.

But she couldn't do that.

She had promised this girl, both her captor and her liberator, that she would help her get away from this boy and she intended to keep her promise.

Grabbing up a handful of rope from the floor of the van, she twisted the unknotted end around her hand. She swung the heavier knotted end toward Bones' face, aiming for his eyes. He fought this attack off with his right hand and frantically tried to grab the knife out of Rain's hand with his left, shouting desperate curses all the while.

Rain managed to drag the knife across his chest but, mostly, all the blade got was leather.

But she had broken from his hold.

With her left hand, Rachel grabbed Rain and, with her right, she grabbed the long handle for the sliding door and yanked it back. The door slid open, Rachel simultaneously falling out of it and dragging Rain behind her.

Together, they were out into the night, in some kind of small hollow, running up a hill from the direction Rachel presumed they had come.

"You two better get back here!" Bones shouted, his breath rasping as he ran behind them.

"Run faster!" Rain hissed.

Rachel heard the loud report of a gun and half expected to feel a bullet bite into her back or her leg. But apparently Bones was too full of rage to really focus and take aim. Rain was also unfelled by the shot. It gave Rachel impetus to run even faster and find some cover but here on the side of this hill, cover seemed to be somewhat absent. The woods were just over the ridge.

She ran in a crazy zigzag pattern, not sure if Bones was following them or not. Another shot went off and Rachel would have sworn she heard the bullet whistle past her ear. That would be great. Come all this way just to get shot in the head.

When they reached the road at the ridge, Rain threw herself down into the gravel. Not knowing what else to do, Rachel did the same.

Here, the air was a little mistier, a little thicker than it had been back in town. Rachel couldn't make Bones out and figured he couldn't see them either.

"Let's go straight across the road, into the woods. He'll think we stayed on the road," Rain said. "Stay low."

"Right," Rachel replied, admiring the other girl's combat skills.

The woods began immediately on the other side of the road and descended sharply. Running downhill made them much faster. Now Rachel feared flattening herself against a tree more than she feared Bones' gun. It was too dark for him to see. Nearly impossible with the added darkness and occlusion of the woods, she figured.

The two girls continued to run, brambles lashing at their ankles and thorns scraping their faces.

Eventually, Rain stopped.

"I can't run any more right now," she said, panting.

Slowing her breathing, Rain pricked up her ears, listening for any sounds of Bones. Rachel did the same.

Rain pulled a pack of cigarettes from the inside pocket of her leather biker's jacket. Reaching to pull a cigarette from the pack, she flinched and pointed to something on the back of her hand. Rachel squinted her eyes and looked.

"What's that?" she asked.

Rain snorted a laugh. "I think it's his fucking ear lobe."

With the middle finger of her other hand, she flicked it off and said, "Gross."

"He'll never miss it."

Rachel wished *she* had a coat. She was still dressed for bed, without the comfort of shoes. Her feet had to be a bloody mess but she was so eager to get away from the greater danger she hadn't felt anything underfoot.

"Can I have one of those?" Rachel asked, not really knowing why she would want one since she didn't usually smoke, had been nagging Jacob for months to stop smoking, and her lungs were burning from running.

"Sure," Rain said, holding the pack out to her.

"Thanks for what you did back there."

"Yeah. I think we showed him, didn't we? Sorry about cutting you. I had to do it with him looking."

"Don't worry about it," Rachel said. "I'm just happy to have my breasts for now."

"Bones has a real thing for cutting the nipples off. He plays with them for days. Until they get all rotten and smelly."

Rachel suppressed a shudder.

They lit their cigarettes and continued walking in the dark woods.

"What made you change your mind?" Rachel asked.

"What you said... about him messing with you. That's what did it. It's happened before and I didn't even really care if you were lying or not because it made me think about last time and how *that* had made me feel and about how I should have left him then. How I should have just quit this whole thing the minute it started but didn't and I guess that was it. I didn't want to be around him another minute. I've been thinking about it for a pretty long time but I never had anyone I could use as an accomplice or something. I haven't really been myself until recently."

"Do you think he's still following us?"

"Honestly? I doubt it. He doesn't like to leave his van alone and he's... well, he's incredibly lazy for one thing."

"Lazy Bones."

"Ha."

"Sorry."

"No need to be. That's what I think of him as too. To myself anyway."

"So what happened last time?"

Rain took a deep drag of her cigarette. "You really want to know?"

"Tell me some stuff about yourself and I'll tell you some pretty shocking stuff about myself. How's that? Maybe we can try and make some sense of all this."

The girl exhaled and Rachel noticed her breathing trembled just thinking about it.

Rachel reached out and touched Rain's arm.

"It's okay," she said. "Bad stuff happens to everybody. It'll make you feel better to talk about it. Trust me."

The girl took a harsh drag from her cigarette and said, "I guess so," smoke puffing out of her mouth.

"Okay," Rain said. "First of all, let me start by saying this: I don't really know you and what I have to tell you could get *me* in a lot of trouble too. I want you to promise me you won't tell anyone about what I'm about to say. I mean, I'd look like an *accomplice* or some-thing. And I didn't really want to do any of it."

The girls sidestepped a tree and landed on a narrow clearing.

"As much as I would like to promise that, I don't know if I can."

"Then I can't tell you."

"Well, see, my situation's a little more complex than you might realize. A couple years ago, my boyfriend, Jacob, and I had some really strange stuff happen to us and ever since then we've been trying to sort of figure out what it was that *really* happened. So, I can tell you now, whatever you tell me will probably make it back to him because we don't keep *any*thing from each other. Especially not the really strange stuff. Not anything that might help us get to the bottom of this mess."

"Well, I guess it's okay if you tell him if you're sure *he* wouldn't tell anybody else. I was mainly talking about cops or anyone like that."

"Oh, I wouldn't tell a cop." Rachel almost laughed at Rain's nearly naive sense of caution. "Besides, the cops in this town are probably just about the most evil people we have. Besides Them."

"Them?"

"The Devils. Have you ever heard of the Devils?"

"Can't say that I have."

"Well, let me clue you in. They're kind of a legend here in Lynchville. Now, I have family all over the U.S. and I've mentioned the Devils to just about all of them and none of them seem to have heard of them either. The Internet doesn't really help much. The Devils are like the most evil thing imaginable. I don't really know what it is about them that makes them evil or what they're trying to do. Legends are the typical boogeyman type of stuff, you know. Sometimes they're vampires. Sometimes they're ghosts. Werewolves. Zombies. Just about everything. It's said they're older than the town itself and, through some twisted logic, have like a psychic hold on the town or something. Which explains why people don't really leave. I mean, people move *away*, but no more than usual. Most people don't even really believe they exist. They treat them like an urban legend or something. Hell, me and Jacob *believe* and we're still here.

"Almost everyone I know who lives here has some wicked bad nightmares but you don't really know if that's because of the Devils or if we're all just a little paranoid, you know? And if you don't *believe*, then the nightmares can't hurt, right? Anyway, there does seem to be a higher than usual death rate in Lynchville and of course there's talk about someone somewhere covering everything up because they benefit from the Devils in some way. Or maybe the leaders of the town are Devils themselves. You know, like some ancient council that feeds off the town's energy. Who knows? That's the mystery we're trying to figure out. Mainly, we just want to find out why what happened to us happened. I know it all sounds crazy. I'll tell you more when we meet up with Jacob.

"Do you think I'm crazy?"

Rain chuckled slightly. "Do you think *I'm* crazy?"

"I guess it's all relative."

Rachel's body ached. The cut on her foot, after trodding over dirt and dead leaves and twigs, was now throbbing.

She pitched her cigarette off into the woods.

What if Bones saw the glow from the cigarette?

No. He couldn't have kept up with us, Rachel thought. She

trusted Rain when she said he was lazy. Besides, they were lost in the woods themselves. She didn't have any reason to believe Bones knew these woods any better than the average person.

Rain tossed her cigarette out.

"I'm sorry," Rachel said. "You had something you wanted to tell me and I completely took it away from you. You just seemed so nervous. I thought it might calm you if I talked for a little bit first. Let you know we're all a bit fucked up."

"No. Thanks. It did. It helped."

Rain pulled the jacket tightly around herself and said, "You cold?"

"Surprisingly no. I'm just kind of glad to be alive. In a bit of pain."

"You sure?"

"Sure."

"Okay, well, mainly, I pulled that stuff back there because I just can't take Bones anymore. He's a lot sicker than I thought he was. We've been running for almost a year now."

"Running from what?"

"Well, not really running *from* anything. It's more like we're running towards something only I haven't really been able to figure out what it is, exactly. I think only Bones knows. It gets kind of complicated. It might be the Devils you keep talking about. He says we're gonna be fucking vampires. Anyway, like I said, it's complicated."

"I think we have all the time in the world. We're a good half hour away from any signs of civilization."

"Do you know where we are?"

"I have a good idea. I think if we just stay on this trail, then we'll end up behind the cemetery."

"Great. That's just what I need. A fucking cemetery."

"You think Bones knows this area?"

"Hell no. He's fucking clueless. Spends all his time following other people and never looking out the window."

"Then I think we're okay for now. We can go to Jacob's and get cleaned up when we find our way out of this. Let him know what's going on."

"All right then, since we have the time, I guess I'll start at the be-ginning."

Rain took a deep breath and, for the next few moments, Rachel saw and heard the terrified girl that Rain truly was.

Eight

"Me and Bones went to high school together in California. He was always a pretty bad kid and I was always a pretty good kid until I turned fifteen and then I guess I got a rebellious streak or something. That's when I started hanging out with Bones. His real name's Lonnie by the way. I think part of the reason I did it was because I knew my parents hated him. We started hanging out last summer, not this past summer but the one before that. And we would just, you know, pop some of his mom's pills, smoke some pot, fuck whenever the parents were out of the house. As stupid as Bones is, I would have to say he was a pretty good fuck. Or maybe I was just too stoned to really know what a good fuck was. He was my first anyway. Never mind. That's a whole *other* area.

"So, earlier this year, he comes to my house really late at night and tells me he saw this woman standing out in his front yard like asking him to come outside or something. So Bones goes outside and the stupid fucker doesn't even really remember what this woman says but he walks away from this conversation with what he called his life's mission. He thought the woman was like a vampire or something. And she wanted Bones to bring people to her. That was it, basically. She wanted Bones to bring her meat or blood or whatever so she could feed on like real human people. I thought he was crazy but he just kept jabbering on and on about it.

"I didn't just think he was crazy for taking this stupid bitch seriously, either. I thought he was crazy for all but telling me he had a big crush on this older woman. For like the next week it was all he talked about. I was sick of it after about the first five minutes but, at the time, there was a part of me that really needed him. All my old friends stayed away from me cause they thought I was a pill popping whore, which I guess I kind of was. I knew that if he left, I'd be all alone. And my friends weren't the type of people you could just get back by dumping your stupid fuck of a boyfriend. They were all rich kids, people who place a lot of value on reputation, you know? Besides, by that time, I'd done some stuff with their boyfriends and... I'm getting off track again.

"Anyway, I thought that if we just did more drugs then maybe Bones would forget about this stupid dream or whatever he had but that didn't work. Before too long *I* started believing what he was saying.

"Then one night he came back and said the woman had come again and she wanted him to follow them and he decided he didn't want to follow them without me. And, in my present state, which was pretty fucking blitzed, I thought this was just about the sweetest thing Bones had ever said to me. At the time, it just didn't hit me how crazy and wrong it all sounded. Here my boyfriend was telling me how he was going to follow this other chick wherever she wanted him to go and I went along with it. I guess I had no self-esteem, you know? He did good at making me think I was garbage. He'd bring up the times I'd cheated on him and tell me this was different because he was asking me to come along with him. I guess he was expecting some big wild threesome or something. Anyway, it was all insane. *I* must have been insane."

"Sometimes we do crazy things," Rachel said. She had calmed down somewhat, now realizing just how cold it was outside, feeling the damp rot of the forest floor beneath her painful feet, the chilly mist clinging to her bare arms and legs.

"To say the least," Rain said. "Well, this is when things started to get strange. Like they weren't strange enough to begin with. One day we just hopped into Bones' van and headed east. He was pretty vague about what he was doing. Probably thought that it would freak me out. But I was empty inside. Incapable of being freaked out. The only way he could have done that was to take the pills and the vodka away. At first we had money for cheap motels and that kind of thing so he was able to lock me in these while he went out scavenging in his van. He was taking people out of their homes and from the streets and taking them to these people he had met. I didn't have any idea. It was *Bones*. He would go out and I'd stay in the motel room, crocked out of my head, watching soap operas and heading deeper into oblivion. He would come back and fuck me senseless and that was the day. I thought maybe he was out selling drugs to make a few extra bucks or something like that. Until I saw her, I wasn't going to believe this woman existed. Besides, as dumb as Bones is, I didn't think he was capable of murder. I thought he was essentially a good person. Just like I knew I was, somewhere deep deep down.

"He took his victims to the people in that house. He said they were too weak to go out hunting themselves. That's how I justified it when he finally told me what he was doing and by that time it was too late to get out. I knew that, even if he wasn't like *slashing* anybody or anything, what he was doing was still murder. It's like the Nazis who lined people up for the gas chamber. Even if they weren't the ones turning on the showerhead, they were still killing these people. And I wondered what they did to the victims. Thought maybe it would have been more merciful to kill them beforehand. I saw what some of the corpses looked like when they came back out.

"Like I said, it was too late at that point. There was something about him I was hooked on. He had *changed* in some way or the other. Those people that he had met up with had changed him, I was sure of that. They had some kind of *power* over him and he was able to exert this power over people. That's how he could kidnap them so easily. *That's* how we never got caught. All that shit he told you back there about the van being some kind of a decoy is totally wrong. He had *their* protection. How else can you explain getting pulled over ten times and, each time, you know the trooper who pulled you over was looking for a specific vehicle and a specific person that fit the description of Bones and each time they came to the window, they never even bothered looking at his driver's license? They just took one look into his eyes and told him they had made a mistake and he was free to continue on to wherever he was going. More than once I wanted to cry out to them. I wanted to come clean and tell them what he was doing. Still, though, I went along with it. I figured the only reason I was even able to have these thoughts was because I never came face to face with those people, so their power wasn't as strong over me as it was over Bones. But I wanted to see them. And that was part of Bones' power over me.

"I *begged* him to take me to them. I let him do things to me that he had asked for since meeting me. I let him hurt me more than he already had until I was reduced to a sad lump of nothing. I *had* to meet them. Part of me wanted to be changed in the same way he was but I think there was another part of me that just wanted to be able to go along with this as casually as Bones did. But he wouldn't take me to them. It was like they were *his* big secret. Of course, now I realize what I wanted was change. My brain was telling my body I couldn't go on like this. If I wasn't sixteen and resilient I probably would have been dead.

"So, eventually, we ran out of money and had to start living out of the van which meant that I had to go on these kidnappings with Bones. It also meant that the drugs were gone. Forced detox. Not fun. I was able to deal with it, with what Bones was doing. Detoxing like that, I was totally out of my head. I felt psychotic. I *liked* seeing other people in as much pain as I imagined I was in. I even helped out from time to time. He would take them somewhere, always making me stay in the van, and come back empty handed... *most* of the time. But these strange people were selective about who they would take and sometimes they would turn him away with one of them. I don't know why. They murdered them, maybe drank a little of their blood, but they didn't want to keep them. So Bones would drag these corpses back into the van and then *we* would have to get rid of them. But even that's not what made me finally decide to leave Bones.

"Even though things just kept getting worse and worse. We hardly fucked anymore. We never bathed so even the idea of fucking was sort of gross. The van smelled... Well, you know about the van. Everything that had seemed so shiny and new just a year ago had deteriorated. Gone *way* past deterioration, actually. I'd find myself at a truck stop while Bones was off and I'd try and hook up with some of the sickest looking truckers there. Just to satisfy *something*. One of the many desires I had. Most of them wouldn't even look twice at me. How bad is that? I was *that* crazed and smelly and disgusting. Still, I was there with Bones rather than on the phone to Mommy and Daddy... It was like some part of my brain was still stuck in an unusual place. So I guess you're wondering what *did* make me leave, huh?"

"A little," Rachel said, but she didn't know if she really wanted to or not. Already, she had found herself grimacing with nearly every sentence from Rain's mouth.

"About a month ago, he kidnapped this girl. She was about our age, maybe younger. Beautiful. Even me, jealous as I am, could admit she was beautiful. So Bones took her into these people and came out a little bit later with the fresh corpse of this girl. We had to go somewhere to drop the body and I must have fell asleep or something. Anyway, when I woke up, I could hear Bones grunting. I was in the passenger seat and when I looked back at him he was on top of the girl, fucking her corpse. Her dead eyes were all filmed over and staring right at me and I... I just felt something whoosh out of me. I wanted to throw up or scream at him to stop or something but I just turned around and pretended to be asleep because I thought he would get really mad if he knew I saw him doing that.

"After that, I couldn't look at him the same way again. There were just so many things wrong with that. I didn't know him anymore. Didn't *want* to know him. So I had my revelation. Maybe it was because the drugs were out of my system or something. I knew I was part of the reason that girl was there. She had died, in part, because of me. Worst of all, I realized that she *was* me. A beautiful girl of fourteen or fifteen. I thought of the way I had looked before Bones and the drugs and all the other guys... I wanted that. I wanted to be that way again.

"Mostly I just avoided him, waiting to meet up with someone who could help me. I started stealing clothes from thrift stores and at least bathing in the truck stop restrooms. I was tired of being a pig. I was tired of... everything."

"Jesus," Rachel whispered.

"That's pretty much it."

"I would hope so."

Rachel reached out and grabbed Rain's cold hand, trying to comfort her in the only way she really knew how.

"Rain, Bones is behind you now. All of that's behind you. Maybe you can help me and Jacob. I think the people who got their claws in Bones might be the Devils. Or, at least what *we* call the Devils. But Lynchville is not like other towns. Never has been. We need people to help us in the fight. We need to get rid of these people."

"I'd like to. I'd really like to do that. I think that if we hadn't found you, then I would have killed myself eventually. Maybe I just felt some kind of connection with you."

Rachel didn't want to elaborate too much on that. She didn't want to explain to Rain how, ever since her encounter with the Devils, she was able to exert a little bit of this power over people as well. How she could kind of feel their consciousness in her fist... and *bend* it, pull it into her. Sometimes. It didn't work all the time. It wouldn't have worked with Bones. She wasn't the only one the Devils had changed. Jacob had had vivid visions ever since that day. He said his psychiatrist called them waking hallucinations. Most of them featured the Devils.

And fire.

And murder. Something like sacrifice.

The girls reached the edge of the woods and the cemetery loomed in front of them, stretching up its broad slope, ground fog wrapping its ethereal fingers around the aged tombstones.

"We're pretty close to Jacob's now," Rachel said, continuing to hold Rain's hand as they walked through the milky night, in between the rows of tombstones where, earlier, two others had coupled on ground meant to cover the dead.

Nine

Jacob stood in the middle of the living room, staring down at the broken twisted remains of the television, blood dripping from his right hand. The beating he had administered to the TV made him a little more tired but it didn't make him feel any less scared. Bad stuff was still coming, he knew. He couldn't put the thought out of his head.

He was restless, wanting to do something but not sure what.

He went into the kitchen to put some coffee on.

While the coffee brewed, he bandaged his wounds.

Once properly, if unprofessionally, bandaged he cleaned up the vomit on the living room and uprighted the corn plant in front of the windows, throwing down some towels where the rain had blown in.

That done, he went back into the kitchen, grabbed a white ceramic mug from the cupboard and poured a cup of very strong black coffee. He filched a cigarette from the breast pocket of his shirt and headed back out onto the balcony.

He sat down on the damp weather-beaten wooden chair he kept out there, surveying the chilly night surrounding him.

How could something so beautiful be so dangerous? He was thinking about both the town and the night.

Smoking his cigarette, he relished the impenetrable silence around him. He tried not to think about anything in particular, tried to go blank, but he couldn't help it. His mind went in circles, continually thinking about the image he had seen on the TV, substituting Rachel for Mr. Leavingworth, flashing back to two years ago... the people in the woods. The whole twisted night. The violence of it all. The Devils.

People could tell him they didn't exist.

They could tell him there were no such things as Devils.

He wouldn't believe them.

He saw more that night, *felt* more that night and every night since to think that it was anything other than something supernatural. The unexplained. Wasn't "supernatural" the word we used to explain the unexplained.

Teenage boys hunting and trying to kill a teenage girl was natural. It was nature. It was nature at its most cruelly debased level but it *did* exist within the realm of human nature.

People who became monsters... who became something else, was not natural. That was what Jacob couldn't explain. That was super-natural—outside the realm of *human* nature.

And there was more.

So much more.

His thoughts were feverish and circular, relentless.

He quickly finished his cigarette and tossed it out onto the street, wishing it wasn't the only thing he could cast away.

He went into the bathroom to take a hot shower and change clothes, wash away the dirtiness of this evening and put on a fresh skin. Might as well start his day early. He didn't think he would be getting any sleep tonight.

Ten

Bones stood in the cold night listening to the sluggish chirping of the bugs in the distant woods.

Fucking bitches, he thought.

After giving chase to the girls and losing them once they got over the road he had come back to this strange little hollow where he had brought the van. The house was in front of him and that meant those people were in there. If they weren't there, Bones knew, he would not be able to see the house.

It never ceased to amaze him, this world of magic these people had brought him into. And this house. This house that followed them like they were turtles and it was their shell or something.

Bones didn't want to go inside but knew he would have to. If he simply tried to escape them, they would hunt him down. They would find him. And then it would be like the last time. The time in Illinois when he could not find a single person to bring to them. The time when he had almost gutted Rain in her sleep just so he wouldn't have to feel their wrath. Just so he could please them. He wanted so much to please them. He loved being in the house as long as he had some bleating, pleading prey in tow.

He didn't want this to turn out like last time.

That wound had not yet healed. It ran, a jagged zigzag down his spine.

They had opened him up, told him they needed blood, and they had suckled from him. The cut was really nothing more than a flesh wound but it stung his pride and it hurt him to sit upright.

Ilya and Ernst. Ernst and Ilya. Anything to please them.

He had never told Rain he knew their names. He didn't want to share with her. And he guessed, deep down, he just hadn't trusted her. He knew she would try some shit like the stunt she pulled tonight. He was certain he would be the one laughing in the end. Ernst and Ilya did not like people to get away. They didn't like people existing who knew their secrets. Or maybe they didn't mind if they existed, they just wanted to drag them down to where they were, somewhere deep within the house, wherever the house happened to be.

That was another reason Bones dreaded confronting them with tonight's escapee. Bones knew all about Rachel Stokes. He had received sort of a briefing before going to invade her house. She had burned them in the past. They didn't go into great detail and Bones had enough sense to know this was because she had somehow put one over on them, making them feel stupid, making them feel less powerful. She had, somehow, *hurt* them.

And he had blown it. Now she would have her guard up. If this girl had defeated them in the past then he guessed it was entirely possible for her to beat them again and this agitated Bones. It meant all the hard work he had put into this thing, all those innocent people he had killed, had all been for nothing. He didn't want to let that happen. He wanted to see this thing through to the end, until he was like Ernst and Ilya.

Powerful.

Bones stopped at the van, reached in, and pulled his pack of cigarettes from the console in between the two front seats. He lit his cigarette and stared at the house while he smoked.

Sometimes he wondered what he had gotten himself into but that was only fleeting. Soon, the world would be his and never mind if that stupid bitch didn't want to come along for the ride. She obviously didn't have the stomach for it anyway. A weak will. She couldn't carry through with anything. He would see to it she died before he left this sad little town that was so important to Ernst and Ilya.

Thinking of how he would destroy Rain diverted him from his doubts and led him through the smoking of his cigarette. It would be beautiful, when he finally put his hands on her again. He knew he would have to fuck her before killing her. He wasn't about to hand her over to them without having at least one last little taste for himself. Rachel Stokes might be theirs but Rain, Rain was his. And he wanted that to be the last thing she remembered before dying so she knew what she was missing by running out on him.

Bones tossed his cigarette out into the oily-looking grass and approached the house.

He walked up the crooked steps and, without knocking, pushed the door open.

Zack slept on the couch.

Bones didn't like Zack at all. He had been with them since California and he was clearly Ernst and Ilya's favorite. Bones didn't have any idea why. The boy seemed so weak, almost effeminate. And he didn't have to kill. He only had to bring people to Ernst and Ilya. Keepers, as Bones thought of them. Those that stayed in the house. Below.

These were not cast-offs. These were going to be part of the army of the Devils, dead souls to swell the ranks and make them more powerful. Bones didn't really know how Ernst and Ilya determined some people were keepers and some people were meat. He figured it wasn't his place to question that. Besides, since Bones had been given his special task, that may have changed. Maybe now Zack *was* doing the grocery shopping.

He wanted to spit on Zack, sleeping so peacefully there on the couch. He hadn't done a damn thing since California. He had merely sat around reading some damn book Ernst had given him, a book Bones wasn't allowed to read. And now he was in the process of seducing some high school girl Bones figured held some interest for Ernst and Ilya. Probably getting a little on the side from her. Fucking fag.

No one was around. What would it hurt? he thought.

He coughed some phlegm into the back of his throat and projected it out toward the sleeping boy. It landed on his shoulder, quivering there with Zack's breathing. He didn't stir and Bones guessed it didn't really solve anything but it made him feel a lot better. Like he had one on Zack now. Next time maybe he would think about slicing his throat while he slept there. That way he could be Ernst and Ilya's favorite and put any question of who was better out of their minds.

Bones knew exactly where they were. They would be under the house. All he had to do was walk to the back of the house and go around to the underside of the staircase. There was a door there that led downstairs. Bones wasn't really supposed to go down there on his own but they had led him down there a couple of times. It wasn't anything spectacular. Of course, the only thing he had seen was the main room, occupied by a large table where Ernst and Ilya took their sacrifices. They never let Bones watch them eat. He didn't even know why this was something he wanted to do other than he thought he could watch Ilya do just about anything.

She was the real reason he was doing all of this.

Ilya had become something like his entire reason for existing these past few months. He thought about her all the time. He wanted to be Ernst just so he could be near Ilya. Everything he did, he did with the hope Ilya would let him touch her. It didn't even have to be in a sexual way. He killed for just momentary contact with her. He didn't know how long he could resist before he might try something that would get him killed. Still, if it meant dying with his tongue in her mouth or his dick between her legs, then he thought it might be worth it.

Bones opened the door beneath the staircase, the blue light stronger down there, coming up to meet his eyes.

He took a deep breath and slowly descended the stairs.

About halfway down, the stairs changed from old worn wood to stone. Bones nearly slipped with the transition. There wasn't any kind of banister to hold onto. He went slowly, feeling the death grow more palpable with each step. That was the only way he knew of to really explain it. Above, in the house, above the ground, things and people were alive. Below the house, there was nothing but death. The smell of it, dark and fruity, seeped from the stones around him.

There were ghosts beneath the house. Or something like ghosts.

Bones had always thought of them as ghosts with teeth. In the end, that was really what Ilya and Ernst were—ghosts with teeth. They were things more than people. Things that had died a long time ago and, having somehow escaped the clutches of death, had also managed to escape many of the physical trappings of life. He had heard their stories. He had heard them from Zack and he had heard them from some of the people he had met while passing through the whole haunted country. While not everyone knew of them as the Devils, he didn't have to go far to find a tale about a man or a woman. A horrifying vision in a nightmare. An eater of the soul. A taker of children. A myth. A legend.

While it was their beauty and their power that had initially attracted Bones to them, it was also their beauty and their power that held him in fear. Whatever they told him to do, he would do it, because he was terrified of them. And as more time passed, as he saw more and more of Ilya and Ernst, the more his fear grew. The more his fear grew, the more his respect grew. The more his respect grew, the more he wanted to be like them.

The stairway ended at a heavy wooden door. This was the door Bones was never allowed to enter without knocking. There were many times he had wanted to brazenly swing the door open, trying to catch them at something they didn't want him to see. To get just a taste of the deeper mystery.

Bones took a deep breath and knocked on the door.

"Enter," he heard Ernst say from the other side.

Bones put his hand on the old iron handle and pushed the door open.

Ernst and Ilya sat at the large stone table that looked like it had somehow grown from the stone of the floor. It never mattered where they were, what state or town they were in, this scene was always the same. There wasn't any explanation for it, Bones knew.

"Hi," Bones said, feeling dumb. He never knew how to greet them.

Neither of them said anything. They simply stared at him.

"You lost her," Ilya said.

Bones nearly corrected her and said, "*Them*. I lost them." But he thought better of that. He didn't want a bad situation to seem even worse.

"Yes," Bones said. He guessed they could tell by his injuries.

"This is unacceptable," Ilya said.

"I know."

"If you know," Ilya said, "then why did you bother coming at all. Why didn't you run off when you had the chance?"

"Because I wanted to let you know I could make it up to you."

Ilya smiled. It was a sick smile. It didn't make Bones feel good at all. It was the kind of smile somebody wore when they were making fun of you.

"I'm sorry to say there isn't going to be another chance."

"Whaddya mean?"

"This is the end of the line."

"But I want to continue on with you."

"There is no continuing on. This is where we stop. This is where we belong."

"Give me one more night. I promise I'll bring you someone to-morrow. Hell, I could even bring you someone by morning, if you give me another chance."

"No. It had to be her. You're finished now."

Bones felt anger flicker up through his body. "It can't be over. Not just like that. Not after all I've done."

"It can if we say that is how it is going to be. What do you expect to get from us anyway?"

"I want to be like you."

"What does that mean?" Ilya asked. "Everyone seems to be say-ing that, 'I want to be like you.' But you don't have any idea as to who or what we are."

"Oh, I think I have a pretty good idea."

Ernst stood up, unfurling his height, and looked at Bones.

"I have something I want to show you," he said.

"I'd like to see anything you have to show me," Bones said.

"Follow me, then."

Ernst turned to his right and walked across the large stone room. Bones followed him. There was a door on that side of the room, to

Bones' left, that he had never noticed before. He wondered what was going to be in the room. He wondered if Ernst was about to show him the big secret, the thing that would help him to understand all of this.

Ernst pulled on the heavy door and it swung out from the frame.

The room was dark, not lighted up in the deathly blue that lighted the other rooms of the house. Ernst walked slowly over to a wall and held his hand up to a candle. He touched his finger to the wick and the candle came alive, bathing the room in a shimmering soft orange light.

Bones heard the whimpers before he saw the other thing in the room.

It had been hiding in the corner and now it half-crawled, half-walked out into the middle of the room.

Bones stared at the thing, trying to figure out what it was. It looked like it had once been human. There was something about it that reminded him of the Elephant Man in that creepy black and white movie he had seen as a child. It just didn't look right. It was like it had all human parts but they were put on all wrong. Its arms dangled limply away from its body. It wore only a tattered old loin cloth of sorts. Knobs ran up its ribs. Its toes curved more out than in while the feet themselves seemed to be going in the opposite directions.

"What do you think of it?" Ernst asked.

Bones didn't know what to say. He thought it was horrible but he didn't know if that was what Ernst wanted to hear. He knew he was already on thin ice and he wanted to think carefully about any questions he was going to answer.

Ernst supplied the answer for him. "Hideous, isn't it?"

"Yeah."

"Do you know who that is?"

"I have no idea."

"That is the last person who messed up."

A sharp spike of terror jabbed at Bones' spine. His throat closed. His heart shimmied. It was like the whole illusion he had been led to believe was now shattered and he wanted to get as far away from it as he possibly could.

"The last person we trusted," Ernst said.

Run, he thought.

He could still do that, couldn't he? Sure, he had never seen Ilya or Ernst move in any way other than that creepy crawly horror movie villain style and he thought if he just turned and bolted then he would be able to make it safely out of the house and into the night and then he could get into his van and disappear completely. Forget he had ever seen the Devils. If he could just get to the van then he could get away from all this. Ernst and Ilya didn't have a van. If he could get there then he had absolutely no doubt he could find safety and freedom somewhere.

Or he could go after Ilya. Leap on her. Press his nose against her scent. Ram his hand up that dress and feel the magic between her legs.

His muscles tightened and he turned, legs already bending to charge ahead.

He ran into Ernst who felt as hard as rock and fell down to the ground, onto the actual rock. Not much difference. Somehow Ernst had managed to position himself in front of the door faster than Bones could have imagined anyone moving.

Ernst bent down and pulled him up, whispering into his ear.

"You didn't want this to be your fate, did you?"

"No. God no," Bones slobbered. All sanity had left his head with the thought of becoming like that thing behind him. And he could see it happening. He knew, in that instant, that he was absolutely nothing to Ilya and Ernst. Little more than a slave.

"I know. It hardly seems fair, does it? But think about it, Mr. Latch needs to eat too. Isn't that right, Mr. Latch?"

"Eeeeeat," the thing grumbled from behind him, drool running down what passed as the thing's chin.

"We have other things planned for you. But, as you may realize by now, you are not just a body, you are also a spirit. Mr. Latch needs some of your body and we need some of your spirit."

Ernst tossed Bones back toward the creature. Bones wanted to fight but Ernst kept talking and the entire time he talked, Bones could feel him reaching into his brain or something, shutting down all of the mechanisms that made him want to kick and scream. While he felt Ernst reaching in, he felt the thing's hands and mouth all over his body. He heard the popping of his skin just under Ernst's whisperings. He felt strips of his skin being pulled away from his body as his head was shoved down onto the floor, there to sniff up this creature's excrement and piss scent.

"Mr. Latch failed us many years ago," Ernst said. "We didn't know what to do with him. At that time, we were not so divided into flesh and spirit. We thought the human body could undergo transformations. We thought we could shape people like clay. Like a sculpture. Something to look at, nothing more. A work of art— beautiful in its brutality. Something to decorate our lives with. We decided to experiment with what the human body could do. And we needed a punishment for Mr. Latch. So we pulled him down here, down into the darkness, where no one could hear his screams as we broke his bones, one by one. But we didn't want him to heal in the way he was supposed to heal. No. We wanted him to heal how *we* wanted him to heal. We wanted him to look different. We wanted him to look not human. So we set his bones nearly oppo- site how they were supposed to grow. I imagine the healing process was twice as long as it was supposed to be and probably twice as painful. But we had all the time in the world. If there is one thing the dead have, it is time. I think it was this vast amount of time that drove us nearly insane, drove us to do some of the things we would not have otherwise done. But we were like morphine to Mr. Latch. We didn't let the pain get too out of hand. Imagine it, Bones, imagine burning up with pain until you feel Ilya's lips on you, her tongue moving over all of the broken twisted places. Imagine..."

Bones wanted to imagine but he could barely think. Mr. Latch's mouth was burrowed somewhere below his arm, in the flesh, and Bones thought he could feel a large snake-like tongue move around the joint of his shoulder.

And then Ernst's hand was wrapped around Bones' bloody wrist and Ernst was dragging him somewhere away from Mr. Latch.

Bones' thoughts became as much blackness as thought.

He remembered the heat of a fire. He remembered being bound by something that felt like a harness. The bone dry kiss of the flame. The hiss of his skin burning up, his blood boiling. The freedom of falling through the air. Falling into fire. He was pretty sure that was when he died. He never really thought of feeling himself die before but he could. He felt his body drop away, drop down into the fire and he felt his spirit lift up from the body, weightless and unrestrained. And he felt his spirit returning to Ilya and Ernst, there to sit by their side, away from his prison of skin. They were his liberators and he was here to do what they wanted him to do.

Quietly, Bones' spirit listened as they told him about the future.

Eleven

Jacob stepped out of the shower, relishing his new clean feeling, and stood amidst the swirling steam in the bathroom. Even though he had lived alone for a while, he still couldn't get used to the idea of showering with the door open. Tonight, he had also locked the door. That was something he never did. Maybe it had something to do with *Psycho*. It probably had more to do with the events of earlier. He pulled on a clean pair of Levis and a black t-shirt, the closest he had ever come to wearing a uniform.

Stepping out into the apartment, he squinted at the harsh lighting. After demolishing the television, he had turned on every light in the apartment, hoping to chase away the twisted horrors lurking in the shadowed corners. He went into the kitchen, poured himself another cup of coffee, tasting slightly burned at this point, and lit another cigarette. He thought he could feel the black bags developing under his eyes.

He crossed the living room and put a compilation CD he had made a while ago into the player. He never marked these things and didn't really have any idea what was on it. After the player took a second to load the CD, a Flaming Lips song filled the apartment. Jacob found this agreeable. Their music had always made him a little happier and, settling back onto the couch, he thought he could almost feel the horrors of the night ease up a bit.

Then his door banged open and everything came back in a surging wave of acidic saltwater. He spilled coffee all over himself, ducking in front of the couch, going down in a sparkle of cigarette ash.

"Jacob, it's me," Rachel said quickly.

He stood up slowly, his clean clothes now soiled with coffee, his heart hammering in his chest. Finding out it was just Rachel didn't make him feel any better. One look at her sent his adrenaline pounding again. He felt scared and angry at the same time.

She looked as though she had been beaten. And there was a stranger with her. He tried to make some things fit together in his brain but he couldn't do it. He stood there, unable to really say anything, shaking with confusion and anger.

He put the now mostly empty mug of coffee on the end table, crushing out the cigarette in the teeming ashtray.

"Who the hell did that to you?" he asked from across the couch, already walking around it, coming toward Rachel.

She sighed. He couldn't see any of the fear he thought he should have seen in her eyes.

"Well, that's a long story."

Jacob couldn't begin to ask her all the questions shooting around inside him. Was it one of the Devils? Had everything come back? Are they still after you? How did you escape? Who is this person you're with? How bad was it this time? What do we need to do to find some shred of safety?

Instead, he said nothing. He approached Rachel and took her in his arms, smelling smoke and outside and blood and grass and dirt.

"Are you okay?" he asked.

"Yeah. I think so."

He released her and held her at arm's length, sizing up her wounds. It was mostly dirt and some sizable red blotches that would probably turn into bruises. Her face was the worst, covered in dried blood. Her feet and legs looked like they had been switched. She favored her left foot, the right barely touching the floor.

"This is Rain..." Rachel said, motioning to the girl beside her, searching her mind for her last name, wondering if the girl had ever given it to her.

"Rain Hanson," the girl said, holding her hand out to Jacob.

Rachel felt a very brief flicker of jealousy.

Jacob took her hand in a gentle shake and said, "Jacob Riley." He normally avoided eye contact but searched Rain's for some clue as to why she was there. He got nothing. Like many people he had come into contact with she had learned to mask her emotions, hide her past.

"Nice to meet you. You have a really great girlfriend."

"I know," he said. "The best."

He hugged Rachel close and said, "So are you going to tell me what happened?"

"Of course I will but there're some things I need to do first."

"Anything."

"Well, I think we'd both like to take a shower. And if, through some divine intervention, you don't have any coffee made, you could put some on. I think we have a lot of talking we need to do."

"Okay," he said. "Go, shower, get clean. You can get some of my clothes out of the dresser in the bedroom. You probably have some stuff in there." Jacob could never figure out how so many of Rachel's clothes ended up in his apartment. She had never officially moved in, bringing over her wardrobe and all that but, to the best of his knowledge, she had never gone home naked either.

"Come on," she said to Rain, pulling the girl behind her.

He watched them retreat into the bathroom and went into the kitchen to make a fresh pot of coffee, amazed at how much more comfortable women seemed to be around each other. While in the kitchen, he found a dish towel and swabbed off some of the wetter areas of his clothes. Lighting another cigarette, he sat on the first couch and listened to a Leonard Cohen song and the soft murmur of the shower from the bathroom. Of all the things he could have thought about, he found himself wondering if they would have enough hot water to last them an entire shower. He figured Rachel must have had a rough night. She didn't even notice the state of his apartment. Namely, the TV that was piled up against the wall across from the couch.

He would wait until Rachel came out, then they could exchange their nightmares as they had on so many other evenings.

The terror had come back. He could feel it beating a tattoo against the back of his brain. Curiously, he felt more alive than he had in over a year.

Maybe this feeling of aliveness was coupled with the fact that he knew Rachel was all right. Knowing that seemed to remove at least one major burden from his psyche, never mind that her current state opened up a whole new level of questions. He sat on the couch, his back to the bathroom door, staring out the windows at the dark night. Birds chirped from out on the balcony. Dawn would be coming on soon. A chronic insomniac, he had seen more than his share of dawns.

First there were the birds. These were followed by the occasional car door slamming, the engine humming to life as its owner warmed it for the drive to work. And then there was the first light of dawn and this seemed to wake everything up. The birds went crazy, screeching and flapping. A steady stream of traffic poured beneath his window. The voices of kids walking to school. The squeal of school bus brakes. He thought of all of these as signals. They were signals telling him he wasn't alone and that there were other people out there. People who did not want to kill him or kidnap him. Kind people. Everyday people. *Alive* people.

Yes. There were alive people out there. He knew it. He heard them every day and he wondered why it seemed that every day, he was just one step closer to death, one step closer to joining the worms in the moist ground.

But those were lonely thoughts and he wasn't alone now. Rachel was in the other room and she had brought a friend and soon the whole town would be awake and swarming on the street below him. That still seemed like an eternity away. He knew it was only then that he would be able to lie down and finally get some rest. So often, the sounds of the town waking up had sung him to sleep.

The gentle gurgling slush of the shower water stopped and the bathroom door opened. He turned to see the girls, wrapped in towels, head into the bedroom. A moment later they came out, each of them wearing a combination of his and Rachel's clothing. Rachel wore a pair of her baggy cargo shorts with one of his t-shirts that looked huge on her. Rain wore a smaller pair of Rachel's khaki shorts and one of Jacob's t-shirts. The girls' legs were pale and bruised. Rachel looked better now that she had washed the blood off but there were still blotches of red on her face and a series of cuts along her legs. She had a gauze bandage around her right foot.

She sat down on the floor in front of Jacob and said, "Give me a cigarette."

"You don't smoke," he reminded her.

"I do now. Don't hoard. Give." She extended her hand.

He proffered the pack to her. She shook one out and lit it up, looking awkward. Rain pulled her battered pack of cigarettes from her jacket and lit up. Feeling left out, Jacob decided to have another cigarette himself.

"We're going to make it smell like a bar in here." He went into the kitchen to get them some coffee.

"Yeah," Rachel said. "Except bars have TVs."

So she *had* noticed.

"Yeah. That…" He handed mugs to the girls.

"You didn't like what was on? Maybe you're a rageaholic."

"Something like that. It's been a strange fucking night."

"Tell me about it." Rachel looked knowingly at Rain.

"So you've made a new friend," Jacob said.

"More like an ally."

Rain nodded.

"To fight the good fight?"

"Is there any other kind?"

"Not that I know of. So, you want to tell me what happened to you first?"

"Sure."

"Well, I guess we should think about things for just a second. Are we safe here? Do we need to disappear? Are you still being followed? Someone did *do* this to you, didn't they? It wasn't like a freak bicycle accident or something, was it?"

"Yes, someone did this to us and, are we really going to feel safe anywhere? Do we have anywhere else to go?"

"Probably not."

"Then I guess this is as good a place as any, wouldn't you say?"

"Yeah, I guess I would say."

"I thought I was safe in my house too but I was wrong." Rachel turned slightly toward Rain. "That was something we didn't talk about. Just how the hell did you and that fuckhead get into my house?"

"I'm a little confused," Jacob said.

"Okay, well, this is how I spent my evening. I went outside because I thought I heard a sound and there was a mangled cat that I fixed up and then when I went back into my house, I was attacked and dragged into my closet. I haven't stopped to think about that yet. How did you know my closet had that... what was it, a trapdoor or something?"

Rain looked guiltily at the floor, taking a hesitant puff of her cigarette.

"Bones said the people told him that would be there. He said these people knew this town better than they knew any other place because they had been here so long. Apparently, they have been making people disappear for quite some time. He said their power and influence is not as far reaching as it once was. Anyway, most of the houses were built by the same builder in this town, over the span of about ten years. The builder was drawn into this thing, this fucking cult or whatever the hell it is. So he built all of the houses with this hidden door in the back of the closet. Essentially it isn't there. It is just a piece of loose drywall that is caulked a little bit and then painted over so, from the outside, you have no real idea that it's there. But all it takes is like a sharp blow to knock this panel off. And that led to kind of a tunnel. There are tunnels running under just about all of these houses. They come out in the river. I'm really quite surprised someone hasn't found out about them. I guess people don't really want to believe evil truly does exist below the surface of their town.

"Probably try and pass them off as historical or something. But really, they were made so the people involved in this cult or religion or whatever could sneak out without being seen. The cult could go out into that field and have a service that involved half the town and the other half would think they were tucked away safe and sound in their homes."

"Wait," Jacob said. "You helped *kidnap* Rachel?"

She took a final drag from her cigarette and crushed it out.

"Yeah," she said, meeting Jacob's accusatory stare. He could see a bit of the rebellious child she undoubtedly had been. "I guess I did."

Rachel interjected. "But I've forgiven her that. In the end, she helped save my life."

Rachel proceeded to tell Jacob about her evening. She didn't like the way his face dropped as she told him more and more. Every word out of her mouth was just further confirmation of their unified suspicions.

As Rachel spoke, she went into the kitchen and poured cups of coffee for each of them, never breaking stride in her narrative. She seemed to have a natural storytelling quality and Jacob found it difficult to look over her objective manner and see the reality in any of this. It was like listening to someone talk about a dream or read a book. Once she was finished relaying her adventure of the night, Jacob immediately set about grilling Rain.

"So you know a lot more about this than we do, at this point?"

"Well, I don't really know how much I know."

"Please tell us what you do know."

"Okay. I don't even know their names. I've already told Rachel some of this but I think she was pretty thorough in her account. I know we started in California. But Lynchville seems to be some kind of final destination. Apparently, it holds a lot of meaning for them. For nearly the past year, they have demanded that Bones bring them sacrifices, nearly every night. Not exactly every night. I couldn't really find any kind of pattern to this. I was messed up for a large part of the time and some of the days seemed to run together and sometimes I think two weeks must have felt like a day and vice versa. When I asked him why he was doing it, he said it was because he had to. Because they demanded it of him."

"Did you see these people he took the victims to at all?"

"No, but like Rachel said, there is a man and a woman."

"So, if most of your boyfriend's attacks had been of random people, why did he choose Rachel? I mean, of all the closets to crawl through, it seems like sort of a coincidence you guys chose hers."

"Oh, well, she was the exception. Bones didn't choose her. He said the people were very specific and he couldn't fuck this up. See, this whole thing started because he wanted to be whatever it is they are and he thought that bringing them Rachel was going to be the thing that would, hell, I don't know, get him into the fold or something like that."

"Did he say why?"

"The only thing he said was that she was a very special person to them and they needed her."

"Do you have any idea what these things are?"

"I haven't really thought about them too much because it scares me. I've seen enough of what they can do, like with their control over Bones and everything, that I've been really really scared. I think fear was one of the reasons I didn't split with Bones sooner. It was like once I knew I was involved in it, I felt like I kind of had to stay."

"But you went with Bones when he dropped his victims off to these people, right?"

"Sometimes. I mean I was never allowed to go in or anything like that."

"Go in where?"

"Where the people stay."

"And what kind of place did these people stay in?"

"I don't know. I never saw it. He would just take the van out to a secluded place and say he was going to take them to the house. I never wanted to tell him I didn't see a fucking house because if you disagree with him then he has a tendency to get really violent so I just pretended I saw a house."

"Do you think that *he* saw this house? Did he ever describe it to you?"

"No, I never had him describe it to me but I'm pretty sure that, if he didn't see it, then at least he thought he saw it."

"Didn't you ever watch him go into the house?"

"No. I was usually in tears at that point."

"Why were you in tears?"

"Because I wanted him to stop. He was okay back in California but now he was just a creepy serial killer. A serial killer who can never be caught because he doesn't really operate in this reality and I was having a hard time just looking him in the eye. I didn't want to watch him do this thing he apparently loved to do. Every night he left with one of his victims, it felt like he was leaving me and I guess it just made me kind of mad. I didn't want any part in it."

"Now I think *you* have some talking to do, TV-buster," Rachel said, disrupting his assault.

"Wait, wait, I'm not finished just yet. Now's the part where we talk about her like she isn't even here, okay?" He looked at Rain and said, "So... pretend you're not here."

"Am I allowed to defend myself?"

"Could you defend yourself if you weren't here?"

Rain shook her head.

"Then no," Jacob said, turning to where his back was nearly to her, even though she sat right next to him on the couch. "Okay," Jacob asked Rachel. "What do you know about this Rain character?"

Rachel slipped into her mock serious tone. Anyone else would have thought she was humoring Jacob but he knew this was how she sounded when she was being completely honest. "Well, Jake, to be perfectly honest with you, I don't really know that much about her at all."

"She tried to kill you."

"I don't think she really tried to kill me. She was just, you know, *in love.*"

"Then what was she trying to do?"

"She was helping her boyfriend."

"Do you think she still has feelings for him? I mean, how do you know it wasn't just some kind of ruse so she could, ultimately, get to the both of us? You know how much they would like to get to the both of us."

"You heard her say she was hammered half the time. Once the magic of the drugs wore off she saw him for what he really was and, believe me, it wasn't pretty. So I don't think it's just that she fell out of love with him. I think she was very smart. Biding her time. It's all about self-preservation. In the end, if we bring those fucks down, then a lot more people will end up safe than would have if Rain had been killed when she wanted to first get away from him."

Jacob continued haranguing Rachel in this fashion, staring at her all the while.

Rachel stared at Rain.

Rain stared at the floor.

"Jesus, Jacob, you're starting to sound paranoid," Rachel finally blurted.

"I've been paranoid my whole life. You know that. There isn't a reason to change now."

"To answer your main concern—once again: No. I don't think she just came along because she has grand dreams of finishing what he started."

"But how do you *know* this?"

"She tried to *stab* him."

"Sometimes we hurt the ones we love the most."

"Now you're just being facetious."

"I don't know what that means."

"Neither do I."

"So," Jacob said, letting the word hang in the brightness of the room. "The real question is this: *Can we trust her?*"

Rachel paused for a moment, looking hard at Rain, who sat on the couch with the grave look of a defendant awaiting a jury decision.

It was actually a pretty good question. Rain had not painted the most flattering portrait of herself. She ran away from home. She got hooked on drugs. She fucked other guys while she was with Bones. Sometimes for drugs. She had initially gone along with the murders. Could she be trusted to focus on the task at hand? Could she be trusted not to sneak into Jacob's bed and fuck his brains out at night? The real question, she guessed, was: Could Rain be rehabilitated? Could she actually be among a minority of people who had actually decided to make a change in their lives?

"Yes," Rachel said. "I think we can trust her. She has pluck."

"We need pluck."

"God knows you don't have any."

"I mask my pluck in a deep layer of sloth."

"You mask it in a deep layer of shit."

"Such language."

"The TV. It's broken. You were still awake when we got here. Look like you haven't slept much at all. Explain."

"It's not pretty, subject-changer."

"I need to hear."

"And you will. You'll hear everything. I think maybe we should rest first though." He gestured over toward Rain, now reclined against the arm of the couch, taking one very slow blink. "I think our guest might be tired."

"No, I'm okay. I'm awake," she said. "I just feel kind of beaten."

Rachel smiled and Jacob knew they were not going to sleep without him telling his end of the story. "It's settled then," she said. "It'll be a bedtime story."

"You won't like this bedtime story."

"Then I just want to hear the sound of your voice. Fucking humor me."

"Fine," Jacob said, launching into his account of the whole strange evening, beginning with how he came home to the crazy landlady and carrying them all the way up to when he decided pne television must be stopped, lest it strike again.

While Rachel stopped him every now and then to make witty, pithless little interjections, Rain was totally silent but awake and more alert than she had looked a few moments ago. Jacob stood up, pulled another cigarette from the pack and handed one to Rachel saying, "You're gonna get hooked."

"I've been hooked before. At this rate, I don't think I'll live long enough to get lung cancer. I have to pee."

She went into the bathroom and Jacob motioned for Rain to stand up from the couch.

"You're sitting on our bed," he said.

"Oh, sorry." She stood up and moved out of the way while Jacob threw the cushions off the couch and pulled out the mattress.

"Quaint, isn't it?"

"Very."

"So, you were pretty quiet during that whole thing. What are *you* thinking?"

She kind of shrugged, looking resigned. Rachel came out of the bathroom and Jacob knew that, by the sheer small size of the apartment, she had heard his question.

"I don't really know what I think just yet."

"Come on," Rachel said. "Now's a good time for honesty."

"Well, have you ever heard the expression, 'Out of the frying pan and into the fire'?"

"Something like that, yeah," Rachel said.

"Well, I got away from Bones thinking I could get back to some kind of semi-normal life and now I seem to be in the middle of everything."

Jacob, standing in front of his busted television at six o'clock in the morning said, "What? This isn't normal?"

The girl tried to chuckle.

Rachel sensed the doom weighing down Rain's shoulders. "Look," she said. "Don't feel like you have to stay and help us. This isn't personal with you. If you wanted to go, you might actually be able to get away from them. They might not want anything to do with you. And Jacob and I could help you get out of Lynchville, if that's what you want. You can stay here for as long as you need to and we'll help you get away. If you want to leave tomorrow, we'll drive you out of town."

"No," Rain said. "I can't do that."

"Then you'll stay?"

"Of course I'll stay."

"Why?"

"Because it *is* kind of personal with me. In a way, they took Bones from me. I know he was kind of a loser and everything but nobody should have that done to them—promises without results, turned into a killer, which he most definitely was not before. And they are definitely responsible for stealing away the last bit of innocence I had."

Rachel went to the closet and brought out some blankets.

"I can just sleep on the floor," Rain said.

"Nonsense," Rachel said. "This bed can comfortably sleep three, I'm sure of it. I'll sleep in the middle so Jacob doesn't hump you while he's asleep."

"Thanks," Rain said, smirking.

Jacob cleared his throat, crushed out his cigarette and said, "So, I guess I'll be the one to ask what we plan on doing."

As if the answer was obvious, Rachel said, "We wake up and then we go hunt them down."

"Okay," Jacob said. "I guess that's resolved then."

"We'll work out the details later."

Jacob went around the apartment and turned off all the lights except for the one above the kitchen stove, throwing a faint bluish glow over the apartment, complementing the nearly same color glow given off by the newly birthed morning.

Twelve

Daniel Clock lay in bed counting his wife's snores. They were not loud and grating things. They were not unpleasant. He found them rather comforting. Especially on nights like this. Not that he really had too many nights like this.

He was an insurance agent who worked out of an office in Bryton. He lived in the nicest neighborhood in Lynchville. The only neighborhood that could be considered affluent. Aptly called The Oaks, it had been built at the edge of the nature reserve. Every year, a couple of new, large houses were added to the street. So far, they were up to ten. Acorn Lane was a comfortable place to live. Daniel Clock liked comfort. There had been times in his life when he had not felt so comfortable. There had been times when he didn't feel like he was making enough money; when he felt like his wife, Julia, might be cheating on him; when the fact they could not have any children bothered him. That was when Daniel decided to see the psychiatrist, Dr. Bettermore. The Comfort Doctor. That was how Daniel thought of him. Dr. Bettermore had given him these wonderful pills and told him he didn't have any reasons to really worry. The good doctor pointed out how financially stable Daniel and Julia were. How they were pretty much set for life. The doctor told him the only thing that could harm him was whatever his mind could conjure up.

Daniel had practically begged him for the pills.

He didn't like to think about killing himself. He didn't like to think how meaningless his life seemed at times. The Suicide Card, Daniel called it. He had never really thought about killing himself. Not seriously anyway. He just wanted to be comfortable. He just wanted the nightmares, both waking and sleeping, to go away. So the doctor had given him the pills and Daniel, once again, became a very comfortable man.

Julia's snores were the only things making him feel comfortable at this point.

Daniel was convinced there was someone else in the room with him. Well, he didn't really think it was another *person* in the room with him. He thought it was some*thing*. A Devil.

He wanted to laugh about this. He knew they were only stories. He knew the nightmares and the legends weren't real but goddamn if there wasn't a peculiar shape on the far wall, up in the corner near the ceiling. And goddamn if that shadow wasn't staring at him.

Shadows don't have eyes, he told himself.

But, then again, shadows didn't breathe either. They didn't whisper. They didn't say things like they were going to come inside his head and eat him alive. They didn't say they were going to tear him apart. They didn't say they were going to make his heart stop in his chest. No. A shadow was just a shadow. A blockage of the light created by an object.

That was how he knew the thing in the corner wasn't a shadow.

Daniel had watched it for some time, his mind circling back on itself, creating dilemma after dilemma. He couldn't just get out of bed and leave Julia behind. But he couldn't exactly wake her up and tell her there was a shadow in the room, watching them, and that he was pretty sure it wasn't a shadow at all but a Devil. No. He couldn't do that. She would laugh in his pudgy face if he did.

Sweat glistened on his skin despite the coolness of the room.

His heart hammered in his chest beneath his pajama top.

The bed sheets were balled up in his fists.

"I know you're up there," he whispered at the shape, half to himself.

He swore he saw it move down the wall, snake-like. It was the size of a human and a more rational part of his mind told him the movement could have been created by a passing car.

The thing whispered inside his head.

"I'm going to cut you out," it said.

Fear clenched Daniel's muscles. He was beginning to think the fear paralyzed him. That he wouldn't be able to move if he wanted to.

"Please. Just go away."

"Not without you," the thing whispered, slithering farther down the wall.

Tears rolled out of Daniel's eyes. He didn't know how he was going to solve this problem. He didn't feel very comfortable right now.

He put a sweaty palm on Julia's hip. She was turned with her back toward him.

"Don't hurt her," he said.

"I don't want *her*," the shadowthing hissed, sliding onto the floor now. "She's a stupid cunt. I want you. I want to crush your brain."

"You're not real."

Even after saying that, Daniel had to repeat the phrase in his mind, a childish mantra. Not real. Not real. Not real.

A very real, very cold hand touched his cheek.

Daniel was out of the bed with a bolt, running for the bedroom door. He turned the knob and dashed out into the hallway, his pajama bottoms flopping around his ankles. He reached the top of the stairs and felt the thing's hands on his back, shoving him.

He went tumbling down the stairs, the sound of his skull whacking the stairs and the wall and the railings ricocheting around in his head.

Collapsed twitching at the bottom of the stairs, he felt the shadowthing on him and then, yes, then he felt the shadowthing, the Devil, *inside* him, sliding up his nostrils and into his ears, a slow burn hiss through his short circuiting mind.

And then the thing was completely inside him, reanimating a body that should have been dying, canceling out his thoughts, scorching the inside of his skin.

Daniel had a thought. A very real thought. The last comfortable thought he ever had.

He thought the Devils were real and everything he had heard about them was true. He thought he now knew the mystery. He thought everything was now exposed to him and just before he could figure out what that was, he went screeching into insanity and death.

Entering the man felt like a sexual climax, like a bucket of come shooting from his balls. Only Bones no longer had balls to manufacture come or a penis to come through.

The resulting feeling was more intense than anything he could have imagined. He was now just a floating spirit and when he squeezed, *insinuated,* that essence into the body of Daniel Clock, it was like every nonexistent molecule of his ethereal body swelled, nearly exploding, wracking him with shivers. Once inside the man, Bones began to eat what was there. The only things he could remember about Daniel were his last dying thoughts, the shrieking madness, the fear of death. And, while the soul of Daniel Clock no longer existed, his body did, and Bones went about reanimating that with his own soul. Of course, this was not the body Bones would have chosen but he knew it was just practice. It was just part of the teaching before he could take over someone more powerful. Before he would be able to enter someone without that person realizing it and lie dormant like some hereditary disease that has yet to flare up.

Daniel Clock's body uprighted itself, somewhat jerkily. It had a broken neck. Several vertebrae had slipped out of place. Its leg was broken. But as long as it had muscle and bone for Bones to tug on like puppet strings, the body could move. Julia, the man's wife, still slept upstairs. She would sleep well into the morning. When she woke up, she would miss her husband but just the mere thought of him would send some inexplicable fear throughout her mind. Once he failed to come home after work, she would be vaguely curious but wouldn't think much of it. In a few days, she might call the police if her conscience got the best of her. It would end there. Missing persons claims were hardly given the attention they deserved in Lynchville. Maybe, if things got really bad, she would go see Dr. Bettermore. He would assure her that either she never had a husband named Daniel or that husband had abandoned her. Within a month, she would have her lover moved in. He will be an out-of-work construction worker who lives in a ramshackle trailer park on the outskirts of Culver.

And if she still can't get Daniel out of her mind. If she has the nightmares that so many folks in Lynchville have, then Dr. Bettermore might recommend she be placed in the Signal Point Behavioral Healthcare Center, which was really just a politically correct way of saying the insane asylum. Never mind that Lynchville wasn't nearly large enough to warrant such a facility. It was simply understood that the town liked to take care of its own problems.

Eventually, if a body ever turned up, it would be put to rest in Lynchville Memorial Cemetery. The name on the headstone may or may not be accurate.

Bones left the house through the back door, getting used to the extra girth he now carried. It was almost dawn. He knew he had to find a place to hide until the sun went down again. This is what he was told by Ilya and Ernst. He didn't ask questions. It was all part of the learning. He would find out the reasons for things later. Not that he necessarily needed reasons. He had power now. More power than he could ever have imagined and, all in all, he felt pretty good. Maybe he wasn't just like Ilya and Ernst. Maybe he didn't get everything he wanted. But maybe this was even better.

This neighborhood was built on the edge of the reserve and

Bones went toward the woods, eager to put his screaming soul to rest for the evening.

It was funny how some days went. When he woke up that morning he had been alive and with Rain and doing what he had done for the past few months which, even though it might have been sick and wrong, was what passed for normal these days. The day took a strange turn and he ended up dying at the hands of the very people he sought to please. Only to be given this exotic second life. This life after death. This freedom and power he had searched for his entire life. The gift of being a soul unburdened by any type of human body. The human body was now merely a host and he was there to use that host to serve whatever function he needed. Above human law. Above human punishment.

Once in the woods, he found a place where the earth was soft and began digging. He got down on his hands and knees, his new sizable buttocks pointed up toward the sky, grabbing handfuls of dirt and throwing them around him. He worked incredibly quickly, unaware of how that much effort should have caused his muscles to burn, oblivious to the small stones and thorns and little pieces of glass scraping against the tender pink flesh of his insurance agent's hands. He was like some kind of burrowing animal. A mole perhaps. A big, fat mole. Digging out the dirt and simultaneously pressing himself farther down into the ground, almost like he was making his own grave.

Only until the sun goes away.

When it was dark again, that was when he could rise and begin to search for new prey. That was when he could begin to further his learning.

Within an hour, he was lying in the ground, reaching out his arms to bring the earth onto his body, to give him coverage from the first rays of the sun. He felt worms and bugs wriggle against his skin. He liked the feeling. The smell of the earth caking his nostrils, dark and rotting yet teeming with life, was something he also liked.

When he finally put his soul to rest, he thought about how it had turned out to be a pretty nice day after all.

Thirteen

Friday morning in Lynchville and Autumn Jackson awoke to the sound of her clock radio bleating to life at 6:37. She was glad the alarm woke her up when it did. She was having a wicked nightmare. In the nightmare, a huge black dog had her pinned to the bed and she was staring at its dripping and snarling maw, preparing for its teeth to rip the flesh from her throat.

But now her eyes were open and there was weak October sunlight streaming in through the window and the deejay from the college radio station in Bryton was telling her it was an unseasonably warm fifty-two degrees outside and they were expecting a high of sixty-three before giving way to the Pixies' "Debaser." Never one to lie in bed or hit snooze, Autumn was up, wrapping her terry cloth robe around her scantily clad body, dazedly wandering over to the closet to pick out some clothes for another rousing day of her junior year at Lynchville High. Seeing that it was going to be warm and seeing that she had seemed to grow a nice pair of legs over the summer, Autumn selected a short gray tweed skirt and a black button down shirt. She was going to look sharp today, she thought, even though her skirt was probably going to be too short for the high school's dress code. She didn't think any of the administrators would care. She was and always had been a straight-A student and they tended to turn the other cheek on a lot of things she chose to do and say.

While showering, she knew her nightmare was going to linger with her all day, throwing a pall over everything she chose to do. And just what would she do today? Probably the usual. There wasn't a lot for teenagers to do in Lynchville. Football, drinking, and fucking seemed to be relatively standard fare for most of the students. She didn't go in for the football part and hadn't really found anyone she thought worthy of fucking just yet. That left drinking and she figured she and Charlotte Black could probably manage to do a little of that. Maybe they would go to the Wake Up Screaming Cafe after school, possibly browse through the Den of Iniquity bookstore, both owned by the strikingly gaunt Mr. Stoop, before heading over to Charlotte's for a campfire and some wine pilfered from her parents' not extensive but always reliable wine cellar.

She ran the water in the shower until it was nearly scalding, letting the steam fill the bathroom and her head, hoping it would take away some of the icky feeling rattling around inside her. After showering, she wrapped herself in the robe and went into her room, smelling her mother's morning coffee as it drifted up the stairs. Once dressed, she went downstairs. Her younger sister, Ashley, sat on the couch watching the Disney channel and eating a Pop Tart.

"You look pretty," Ashley said.

"Thank you, Sis." Autumn bent over the couch and pecked Ashley on the head. She was in the seventh grade and was continually enamored with her older sister. It made Autumn feel good. She was sure Ashley would grow up to be a great person.

Autumn went into the kitchen where her mother sat at the table reading the skimpy *Lynchville Chronicle*.

"Anything interesting happen in Lynchville this week?" she asked.

"Does it ever?" her mother replied. She looked up from her paper, over her tortoise shell reading glasses. "You look nice."

"Thanks."

"Could that skirt be any shorter?"

"That's how all the kids wear them these days."

"I guess. It's a good time to be a boy. No wonder they're getting dumber all the time. They probably have trouble concentrating."

Autumn poured herself a cup of coffee, dumping a generous amount of milk and sugar into it. She leaned back against the counter. "So I might go over to Charlotte's after school today."

"By that you mean you won't be home after school."

"Right."

"Be careful. Call if you're going to be late or staying overnight."

"When's Dad getting back?"

"I don't know. Monday, I think."

"Have you talked to him?"

"He called last night. Having a wonderful time, I'm sure."

"I think there's a hint of sarcasm there. Are you implying that lecturing about postmodern pedagogy in North Dakota could be anything other than entertaining?"

"That's exactly what I'm implying. Sometimes I think *he* doesn't even know what he's talking about."

"I think he's trying to figure it out."

David Jackson was the head of the English Department at the college in Bryton. Currently, he was hopping off to various remote and relatively dull areas of the United States, preaching about the integration of technology into the education system. Autumn had tried to read his lecture. It had nearly put her to sleep. He seemed to take a very basic concept and infuse it with lengthy arcane words and wild abstractions. Whatever made him happy, she figured.

"I might go to the bookstore after school. Anything you want me to look for?"

"No. I think I'm okay. Besides, you would probably just ridicule me for my tastes."

"Why would I do something like that? Everyone needs more Nicholas Sparks in their diet."

"Now I haven't read one of his books in a very long time."

"That's right. You've graduated to the college of Oprah."

"Some of those books are good. *You* even read that one."

"That's different. That was Cormac McCarthy. It had cannibals in it."

"And that guy who works in there, what's his name, Mr. Stump?"

"Stoop."

"Whatever. He gives me the creeps."

"I think he wants to give people the creeps. And he doesn't just work there, he owns it. And the coffeeshop next to it."

"So he's an entrepreneurial creep."

"He's a nice guy."

"So was Ted Bundy."

Autumn downed her coffee and put her cup in the sink.

"Aren't you going to eat anything?" her mother asked.

"Mom, if we're going to wear skirts this short then we're not allowed to eat."

"That's right. I forgot that anorexia was cool."

"I'm hardly anorexic."

"Not yet. Just wait until your hair starts falling out."

"I'll have a big lunch. I promise."

"I don't believe you."

"Have I ever lied to you before?"

Her mother raised her eyebrows and went back to reading her paper. "You and Charlotte have a good time tonight. Call me if you're out too late."

"You already said that."

"Did I?"

"Yep."

"Jeez. I guess hot flashes are probably right around the corner."

"Undoubtedly."

"You have your phone?"

"Of course."

"Make sure it's turned on in case I need to get hold of you."

"You're so protective."

"I just like to keep tabs on you so you don't end up strung out and pregnant."

"Don't worry, I have plans other than abortions and rehab."

"It's good to have goals."

"I'm leaving now," Autumn said, realizing she and her mother could banter like this all morning.

"Fine," her mother said. "Be gone with you then."

In the living room, Autumn pulled her black wool coat from the coat rack in case she needed it and said goodbye to her sister.

When she walked out the door, into the refreshing sunlight, she still had that weird feeling all around her. She didn't take it very seriously. She had these feelings all the time and nothing ever came of them.

Her Honda was parked out on the curb. She still had to swing by her friend's house. Gretchen Smith was one of the only other high school kids who lived on her block and she didn't have her license yet. Last year they had been close friends but Gretchen had found a boyfriend, total scum, and now the only time they ever really talked was in the car on the way to and from school. Usually, Gretchen ended up getting a ride home with the aforementioned scum.

Pulling into the other girl's driveway, Autumn honked her horn and Gretchen came bouncing out. The high school was not in town. It was out in the middle of a cornfield and neither of the girls said much.

"You're quiet," Gretchen said.

"Yeah. I have this strange feeling."

"Maybe you're getting your period."

"No, I don't think it's that time yet."

"Well, maybe not for some of us."

"I'm sorry."

"You'll get yours," Gretchen said.

"Yes, I suppose I will. I had this strange dream last night. I barely even remember it now. But I just... have this feeling something *bad* is going to happen."

"Well," Gretchen said. "How much good can happen? This *is* Lynchville."

And the girls left it at that. The name of their town hanging between them like some black splotch of malignant cancer.

Fourteen

Charlotte muddled through the school day. Waking up too early after staying up too late. She regretted taking a shower because it washed the smell of Zack from her skin. She regretted brushing her teeth because it took the taste of him from her mouth.

She couldn't describe it. She felt out of sync with her day. Like the day wanted to pull her one place and she was trying to run in another direction entirely.

She dozed off for a few seconds in her first period Economics class and spent English exchanging knowing glances with Autumn Jackson. What was it they knew? They knew the teacher was a windbag. They knew that, just because the teacher understood Shakespeare and had had a poem published while she was in college, she thought it made her an authority on Literature. The capital letter was how the English teacher, Ms. Gaffney, always said it. The way she said it, you could feel that capital. Third period was History and while she usually found this interesting it just seemed dreadfully boring today. Lunch was next and she needed to go to the restroom before going into the cafeteria where she would try and cook up some plans with Autumn for this evening. Autumn usually had good ideas for what they could do. If it wasn't for Autumn and her plans then Charlotte would choose to sit at home and wait for Zack to mysteriously appear and wonder just what the hell or who the hell he was.

Swinging the bathroom door open, she was glad to see she was the only girl in there. Maybe she could splash some water on her face, wake herself up, without anyone really noticing or asking if something was wrong. She didn't want anyone asking that because she didn't really know the answer. Something *could* be wrong. Something could most definitely be wrong. What, exactly, she wasn't sure. She just felt like it was entirely possible she was in way over her head. Previous affairs had been with simple-minded high school boys who wanted her for all the obvious reasons. And while she had acquiesced to their wants on a number of occasions, she had never really felt anything for them. She had never really *fallen* for one of them. They bored her. The sex was okay at best. Mostly she thought she liked the idea of the act, the idea that it was doing something she wasn't really supposed to be doing, more than the physical feeling of the act itself. With Zack, she liked all of it. It left her shivering and it left her wanting more.

The lights in the bathroom seemed too harsh, as though they had to be extra bright to compensate for the lack of windows. One of them buzzed loudly overhead, that irritating buzz of fluorescent lights she never noticed until it was completely quiet. And the bathroom, cut off from the noise of the cafeteria and the halls, was indeed completely quiet.

She looked at herself in the row of dirty mirrors on the far side of the bathroom. She looked gaunt—too pale, dark circles under her eyes. Her dress seemed to accompany this feeling. It was a long black hippie dress, reaching nearly down to her ankles, worn low on her hips. She wore a tight button-down shirt, a flash of white skin visible between the shirt and the dress. If not for that inappropriate bit of skin, she could have been dressed for a funeral.

Turning to her right, she threw open the far stall.

Startled, she exhaled air that seemed like it was held in precisely for this moment at the sight of Zack, standing in the women's stall.

She nearly laughed with her reaction to it all.

She smiled, holding her hand to her pale chest.

"What are you *doing* in here?" she asked.

He didn't say anything.

"Are you okay?"

He leaned into her, whispering into her ear.

"Get on your knees."

So this was what he wanted. At first she didn't want to. It seemed filthy, here in the bathroom, and there was the chance of being caught. She didn't think any of the students would say anything, probably wouldn't pay any attention, but what if a teacher came in to see one pair of feet on the ground and one set of knees.

"Do it, Charlotte," Zack said.

She liked the sound of her name coming from his mouth. She met his gaze. If this was what he wanted... If this was what it would take to bring him back then she was going to give it to him. And she was going to make it worth his while. She hoped her eyes told him this.

Slowly, rubbing her hands down his arms, she slid down onto her knees and looked up at him.

He unbuckled his belt, unbuttoned and unzipped his pants. Then he pulled down the front of his underwear, as black as his clothes, and his penis sprang out. She rubbed her lips against the tip of it, smelling herself from last night. It didn't matter if she liked the scent or not. There wasn't anything she could do about it.

He grabbed the back of her head, forcing his penis against her lips. She took it into her mouth. He forced the entire length in and she gagged. He continued to thrust against her mouth.

Then he brought her head away from him. She licked her lips and wiped saliva from her chin. She rose to kiss him.

He kissed her forcefully, quickly, and turned her so she was bent over the toilet.

Not wanting to, she gripped the cool reservoir, trying to stare at the wall rather than the bowl.

He yanked her dress and underwear down to her knees. Pulled her hips up so she was exposed to him.

"Play with yourself," he said.

"Zack..."

"Do it."

"What if..."

"Do it."

Tentatively, she reached between her legs with her right hand, bracing her weight on her left. She heard Zack slide his belt from his pants.

She moved her hand faster, feeling the growing moisture on her fingertips. If they got caught, she wouldn't care. This was so crazy it was worth it.

He brought the belt down on her ass.

She came. That sudden. The shock sent her sex into spasms, gripping against her fingertips as Zack lashed her again and again.

"Oh, God," she said, still coming.

Her legs were shaking.

Now Zack was behind her, jerking himself off.

She felt his come splash her burning buttocks. It felt cool and soothing. She pulled her sticky hand from between her legs.

"Pull yourself up," he said.

She did so, conscious of the wetness spreading between her panties and her skin. She felt humiliated and small. She was in pain. She felt dirty. She loved it. She felt great.

She turned to face him and started to say something but he put a finger against her lips. Continuing to stare at him he grew fainter. Became less substantial. It took her a moment to realize what was going on. He was disappearing. He was actually disappearing right there in front of her eyes. That freaked her out even more than the things they had seen last night in the cemetery.

Once he was gone, she doubted if he was there at all. She thought she could feel his come on her bottom but she couldn't be sure. Reaching back to feel it, she thought it could just as easily have been sweat. She almost wished someone *would* have been in the bathroom with her just so she could question them about it, but what would she say?

"Excuse me, did you happen to notice me down on the floor in the stall there? Yeah, on my knees, giving head to some guy that might not be real at all? Did you hear him hitting me with his belt? Did you see another set of feet or was I just blowing the air because that... boy, *that* would just be sad."

No. She wouldn't have been able to do that either. That would have been retardation. She could have written her own ticket to Signal Point after doing that. She figured, if one was to go mad, it was better to go slowly mad in one's own mind rather than to announce that madness to the world.

Why did he always have to leave like that? With so many unanswered questions. Why did she feel like she was being used? Why did she immediately want to do it again?

She pulled up her dress and lowered her underwear once again and did what she had come to the bathroom to do in the first place. Then she went over to the sinks and the dirty wall of mirrors and splashed some cold water on her face before going to the cafeteria where she could sip a Diet Coke and talk to Autumn, neither of them eating anything.

Fifteen

Jacob woke up around noon, fully-clothed, covered in sweat, and slightly confused. He was not used to waking up next to Rachel or on the couch pulled out into a bed. He felt strange. Despite last night being the most openly traumatic evening he had experienced in nearly two years, he had slept soundly, without a single dream or nightmare.

Rachel and Rain continued to snooze, looking almost childlike, facing each other, their knees nearly touching. Jacob wanted to take a picture of them but knew they had things to do. He had shut the windows before going to bed and now the sun poured in and the apartment was hot. Crossing the room, he opened the windows, letting the fresh breeze stream in. Reaching over the couch, he tapped Rachel awake.

"Morning," he said.

"Good morning," she said. "What time is it?"

"Just after noon."

"Fuck," she said, hopping up out of bed. "I need to call my parents."

She grabbed the phone from the nightstand and went into the other room to talk to her parents, probably to apologize for not being there when they woke up and probably to apologize in advance for not being there the rest of the day. Of course, she wouldn't be able to tell them *why* she wouldn't be able to be there.

Rain woke up while Rachel was in the other room.

"Good morning," Jacob said.

"Morning." She wiped the sleep from her eyes.

"Sleep well?"

"Surprisingly, yes."

"Are you still coming along with us?"

"Of course. I think you guys'll need the help."

Jacob nodded.

"Got any plans?" she asked.

"How do you plan against something that may not exist?"

"Good point."

"So my plan is this: As soon as Rachel gets off the phone, we three will hike down to the Wake Up Screaming and grab the only decent coffee this 'burg has to offer. There, we will sit down and talk. And then we will go hunting."

"It feels like we need supplies or something."

"What? Like silver bullets and holy water and all that shit?"

"Maybe."

"Don't think it would do any good."

"Me either. But if Bones is out there... I'm pretty sure a gun could stop *him*."

"You're probably right. Sometimes I wish I was a gun enthusiast."

"I take it you're not?"

"There's not a firearm in the place."

She looked puzzled.

"I know... Maybe Rachel told you a little bit about what happened before and you think maybe it's stupid not to have one around but, well, first of all, what good would it do and... if she had told you the *whole* story then you would know."

"She didn't."

"She didn't tell you the whole story?"

"Any of it."

"Well, then, I think we have some brunch conversation."

Rachel came back into the living room and put the phone back on its charger.

"They're pissed," she said.

"Aren't they always?"

"I'll never quite figure them out."

"You're their little girl. They're worried about you," Jacob said.

"Sometimes I wish I had a sister."

"I'll be your sister," Rain said.

Rachel let go a sinister chuckle. "You should probably meet my parents before you say things like that. You may not know what you're getting yourself into."

"That bad, huh?"

"That bad," Jacob answered for Rachel. "They do, however, have a soft spot for orphans." Jacob was thinking about the weeks they had taken him in and parented him after his own parents had died, patiently, even though they were probably well aware he was fucking their daughter every time he was given the chance.

"So... plans?" Rachel said.

"Ah, yes, I thought we would retire to the Wake Up Screaming and clear our heads. Fill our new friend in on some of our glorious past."

"That's a good idea."

"Let us go then."

Rain got up from the bed and announced she should probably go to the bathroom before leaving. Rachel and Jacob also found this a good idea so they all took turns before filing out of his apartment and down the dimly lit stairway.

Outside, the air was brisk and bright. It didn't seem like the right day to hunt the Devils. Jacob was infested with a mingling of fear and exhilaration. Part of him wanted to be on his way, toward the Devils, hunting *them* rather than the other way around. Another part of him felt hopeless, like they could hunt all they wanted to and not turn up anything. He knew the Devils liked to strike when you least expected it.

They walked the two blocks down Main Street until they reached the Wake Up Screaming. It was a good time to go. It was after the breakfast crowd and before the high school crowd. But, in Lynchville, a crowd was never really that much of a crowd. Stoop's cafe had a very old fashioned wooden sign hanging over the sidewalk. Both the cafe and the bookstore seemed slightly out of place in Lynchville. The sign for the cafe had a large painted bloodshot eye carved into the wood. One could see the eye as someone in the throes of a caffeine high but Jacob had always thought it looked more like the eye of someone gripped in fear. Like something you would see on the cover of a horror novel. The sign for the bookstore, Den of Iniquity, featured the Devil sitting on a chair and holding a book with his left hand, his pointed tale wrapped around his hooves, his right hand adjusting a pair of very studious looking reading glasses. Jacob was amazed the Baptists hadn't cried for the sign to be torn down yet.

Jacob opened the cafe door and held it open for the girls. It was a heavy wooden door and you had to step up a concrete step to get inside. Once inside, he followed Rain who followed Rachel to their customary spot in one of the booths toward the back. Rachel and Rain sat down, sitting next to each other so they faced the front door and the window overlooking the sidewalk. The barista would come to the table and take the order but Jacob didn't really like to be waited on so he went to the bar and got three coffees. The mugs were large black heavy things, indicative of the coffee contained therein. Each mug was printed with a big white eye. The creamer and sugar were kept at the table.

The boy behind the counter, after waiting on Jacob, went back to leaning on the counter. He sat down on a stool and put Beck's *Sea Change* into the stereo. This was one of the reasons Jacob always loved Stoop's. Nowadays, it was nearly impossible to find a cafe where you could listen to semi-decent music.

Jacob sat the mugs down at the table and slid into the booth, his back to the window, feeling slightly hunted.

Rachel added an abundance of cream and sugar to her coffee. Rain drank hers black like Jacob.

They sat for awhile in the dimly lit cafe, the somber music playing around them, not saying much and sipping their coffees.

"On Halloween night, nearly two years ago now," Rachel said. "I made a big mistake."

Sixteen

A Halloween Interlude

1.

Two years ago and it still amazed Rachel how fast it could all come back to her. Just a second of thinking about it and she was there, standing on her front porch, watching the costumed children parade through the dead leaves of the neighborhood.

And it smelled just like every Halloween she could ever remember:

Candle wax.

The latex of the masks and the weird smell of the greasy make-up.

The smell of sugar, drifting out of mouths and from cotton pillowcases and crinkly plastic bags and hard plastic pumpkinhead buckets.

Fires, burning off in the distance. Fires that burned for the children to come home so the whole family could gather round and have one last weenie roast, one last marshmallow roast, all gathered round and sipping cider and waiting for the bitter winter to come on.

Clean air, always so crisp. Always so perfect for this day.

And the smell of dead leaves, the cold damp coming up from the ground. The smell that, to Rachel, symbolized Halloween more than anything else.

The fallen leaves.

The fallen leaves were everywhere.

She could smell them. She could *hear* them, crunchy and brittle as the trick-or-treaters went from yard to yard.

The leaves were beautiful. They looked beautiful. They smelled beautiful.

The leaves were dead.

This was the peculiar thought she recalled with perfect clarity as she stood there and watched two gorillas, much bigger than the other trick-or-treaters, march up the walk to her front porch.

They weren't *completely* gorillas.

They only had gorilla heads.

The rest of them: the leather jackets, the jeans, the black combat boots, were more recognizable.

Dave Gross and Steve Kenyon.

It had to be.

Dave was the shorter and stockier of the two. He was on the left.

"Trick-or-treat," he said gruffly.

"My," Rachel said. "You're a big one. Aren't you?"

"Growth disorder," the gorilla huffed. "Trick-or-treat."

"Do you have a bag or something?"

"Trick-or-fucking-treat," Dave said.

"Dave!" Rachel said. "There are kids behind you."

"I'm not Dave."

"Sure."

"What are you doin?"

"What's it look like I'm doing? I'm trying to give out some candy but there are two big effing gorillas in my way."

"Huh-huh," he laughed. "'Effing.'"

"Will you guys move?"

The gorillas moved off to her right. She sat on the top step of the porch. They leaned against the base of the porch. An alien approached her and she tossed a couple of bite-sized candy bars into his pillowcase.

"You wanna come out?" Steve asked.

"Not right now. I'm passing out candy."

"We could go out later."

She tossed some candy into a little girl's pumpkin pail. She couldn't tell if the little girl was supposed to be a princess or a hooker. A princess, she figured.

"I don't know. I'd have to ask Mom."

"No problem," Steve said.

He climbed the porch steps beside her, hoisted open the storm door and called, "Mrs. Stokes! Mrs. *Stoookes!*"

"Yes?" she heard her mom's voice call from inside the house, probably the kitchen.

"Can Rachel come out after she's passed out all the candy?"

Now her mom had come to the door. She was covered in blood from head to toe. Rachel had told her she was too old to go to their Halloween party as Carrie and her mom had told her to get bent.

"Sure. We're not going to be here to entertain her. What are you guys going to do?"

"Oh, Dale Septum is having this Halloween party at his house. He invited just about everyone."

"Is there going to be drinking there?"

"You bet. Drinking, pot, sex... someone was even talking about scoring some crack."

"You're such a goof."

"I know. It's totally punch and cookies. Supervised and everything."

"Yeah, right. You were probably closer the first time."

Except there is no one in our school named Dale Septum, Rachel thought.

Rachel's mom leaned her head out the door to address her, "Be back by one?"

"Yes, Mom."

"I mean it. It's best to get home before all the drunks are on the road."

"You mean like you and Dad?"

"We're meth-heads. You know that. It helps the concentration. At first anyway... You'll have your phone. Call if there's an emergency."

"There won't *be* any emergency," Rachel said, exasperated.

"Fine, fine. Just make sure it's charged."

"We'll take good care of her, Mrs. Stokes."

"All right. Poke your head in and holler before you go. And there's still a half-hour left so don't just dump all the candy on the next kid who comes. Or else his diabetes will be on your hands."

"Yes, Mom."

"Have fun."

Her mom, thankfully, disappeared back into the house.

"Your mom's kinda hot when she's all covered in blood," Dave said.

"If I give him a sucker, will he shut up?" she asked Steve.

"Only if it's the kind with gum in the middle," Dave said.

Rachel rummaged through the bowl until she found a cherry Blow Pop. She threw it at Dave. It plunked against his jacket and he trapped it with his hands, greedily unwrapping it and pulling off his gorilla mask so he could suck on it. Rachel noticed he had a huge black eye.

"What the hell happened to you?"

"Car accident."

"Well then *you're* certainly not driving."

Rachel deposited a random handful of candy into a Day-Glo plastic bag held by a pudgy kid in a Jason mask. Hopefully, the sugar wouldn't send him into a homicidal rage.

"He's shittin you," Steve said, still wearing his gorilla mask.

"No accident?"

"Not a *car* accident," Steve said.

"She doesn't have to know..." Dave said.

The next handful was larger. This one to Harry Potter.

"We're buds. We tell each other everything," Rachel said.

"See, Davey here had a run-in..."

"Man, it's embarrassing."

"With Bryan Adams and Darryl Hall."

"I can't believe those two guys hang out with each other. I mean, they *know*, right? About their names."

"At least one of them isn't named Oates. I don't remember his first name," Steve said.

"See, now why'd you have to tell? Feel better now?"

"It's just Rachel," Steve said.

"Thanks," Rachel said.

Double-handfuls to Osama bin Laden and Saddam Hussein. It wasn't until they were walking away Rachel noticed they had nooses around their necks. She rolled her eyes.

"You know what I mean," Steve said.

"Yes, I'm too short and pudgy and don't buy my clothes at the mall and until I do I'm just Rachel."

"I'm sorry."

"I'm just kidding." She was, too. She didn't mind being "just Rachel." At least, not around Dave and Steve anyway. To her, they would always be just the boys down the street. The ones who went way back to when boys were kind of icky.

"Besides," she said, "don't feel sorry for me. I'm not the one who got beat up by Darryl Hall and Bryan Adams."

"Real nice. Good going, Steve. Well, I'm not the only one," he said, yanking Steve's gorilla mask off. His top lip looked kind of mashed and swollen.

Rachel, knowing she probably shouldn't, burst out laughing.

"You're on thin ice, Missy," Steve said. "We don't have to take you anywhere."

"Fine. Then I'll just call Anna and we'll have our lesbian sleepover lingerie party and you losers will most definitely not be invited."

"Where is hottie Anna, anyway?"

"I don't know. I left a message but she wouldn't call back. Probably out getting an abortion or something."

A kid dressed like Jesus came up and handed her a Jack Chick comic. Rachel smiled and dumped the rest of the bowl into his brown paper sack, figuring he was going to need it, diabetes be damned.

"I didn't think Jesus freaks were allowed to go trick-or-treating," Steve said.

"Well, he's not the Jesus freak. His parents are. We ready to go?"

"Whenever you are."

"Let me grab a coat and compliment Mom on her dirty pillows."

"Right on. Tell her what I said about the blood," Dave said.

Rachel snorted. "Come back next week. I think she's on her period then."

That shut him up.

2.

They walked to the corner of Maple Street, to Dave's house.

"We takin the van?" Rachel asked, the contempt naked in her voice.

"Ah, the Shaggin Wagon, of course."

"You know," Rachel said. "I had a little more faith in you than that. Every pathetic teenage boy who's left with his soccer mom's hand-me-down minivan calls it his 'Shaggin Wagon.' Ironically, you're usually all virgins."

Dave pulled open the driver's side door. Rachel called shotgun and went over to the passenger side. Steve quietly got in the back, looking embarrassed to be anywhere near a minivan.

"I'm not," Dave said.

"Not a virgin?" Rachel asked.

"Yeah, right," Steve said from the back, yanking his door closed.

"Really," he said.

"Yeah? Who would fuck you?" Steve asked.

"Kyla Richards, that's who."

"She's like twelve!" Rachel said.

"She's thirteen. Well, she was thirteen, anyway. That's only four years difference, you know."

"Oh God," Rachel said. "What did you do? Play Barbies with her first?"

"She was very adult about it," Dave said.

"You're full of shit," Steve said.

"I don't know," Rachel said. "From what I've heard, she's screwed just about everybody else."

"Not Steve," Dave said. "Besides," he said, casting a glance into the rearview mirror as he backed out, "she's a little too young for Steve. He likes em, ah, *older*."

"Oh, keep your fucking mouth shut, fucker."

"I don't know. I asked you not to talk about the fight."

"You have a fuckin black eye! Eventually, the truth was going to come out."

"Mrs. Jenkins," Dave coughed.

"Fuck you," Steve said.

Rachel turned around in her chair. She was actually surprised. Mrs. Jenkins was married to their science teacher. She lived a couple streets over. Not bad looking but she had to be like forty.

"Really?" she said. "Why didn't I know all this stuff? I would have reconsidered spending my evening with the Pedophile and the Graduate."

"It wasn't sex anyway. I never had sex with her," Steve protested.

"Why not?" Rachel asked. "If you had the chance? She's not hideous."

"She wouldn't. She said it was too much like cheating. But she did give me a blow job."

"Really?"

"Yeah. I didn't come though. I was too nervous or something. I cut their grass last summer, by the way. That's how it happened. I wasn't trying to seduce her or anything. She couldn't find her checkbook one day. She drinks a lot and she was pretty sauced so I jokingly told her she could pay me with a blow job. And she did. It was nice. Besides, come on, spending the evening with us'll be better than the Big Green Monster, right?"

Rachel flushed.

"That was in strict confidence."

"Dave knows. He was there. He was the one who tried to get you to demonstrate it."

"You were never supposed to bring it up. I was very drunk."

"Okay. Okay. At least you *didn't* put on a demonstration."

"I didn't want to make you guys wild."

"Just talking about it makes me kind of wild," Dave said.

"Gross," Rachel said.

"That's okay," Dave said. "I'm sure neither of us could live up to the Big Green Monster."

"Speak for yourself," Steve said.

"Enough," Rachel said. "That night didn't exist." Then, looking at Dave, she said, "I guess we'll have to ask Mrs. Jenkins to find out, anyway."

"Nah. You just have to be real nice to me."

"Gross," she said.

"Big Green Monster!" Dave shouted, just so he could try and get the last word about the whole thing.

They navigated from downtown Lynchville and through the neighborhoods, driving slow and braking for the costumed trick-

or-treaters. Now it was just the older ones and the die hards. The herd had thinned. Eventually, they were on the backroads. The backroads were plentiful in Lynchville.

"Well," Rachel said, "what do you guys have planned for us?"

Steve reached under the seat and pulled out a bottle of Jack Daniels.

"Drinking and driving," Steve said. "The hobby of teenagers the world over."

"Oh, God, I'm not *touching* that stuff," Rachel said.

"And for the lady..." Dave said, twisting a knob that released the console between the seats.

Nestled in the console was a bottle of strawberry Boone's Farm.

"That's just as gross," Rachel said.

"Gee, 'Thanks, Dave. Thanks, Steve. Thanks for thinking of me,'" Dave said in a voice that sounded like a petulant transvestite.

"Well, I guess it won't make me throw up."

"That's more like it," Dave said, gently slugging her in the arm.

They drove around the reserve and the backroads, Rachel nursing her bottle of strawberry beer and the boys slugging back hits of Jack, all of them on the lookout for cops. But, as they had often speculated, cops seemed to be mostly absent around Lynchville.

3.

Eventually, Dave was too drunk to drive, swerving all over the road, so Rachel took over.

"Shit, man, he's wasted," Steve said from the backseat.

Dave fidgeted with the radio dials and laughed a lot. He could hardly keep his eyes open. Rachel figured, if they were pulled over, the fumes alone would get their licenses revoked.

"What now?" Rachel said. "Maybe we should get him home?"

"Aw, fuck that, the fat bastard'll be okay," Steve said. "How 'bout you drive us into the woods and let us double-team you."

"Gag," Rachel said. "Think again."

"We could go out to that house that's s'posed to be haunted. The Sad House? Good night for it."

"That it is. The one on Barker Road?"

"No. The other Sad House."

"There's more than one?"

"Sar-casm."

"Oh. You ever been there?"

"Nope."

"I heard it's not there all the time."

"I've heard that too but, what I figure is, people like us come out here too pissed to really know where they're at and just get confused, you know? All these hollows and valleys and shit all look the same."

"Good point."

Steve stood up and stumbled to the front of the van. Tapping Dave on the shoulder, he said, "Hey, man, go lay down in back."

"Fuck off," Dave said, drunkenly swatting at Steve's hand.

"Come on," Steve said. "You'll feel better if you go lay down."

He pried the bottle from Dave's grip and chucked it out the window.

"Why'd ya do that?"

"'Cause you don't need any more, ya fat fuck. Now go lay down."

"You gonna bang Rachel?" he asked.

"No. I'm not gonna bang Rachel."

"Can I watch? Can I bang her too? I've always wanted to fuck Rachel."

Steve looked at Rachel as though this were all a revelation to him. He pried Dave a little out of the seat and said, "Come on, go lay down in back before you embarrass yourself any more."

"Okay. Okay," Dave stood up from the seat and Steve moved out of the way.

Dave didn't make it to the back. He sprawled down on the floor in between the two middle seats.

Steve sat down in his spot and said, "You know where it's at?"

"Yeah, I think," Rachel said.

Steve found a decent station on the radio. Dave had turned it to static. Rachel was a little buzzed and had to concentrate on driving.

Soon the asphalt ended and they were on a gravel road. Some misty fog had gathered here and Rachel wondered if they were the only people out here. It seemed like it would be a popular place to go on Halloween.

It was all a little eerie.

She became a little paranoid.

The road was narrow. What if another car full of drunken teenagers came barreling around a turn? It was so foggy that, by the time Rachel could do anything, it would be too late. She jokingly wondered if all the stories about the Devils were true. She didn't believe them. If she believed them, she wouldn't be here.

Earlier, she had tossed her coat onto the floor beside her seat. She reached down, careful to keep her eyes on the road, and fished out her cell phone.

"Hm," she said. It was dead. She thought she had just charged it last night. "Do you have a charger in here?"

"A what?" Steve said.

"Does Dave have a charger in here? For his phone?"

"Dave doesn't have a cell phone. Neither do I. They're for losers."

"Yeah, well, we'll see who's the loser when we need to call someone to get us when we run into a ditch."

"We'll be okay," Steve said. "I've managed to go seventeen years without one and I'm still here."

"Good thing you have survival skills."

"It should be up here on your left."

Rachel slowed down.

Gradually, the wall of woods on her left faded and then fell away completely. They were on a ridge overlooking the hollow. The house was there, shrouded in misty fog and milky moonlight. Rachel stopped the van.

"Creepy place, huh?" Steve said.

"Certainly," Rachel said.

"Oh, God," Dave called from the back. He had risen to his knees and thrown open the side doors, throwing his head out just enough to spew his vomit outside.

"Thank God he made it out there."

"Yeah. The fuck. So are we gonna go in or what?"

Rachel thought about this for a minute. Another wet heave came from the back.

"I don't really want to."

"Why'd we come out here for?"

"Just to see it, I thought. I feel like my Halloween experience is complete. We can go home now."

"Come on. I dare you. I'll go with you. We can just open the door and run in and then out."

"I can think of *soooo* many reasons why that isn't a good idea."

"You're the smart one. Let's hear em."

"Okay. Well, for starters, it might belong to someone. We're drunk. We're all drunk. If we get caught it's going to go beyond simple trespassing. We're going to be in huge trouble if we get caught. And that's if we're lucky. This is *Deliverance* country where crazy hill people like to solve things their own way. This should frighten you just as much as me. I don't think you want your butt seal broken any more than I do. And Dave is sick. We should take him home so you can tuck him in and give him a little kiss good night."

"Your reasons are shit," Steve immediately refuted. "First of all, if someone *does* own it, they sure as shit don't live in it. Which means no one would notice if we just ran up and had a look. I don't think the cops are any worry because I've *never* seen a cop outside the town itself. And if just me and you go down, it'll give Dave a chance to collect himself."

Dave punctuated this with another heave.

"Come on," Steve said. "We don't even have to go into it. Let's just run down and touch it. That's all. It's either the house or your tits."

"What?" Rachel said.

"Yeah. Either go down to the house with me or show me your tits."

"Fine. I'll race you down there. I win, you show me how you compare to the Big Green Monster."

Steve rolled his eyes.

"Okay, go," he said, springing out from the passenger side.

But Rachel had already taken off, barreling down the slope, the dew-slick grass wetting her shoes.

Steve had a longer stride but she was quicker and more sober.

She bounded up the steps and put her hand on the front door. A bad feeling surged through her body but she tried to ignore it. Steve stood in front of the porch, hands on hips, pouting.

"Okay," Rachel said. "Drop em."

"No. We gotta go in... if you want to see it."

But Rachel was already descending the stairs of the porch. "No way," she said. "You couldn't *pay* me to go in there."

"Then no cock for you."

"You promised."

"You cheated."

"You're such a bastard. You ready to go?"

"I guess," Steve said.

She could almost sense how much he wanted to go into the house, see what was in there, snoop around a little bit. Probably just so he could brag to Dave that he had gone in. He'd probably tell him that they went in there and he fucked her in every room of it.

She couldn't bring herself to go in. She didn't like the way it felt. It had an odd smell to it.

They began walking toward the van.

That's when they heard Dave scream.

4.

After starting out at a run, Rachel and Steve almost immediately held up, simultaneously realizing they didn't know exactly what they were running toward.

Or, perhaps, it was that they both simultaneously spotted the other car, a beat-up old thing, behind Dave's minivan.

"Shit," Steve asked.

"What?" Rachel said.

"I think it's Bryan and Darryl."

"*What?*"

"All we said was we got in a fight. We didn't say we necessarily lost. I think maybe they're trying to get back at us."

He began walking up the side of the hill.

"Just stay behind me," Steve said. "I don't think they'll try much with the both of us. Maybe they thought they had Dave alone."

Rachel saw the boys at the top of the ridge, dark silhouettes against the light of the moon, surrounded by the swirling mist. They spotted Rachel and Steve and threw something at them. Rachel had no idea what it might be. She ducked, half-expecting an explosion.

She heard whatever-it-was thud against the ground and Steve said, "Aw, fuck!"

"What? What?" Rachel asked.

Steve grabbed her arm harshly, pointing at the ground before them.

Dave's head stared up at them. Tendons, veins, and bright white bits of cartilage hung from the tattered flesh. One eye was open, wide and bright blue. The other one was mostly closed. His mouth was open, blood all around the lips. Rachel was pretty sure his tongue had been removed.

She burst into tears, panic shuddering through her body.

"Oh, *God*," she moaned. "Would they do that?"

"Hell, I don't know. We gotta get the fuck outta here."

He grabbed her arm and turned her back toward the house.

But she couldn't go in there. She didn't care how scared and panicked she felt. She couldn't go into that house.

Because something in there wants to kill you.

The thought came completely out of the blue.

Why would something in there want to kill her? She'd never even seen the goddamn house before.

"Fucking come *on*," Steve said, giving her arm another yank.

They ran to the house.

"Not in there," Rachel panted.

"Shit no," Steve said. "That'd be like a fucking trap."

They ran past the house, hearing something behind them.

The house was positioned almost exactly in the center of the hollow. On the other side, woods began at the base of the hill and climbed to its top. Rachel thought that seemed almost as suicidal as the house but she followed Steve as he plunged in.

The people following them seemed impossibly fast.

They hit the woods. Navigation was nearly impossible without any trails. There were sticks and thorns and branches everywhere.

And the sound of the leaves.

The sound of those leaves would make it nearly impossible to hide.

She felt what she had dreaded.

A hand on the back of her neck.

Dragging her down.

Separating her from Steve.

The body above her turned her over onto her back and, looking up at it, she thought, I guess it *could* be Bryan.

But he looked all wrong.

Everything seemed sharper and more elongated. She thought of a hairless werewolf.

Bryan pulled her to her feet.

"She the one?" it asked Darryl. It looked like Darryl had been transformed in much the same way.

A simple thought ran through her head:

It's true. Everything I've heard about the Devils is true.

The Darrylthing lifted Steve by the throat. He chokingly shouted, his legs kicking in mid-air. The creature flung him to the ground and said, "Make sure she doesn't go anywhere."

"Got it," Bryan said.

With his left hand, he grabbed her right wrist and dragged her to a tree. Reaching into his back pocket, he pulled out a small hammer. Rachel kicked. She screamed. She clawed.

It was all useless.

Holding her wrist against the tree, he transferred a large nail from his right hand into his left. Simultaneously, he braced her wrist against the tree and poked the tip of the nail against her palm.

"No," Rachel said. "No. I know who you are. You guys can't get away with this. We know what you did to Dave."

"Dave was a dick," Bryan said.

Then he drove the nail through her hand. She heard it pop through the flesh and delicate tendons.

The pain was excruciating.

She wanted to drop to the ground and curl up into a fetal position but the nail kept her standing nearly upright.

"You sure she's the one? A pudgy skank like that?" Darryl said, his arms closed around Steve's chest.

"That's who he said. I'm sure," Bryan said, the newly acquired snout altering his speech. "Let's go to work on this guy. Ain't he the one who fucked you up?"

"Yep."

"Fuck you!" Steve shouted.

Rachel wanted to tell him to be quiet. Anything he said was going to make the beating that much worse. She didn't want to see Steve without a head.

Darryl threw Steve to the ground.

Bryan turned his attention to Rachel. He unfastened his jeans, pulled out his cock, and pissed on her. The warmth splashed her jeans, sinking through so she could feel it running down her lower legs. He moved closer to her and she could see his penis was huge and erect.

Steve cried out behind him. Darryl had him on his stomach, raking claws across his back.

Bryan reached out a clawed finger to flick one of Rachel's fear-hardened nipples.

She closed her eyes, the tears rolling out.

"Don't," she pleaded. "Don't do this."

And still she was wondering if the Devils really had gotten hold of Bryan and Darryl or if they'd just had like a professional special effects person apply their costumes.

Bryan reached out a hand, grabbed the bottom of her shirt and lifted it.

A gunshot blasted through the night.

Bryan went sideways.

Rachel looked down at him. His left leg was separated at the knee. He howled in pain. Darryl, distracted, looked up from Steve.

His face exploded.

Another shot punched away what was left of his head. Each shot made Rachel jump. She heard Steve moaning in pain.

Bryan struggled to stand up. Another shot separated that leg.

Steve pushed Darryl off of him. He landed in a heap on the ground.

A man came out of the darkness, holding a pistol and carrying a can of gas. He splashed it on the crawling twitching things that were Darryl and Brian. Then he tossed a match and they went up in a perfect blaze, screaming their shouts to a lost night.

Seventeen

The three of them sat around the table sipping their coffee. The storytelling finished, Rachel took her hands away from Rain's. She didn't have to open her mouth to give Rain the past. It was there, fed through her. Jacob had simply looked around the coffee shop while Rachel transported Rain back to that Halloween night.

One he remembered very well.

Sipping her coffee, Rachel said, "After the nail was removed, the hand healed immediately. And ever since then, I've been able to do things... move people's minds. Transport them. Heal things."

"I'll say," Rain said.

"How's that cut on your foot?" Jacob asked.

Rachel slipped off the too large Converse (she had a shortage of shoes at his house), turning it so Rain could look down and see that the cut she had inflicted was completely gone. Gone also were all the minor cuts and scratches that had blemished Rachel's face, legs and arms.

"But," Rain said, "why was Jacob there?"

"Me," Jacob said. "I was out there to kill myself."

"Jesus," Rain said.

"Rather fortunate now that we look back on it though. I was going to douse myself in gasoline, hang myself from a branch and, if that didn't work immediately, I was going to blow my brains out."

"You were serious about it?"

"Yeah. Remember when I told you there were other reasons we didn't keep guns in the house?"

"Yeah, but..."

"Well, we're all here now," Jacob said.

"What happened... after?" Rain asked.

Rachel, already somber, grew more so, leaning her head down to inspect the wood on the table.

"Jacob and I both changed. I already told you about mine. I can do more than just give people visions. I can use it as a weapon."

"Torment them," Rain said.

"I guess, yeah. And Jacob has these wild hallucinations."

"Most of them don't make much sense. Maybe on some symbolic level, like what I saw on the TV last night."

"What about... the other guys?" Rain asked.

"Steve didn't fare so well. Physically, he was probably better off than me. Or *should* have been better off. But, mentally, he was gone. I've never seen him since that night. He's been in Signal Point..."

"The insane asylum," Jacob said.

"I was trying to be polite about it. But, yeah, he's been there since that night and I just can't bring myself to go visit him. Don't even know if I'd be *allowed* to visit him."

"What about the police and stuff? Surely you went to the police?"

"We did," Rachel said. "Jacob and I both went in and filled out the whole crazy report and neither one of us have ever heard anything else about it."

"That's crazy," Rain said.

"About as crazy as you going on a yearlong killing spree with a half-wit and never coming close to being caught," Jacob said.

"The Devils have a way of doing things," Rachel said. "Like maybe you've wondered why we didn't call an outside newspaper or contact some authority outside of Lynchville?"

"Kind of."

"Well, we did. And you call them and they listen to you like you're not a crazy person and then they hang up and you wait for the story to appear in the Bryton paper or something. You wait for a reporter to call you. You wait for something to be on the news.

Hell, like maybe even one of those investigative journal pieces? And nothing happens. I'm guessing that, as soon as they hang up the phone, they have no recollection of ever speaking with anyone. And, yeah, maybe we could go there in person but something tells me that, even though I leave Lynchville nearly every day to go to work and school, if I was to ever leave with the hope of going somewhere and telling them our story, I don't think it would let me out."

"That's fuckin crazy," Rain said. "And I'm sure it's true. Have no doubt."

"On the bright side," Jacob said to Rachel. "It looks like they've come back."

She wanted to throw her coffee in his face.

Eighteen

Silence wrapped itself around them. It was the kind of silence made quieter with the knowledge that something should be said. They all knew that. Rain sipped her coffee and stared absent-mindedly around the cafe. Jacob drummed his fingers against the worn table. Rachel stared into the dregs of her cup.

"So," Jacob said finally. "What are we going to do?"

"I don't know," Rachel said. "Do you have any ideas?"

"Ideas about what?"

"I don't know. Ideas about how to wipe your ass. What do you mean, 'Ideas about what?'"

"I guess it seems simple, doesn't it?"

"It's never seemed simple."

"Yeah." Jacob took a sip of his coffee, now cold.

"What about you, Rain? Do you have any ideas?"

"I think we need some plan of attack."

"A plan of attack is good," Jacob said.

"So let's use what we know about them…" Rachel began.

"And," Jacob interrupted, "remember that everything we know about them might be wrong."

"Right. Well, if it *is* them, we know where they should be. Out on Barker Road. Bones took us to the same place last night we were two years ago."

"Except we might not be able to see where they're staying. Their house," Rain said. "I mean, I didn't see it last night. Did you?"

"No," Rachel said. "Besides, we *might* not be talking about the same people. It would be one *huge* fucking coincidence if it wasn't, but it is a possibility."

"True," Jacob agreed. "So I think we need to get there during daylight. That way, if we *can* see the house, if it *is* visible, we can try to get in and do some exploring. I know for a fact their powers are not nearly as strong during the day. Whatever they are, you have to admit there is more than a little vampire in them. There's also maybe a little human in them and anybody who operates mostly at night has to sleep sometime."

"Yeah," Rachel said. "I'd be the first to agree with you on both counts."

"I'd probably be the second," Rain said.

"Okay. So what do we do when we get there?" Jacob said.

"Do you want to know what I think we should do?" Rain asked.

"Well, that is kind of why we're having this little pow wow here," Jacob said.

"I think we should burn the fucking place to the ground."

"Oooh," Rachel said. "I like the way this girl thinks."

"So we need to make a stop at the gas station," Jacob said. "I have one of those big five gallon things. If it is off Barker Road then we won't have to deal with trying to carry it all that far. And I think it's safe to say that I'll have a lighter. I don't think a little fire is going to be the end of them but I guess it'll be a good place to start anyway, burning them out of house and home."

Rain took a sip of her coffee and said, "I have to tell you guys I'm scared out of my fucking mind."

"How so?" Rachel said.

"Well, you just both seem so casual about this. These people are powerful. I saw what they did to Bones. I saw how much he *wanted* that to happen and it makes me kind of worried about what will happen to us if they're that destructive towards someone who just wants to be one of them. They almost got to me. I mean, Bones wasn't afraid of anything, but as much as he admired these people, I have no doubt it was just as much fear that made him do the things he did. How is it possible to destroy one of these things?"

Jacob ran his finger along the rim of his mug, looking at Rain. "Rachel and I have thought a lot about this over the past couple of years. My brother, James, left to find out about the Devils. He was convinced they were behind what happened to Rachel. Hell, by the time he left, he even blamed them for Mom and Dad's deaths. I haven't heard from him since but Rachel and I have a lot of theories based on our past experience with them. And just things pieced together from what James told me before he left.

"First of all, you have to stop thinking about destroying them. I'm not really sure you *can* destroy them. Whatever they are, they're definitely not human. Think of them like a parasite. A parasite has to feed off the living for survival. There is no other reason for that parasite to destroy human life other than the sake of survival. Plants and animals, what you think about when you think about parasites, are incapable of evil or morals or anything like that. They're merely trying to survive. I think that is why the Devils do the things they do. And I don't think they are all malevolent. I think some of them have found ways to exist without sacrificing humans. Although, they may not be as powerful. I think those are what you would call ghosts.

"So think of the Devils, in their raw form, as spirits. The most powerful ones, like the ones that undoubtedly controlled Bones, are ones that are able to infest a human body and keep it alive, maybe even rejuvenate it. They are capable of insinuating themselves into your thoughts and making you do things you would not otherwise do. But their power is, more often than not, confined to a certain area. This is where their house comes into play. Whatever that structure is, it is not just an ordinary 'house.' It's more like a portal. How else can it move from California to Lynchville? And I think if you were to go down into that house, you would find yourself looking upon a different world entirely and that would probably give you some kind of clue as to how the Devils operate.

"The less powerful ones, of which there are many more, are capable of typical ghostlike activities, showing up in strange places to give people a little fright. I don't think their mind control is any more powerful than giving a person the occasional nightmare or two."

"I don't know if this is helping or just making me more scared."

"Basically, my point was for you to not really think about destroying them. Rather, it will be like we are pushing them back or keeping them at bay. I think that's all we can hope for, right now."

"Yeah, but they *are* here for a reason. All of that stuff that you said about them being like parasites is kind of wrong because these people clearly *can* think and they are very capable of evil and they have to know what they're doing is evil."

"You're right," Jacob said. "They did come here for a reason and it is our goal to make sure that whatever the reason they came stays just out of their reach."

Rain looked down into the emptiness of her cup. "They came for you and Rachel, didn't they?"

"I'm afraid they did. Maybe more Rachel than me. In fact, I think they might just have come for all of Lynchville."

"Why?"

"Because they like it here."

Rain jumped across the booth when Stoop tapped his fingernails on the table. No one had even seen him approach. He was, as usual, dressed in head-to-toe black, looking more like someone dressed for a funeral rather than a bookstore and coffeeshop proprietor. He was well over six feet tall and looking up at him was kind of like looking at the ceiling.

"And how are you all this afternoon?" he asked.

"We're... really good," Rachel said.

"Is there anything I can get you?"

"More coffee?" Jacob asked the table as much as Stoop.

The girls nodded their heads. They were certainly having a two cup discussion. Stoop craned around to face the boy behind the counter. "More coffee, please, David."

"Sure," the boy said.

"Well, just let me know if there's anything you need."

"Thanks," Rachel said. "We will."

Stoop turned to leave, his black overcoat trailing out behind him.

"That guy's creepy," Rain said.

"He's a good guy."

"He needs to dress a little less scary. I think he was wearing eyeliner."

"That's just the way he is. He's always dressed exactly like that. Why change now?"

"Good point, I guess."

David brought over more coffee in a pitcher and went about re-filling their mugs.

"I'm still scared," Rain said after he walked away.

"You *should* be scared," Rachel said. "The point is... no amount of talking is going to make any one of us any less scared. Some strange shit is happening and it's just going to get worse until somebody decides to do something about it. I think we have to be those people. I don't think anyone else in this town is any more equipped mentally to deal with it than we are."

"I guess that's what I'm afraid of. Is it all mental? I have these visions of like some violent showdown. I don't think you can just destroy these people with your mind."

"No, of course not. That would be ridiculous. But there is nothing that can prepare us for whatever that violent showdown is going to be. We just have to do it. We have to try and stay one step ahead of these people. Besides, you'll be amazed with what you can do if you're a little bit scared."

"I guess," Rain said.

"Your life has changed," Jacob said. "And there's no going back to your old life. That's a scary thought too."

Their conversation died down. Two teenagers came into the cafe and sat down near the window. Jacob was too lost in his own thoughts to pay any attention to their conversation but he had seen the looks on their faces when they came through the door. They looked scared. Or at least the tall skinny one looked scared. And Jacob had thought Stoop looked scared also. Maybe everyone just looked scared to him now. Maybe he was the one who was truly scared, only he didn't feel that. He didn't feel that at all. His life, with the exception of Rachel, had become so dreary the past couple of years he almost welcomed this little adventure looming in front of him. And he was happy to see the two girls shared his conviction. Until they had shown up last night, he had thought he had reached the point of madness, the final bend in the road. If Rachel and Rain hadn't shown up with an account of their evening, he would have acquiesced to all of Dr. Bettermore's wishes. He would have started taking the pills. He would have tried to get a job. He would have decided to give his battered mind a little bit of rest. But now he knew he wouldn't be able to do that and he found that thought refreshing because it wasn't something he wanted to do in the first place. Let Dr. Bettermore have his sane little world of perfect mental hygiene, Jacob would take his own world filled with vampires and demons and he would take that world because it was a world that offered hope. With so much terror in front of him, there was also the distant promise of angels. And that promise, ultimately, was what Jacob thought he needed.

Nineteen

"Whose car?" Charlotte asked as the two girls left the high school.

"I don't mind driving," Autumn said.

"Cool."

They got in the car and began the drive toward town, toward the Wake Up Screaming. This had become something of a ritual for them. They would sit at a table they had now sat at enough times to consider it theirs. Then, over some frothy coffee beverages they would talk about their respective weeks at school. They were both fairly studious and didn't really talk that much through the week. When not studying, Autumn read voraciously and attempted to write short stories, maybe the occasional poem that would usually make her wince two weeks later. Said poem usually found its way into the trashcan or fireplace. Most of the stories she hung on to. She wanted to send them out to magazines but she didn't really have any ideas where to send them so she spent a lot of time re-vising. Charlotte played around with painting and photography. She had taken a class her sophomore year and knew how to develop her own pictures. Much to her parents' dislike, she had turned the basement bathroom into a darkroom. Autumn had posed for pictures. Most of them involved fake blood and not a lot of clothes. She wouldn't have posed for pictures if anyone else was taking them but she had learned a long time ago that she had something of a girl crush on Charlotte and would do just about anything she asked her to do.

The drive to the cafe was somber. All day, Autumn had sensed something bothering Charlotte. Well, not *all* day. She had seemed fine in English this morning. She guessed it really started around lunch. Charlotte had come to the table a little bit later than usual looking flushed and distant. And she was quiet. Charlotte was hardly ever quiet. She had even said herself she talked just to make conversation sometimes. She could normally comment on anything, be it the salt shaker at the table or Bobby Saxon's ridiculous sweater. At first Autumn thought she had started her period or something but she knew that was wrong because their periods were during the same week.

Autumn decided to wait until they got to the cafe to talk about whatever was bothering Charlotte. Talkative as she was, she kept things jovial at school. Seriousness—emotions—conveyed some kind of weakness. Autumn knew, if anything *was* bothering her, it would have to wait until after school.

As they drew closer to the cafe, Autumn didn't really know how she was going to broach the subject. She would probably be brash and just come right out and ask her what was bothering her. She lacked subtlety. Or maybe she just lacked social refinement. Charlotte was the only person she really talked to. It was probably just the new boy she was seeing, Autumn thought. She didn't even know his name. She just thought of him as the mystery boy.

Autumn pulled her small car up to the curb in front of the Wake Up Screaming. A dreadful parallel parker, she ran the tire against the curb before backing out into traffic and finally managing to get her car straight enough for it to classify as a parking space, rather than being half in the road and half-parked.

"Good job, little driver," Charlotte said. "That only took about ten minutes."

"You could have driven."

"I don't like to drive."

"I don't like to park."

"I don't like to do that either."

They got out of the car and walked through the afternoon sunshine into the darker confines of the cafe. Autumn recognized David Macklin behind the bar. He had graduated last year and she was pretty certain he didn't have a clue who she was. Not that things

like that really mattered to her anyway. Besides, most of his attention was given to Charlotte. It was like he couldn't look away.
Charlotte dressed and moved like a model. Her dress probably had
the boy wondering how long her legs were.

Autumn ordered a cafe mocha with an extra shot of espresso and
Charlotte ordered a skinny latte. The girls went and sat down. They
knew the boy would bring them their coffee when it was ready. He
moved painfully slow and Autumn thought she would die if she
had to stand there and watch him do this.

They sat in the seat by the window, hardly noticing the strangers
huddled in the back corner of the cafe and only dimly aware of the
sound of hushed, almost conspiratorial, conversation.

"So what's been bugging you?" Autumn asked.

"Nothing, really."

"Is it the mystery guy?"

Charlotte was silent for a minute. "Yeah, maybe it is the mystery
guy... But there are other things."

"Like what?"

"I'll tell you later."

"Wait, you can't say something like that and then say you'll tell
me later."

Charlotte met Autumn's eyes. "Well," she said. "Some of it's
kind of strange and I just think it would be easier to talk about
around a campfire with some wine in our bellies. Not out in public

like this."

"Okay. Well, what kind of stuff is it?"

Charlotte looked at the table and shook her head, knowing Autumn wasn't going to let up easily.

"Is it sexual stuff?" Autumn asked just as David set the tall glasses of coffee down on the table. Undoubtedly hearing what she had just asked, he lingered a little longer than was necessary. In order to shoo him away, Autumn said, "That's all for now. Thanks."

He lowered his head and crossed back to the bar dejectedly.

"Really," Charlotte said. "I promise I'll tell you about it later."

"What if there is no later? What if there is only now? What if the world ends before tonight? What then? Huh? I'll tell you what then. Then I go to my grave always wondering and never knowing what was bothering Charlotte Black."

"Nothing's really bothering me, okay? I've just never really had to deal with things like this before."

"Things like what?" Autumn couldn't really understand what all the fuss was about a boy. At least Charlotte *had* a boy.

"I don't know."

Then it hit Autumn. "Oh, I get it. You *love* him, don't you? Charlotte is in love. Is this your first time?"

"I'm not in love. Love is for desperate people. But I think I'm in something."

"Is it a cult?"

This caught Charlotte off guard momentarily. She almost thought Autumn was being serious. "Of course he isn't in a cult. Cults are so passé. Do you really think I would be some kind of cult slut?"

The people at the other table, two girls and a guy, got up to leave the cafe. Autumn's back was to the door. Charlotte watched them closely. There was something that *wanted* her to look at them. They all looked kind of hodge-podge and disheveled. And they had dark circles under their eyes. They looked like she felt. Too many late nights maybe. She wondered if the guy was sleeping with both of them.

"Okay," Autumn interrupted her staring. "So I guess if you absolutely promise to tell me tonight then I'll stop bothering you about it."

"What are we doing tonight, anyway?"

"The usual sounds good."

"So you *want* to do the wine and campfire thing again?"

"Might as well. It'll be too cold before too long. You don't have any plans with the love of your life do you?"

Not knowing it, Autumn had struck to the core of what was bothering Charlotte. She probably could have told Autumn that and saved a lot of time later. Instead she shrugged and said, "No. We don't go out every night. Hardly ever in fact."

"Oh, I see. It's just sex. You *are* sleeping with him aren't you?"

"But of course. Jealous?"

Autumn knew this was referring to a time earlier in the summer when, very drunk, the two girls had decided to make out. Charlotte had immediately forgotten about it, relegating it to the status of a joke. Autumn had obsessed on it for some time afterward. She had enjoyed it. That bothered her at first but she figured she knew it would before they ever did it and she had come to terms that Charlotte was just not into that sort of thing and Autumn knew Charlotte was the only girl she could ever do that particular thing with. That made it kind of intangible.

Autumn took a sip of her coffee, holding the cup sneakily in front of her face, "Oh, I'll win you back. You'll see."

"Gross."

Autumn laughed at her, hoping Charlotte would think she thought it was gross too.

The girls got away from talking about boys and recounted their week at school, lackadaisically sipping their coffee, two unemployed high school kids killing time. Charlotte thought about the trio that had just left. A quick and uncontrolled shiver ran through her body.

Twenty

Stepping into Jacob's apartment, the gravity of their situation was driven home. In the time they were at the Wake Up Screaming, someone had been in Jacob's apartment. It looked like the work of vandals. The ultimate goal seemed to be that of destruction, the only theft that of the remaining vestiges of security the three contained.

The couch bed was gutted, the stuffing and even the springs from the mattress strewn about the apartment. The stereo was caved in. The windows were shattered. Shelves were tipped over. The coffeemaker was smashed. The door had been ripped from the microwave. The refrigerator and freezer were open, their contents strewn about the kitchen. Even from the living room, Jacob could tell all the books, records and CDs had been pulled from the shelves in the study. Many of them looked ripped and broken. The corn plant Jacob had rescued from outside the previous night had been depotted, its leaves shredded. The clublike trunk lay in the middle of the floor, covered in blood.

Blood.

That was the most disturbing thing. Jacob could have dealt with everything else—it was all just *stuff* when you got right down to it—but the sight of blood immediately shattered whatever stability he had been holding onto.

It was like they all saw the source of blood at the same time.

A dead dog lay against the bottom of the wall that the television had once been against. It was gutted, its fur and skin torn away from its middle in two ragged flanks. Written on the wall above the dog, in what was presumably the dog's blood, was: RAIN IS DEAD.

"Oh God," Rain said, covering her mouth with her hand and going toward the bathroom.

It occurred to Jacob that, even though the girl had shared the bed with a murderer for nearly the past year, she had probably never seen actual gore up this close. She had admitted to seeing the dead bodies but, if Jacob was correct in his assumptions, the bodies would have been somehow *neat*, looking just like alive humans only... not alive.

Rachel looked at Jacob and he knew what she was thinking. She was wondering if whoever did this was still in the apartment. There weren't a lot of places to hide but the bathroom door had been shut when Rain went in. Jacob grabbed the remainder of the corn plant from the floor and crossed over to the bathroom, pounding on the door.

He heard a muffled sigh come from inside.

"Are you okay, Rain?" he said, almost yelled.

He heard her retch and then say, "Yeah... I just... I'm sick. That's all."

Jacob went into the study, wielding the trunk in front of him. He quickly scanned the entire room, subconsciously taking in the devastation that was the result of years of collecting. Turning to his right, he went to the closet and threw the door open, expecting the worst. But there wasn't anything in the closet. After hearing about Rachel's evening, he thought he would always have an even greater than usual fear of closets. He came out of the study and told Rain it was all clear.

"Who do you think did this?" she asked.

"Whoever it was knew Rain was with us. Which means they're a little bit more ahead of the game than we gave them credit for."

"That's a scary thought."

"Damn right that's a scary thought."

"Do you think it was one of *them*?"

"Honestly... no. I don't think it was the two people Rain was talking about. I think it was someone else. Probably Bones or another one of their henchmen."

"You really think they have henchman?"

"I think, if they can manage to control people's minds, then they can pretty much have anything they want."

"Why aren't they controlling us?"

"Are you sure they *aren't* controlling us?"

"Would we be going to hunt them if they were?"

"Think about it... Last night we take in a stranger. I mean an *absolute* stranger. After years of not even letting our friends in on our lives we let someone in, someone who almost tried to kill you, and tell them everything we know. Well, almost everything, anyway. And now, we're getting ready to go visit these fucks. We're walking right into whatever traps they've set for us. Maybe they *are* controlling our minds. Maybe they're leading us right to them."

"But we can't just sit around and let everything explode. And we can't just pack up and get the hell out of Lynchville."

"If we did that I think a whole lot more people would die."

"Whoever it was, they seem to have a particular hatred for Rain."

"Yeah, that was kind of what led me to believe it was Bones."

"Maybe he followed us."

"It's possible."

"Followed us and waited."

"I wouldn't doubt it at all. He doesn't seem the type to let a good thing get away."

Rain came out of the bathroom and mumbled, "Sorry."

"No reason to be sorry," Rachel said.

"I know he did this. That stupid shit."

"You know," Jacob said, "you don't *have* to come with us. You don't have to do this. We can drive you to the edge of town, put you up in a motel..."

The girl shook her head before Jacob could even finish.

"No," she said. "I'm going with you. If I don't help destroy these things I'll never be able to live with what I did. I know it isn't possible to undo what I've done but at least I can make sure it never happens again."

"Stay with us, then," Rachel said. "And if we come across your sweetheart again, maybe you can rationalize with him. Maybe you can bring him around to our side. I think we're going to need all the warm bodies we can get."

"I think he's too far gone to rationalize with."

Jacob said, "I think we should probably get going before it's too late. We've already wasted a lot of time and there isn't a helluva lot of daylight left. I was thinking we could swing by McDonald's and grab something to eat on the way so the coffee doesn't make us all jittery."

"I think we need to be jittery," Rachel said.

"We also need to be strong."

"Are you saying McDonald's makes you stronger?"

"Now is not the time or the place for jokes, Ms. Stokes."

"Fuck off, Riley."

"I love you. Even after that last comment."

"Good. I've got you right where I want you then. And I love you too."

"Let's stop before we make Rain throw up again."

"You guys are nice to see," Rain said and Jacob noticed the look of longing in her eyes. It was the look of an innocent girl who thought, at one time, she had everything Jacob and Rachel had before having it stripped away from her. And that, he guessed, was why she was insistent about coming with them. She might have been interested in righting her wrongs, but she was also mad as hell at the people who she blamed for taking that away from her. "I want to get out of here," she said.

"Let's go then," Jacob said.

They left the apartment and piled into Jacob's battered old Saab, on their way to whatever cruel fate awaited them.

Jacob tried not to think about it. Thinking, he knew, wouldn't do him any good. The Devils had the ability to take everything he was thinking and make it somehow wrong. Every thought he had was a trap. Especially if they *did* have the ability to pick his brain. The goal was to give them an empty bag without any thoughts to pick from, without any conscious or subconscious to warp into their twisted nightmares.

They drove the streets of Lynchville, oddly busy with Friday traffic. The conversation was nonexistent. They drove to the edge of town, first stopping at the gas station. Jacob pulled the five-gallon plastic gas container from his trunk and filled it up. He didn't think this would be enough gas to burn down a house, let alone a house that might not even be there. He didn't even know what it was they were trying to do. Maybe they were just trying to force some kind of confrontation. The thought of how that confrontation might end petrified him.

If they did this, he thought, if they did this right and they were able to flush the Devils out of Lynchville, then he and Rachel would have to leave as well. That was all there was to it. He couldn't live surrounded by fear and that would be what remaining in Lynchville would be like. He already knew he wouldn't be able to live in his apartment anymore. He wouldn't be able to step foot in it without thinking of that ghastly gored dog lying there on the ground and this whole rather ghastly day, spread out both behind and in front of him. He would go back to clean up and collect his things and that was it. That thought didn't comfort him at all. He liked his apartment. And now he was going to have to abandon it just because of them.

Finished with the gas can, he went into the convenience store to pay.

They drove across the parking lot to the McDonald's, getting some food that would hopefully give them a bit of energy. They ate in the car on the way out to the reserve, to Barker Road, to a little valley that maybe, just maybe, contained some portal into an entirely different world. It was both mundane and terrifying. Three young adults sitting in a car, sucking down soda and French fries, heading toward some archetypal nightmare that had, in different ways, haunted each of them.

In the sky, the sun experienced a slow death. Along the twisty winding roads out past the flat farmland, the trees had a strobe effect, filling the car with alternating light and dimness.

That was exactly how Jacob felt.

"It was around here somewhere," Rachel said.

"A little further," Rain said.

Up ahead of them was a sort of clearing in the woods and the road rose while the ground beyond it seemed to dip.

"Okay, up there, I think that's it," Rain said.

"You remember that from last night?" Rachel asked.

"I have an uncanny knack for directions. Going from town to town, I think you kind of develop that. Or else you just spend a lot of time being lost."

Jacob's grip on the wheel had tightened. He pulled the car off the gravel road and onto the grassy shoulder. The sight of Bones' van was the only thing hinting they were in the right spot.

Jacob, not knowing it was Bones' van, said, "Looks like somebody already beat us here."

"That's Bones' van," Rain said. "Isn't it stupid?"

"Well, it wouldn't occur to me to paint a skull on my car but it also probably wouldn't occur to me to kill a lot of people so somebody else could drink their blood, either."

"He's probably in there," she said.

"Wanna see?" Jacob said. "It can be our first challenge. Warm up with the humans before battling the monsters."

"We don't have any kind of weapons do we?"

"There's a tire iron in the trunk. I think that's about it," Jacob said.

"So prepared," Rachel said.

"I don't think we should go down to the van without *some*thing," Rain said.

Jacob, feeling somehow obligated to act macho, said, "I'll get the tire iron and go down. If worse comes to worst, he'll kill me but we all know that no one ever really *dies* here. Maybe it'll be an advantage."

"No," Rain said. "I think I should go down. I know how to talk to him. But I still want to take the tire iron and I want you guys to be close by."

"How 'bout we all just go together?" Jacob said.

"Good plan," Rachel muttered.

They all got out of the car. Jacob went to the trunk and opened it, the smell of gas hitting his nostrils. He took the can out and put it on the ground before reaching in to grab the iron.

He slammed the trunk shut and said, "Am I the only one who fails to see the house?"

"I don't see it," Rachel said.

"Me either," Rain said.

"Okay, so I'm not just blind. Anyway, this is going to make it kind of hard to burn down."

"I think we'll have to wait," Rachel said.

"Wait for what?"

"Dark. I have this feeling they're not going to let us see it until dark, when they're stronger. The darkness is *their* time. But they *do* want us to see it. At least, they want *me* to see it."

"You could have shared this feeling back at the apartment."

"Why? So we could hang around there a little bit longer. I know it's so hospitable and comfortable there right now but I kind of wanted to get out."

"Your sarcasm does not amuse me. I have a tire iron and some gas. I'm heavily armed, you know."

"You don't scare me."

"Fine."

Rain was already walking down toward the van and Jacob thought there had to be a part of her that wanted Bones to be in the van. And there was probably a part of her that wanted to find him somehow transformed into who he used to be, the disillusionment lifted from his brain. Jacob saw the first as a grim possibility but he knew the latter was highly improbable. Wherever the boy was, he wasn't going to return the same person who went into this nightmare.

Rachel and Jacob trailed Rain by about fifteen feet. Rain walked through the knee-high grass until she reached the van. She went to the back of it, her hand on the chrome of one of the back doors. Jacob heard the door click as she depressed the handle.

He took a deep breath as she pulled the door open.

Twenty-one

Rain swung the door open and it seemed to take an impossibly long time getting there and when the door *was* finally open, Jacob could see Bones spring out of the back of the van, a knife in his hand, throwing himself on Rain, savagely cutting her throat before he and Rachel could move toward her.

But that didn't happen.

Once the door was open, the only thing they stood looking at was the empty black mouth of the van.

He breathed a tentative sigh of relief. Tentative because it now meant they didn't exactly know where Bones was. He could be anywhere. He could be coming up behind them right now. Jacob had known weapons wouldn't work against the Devils but he had forgotten about this potentially treacherous human element.

"He's not here," Rain said.

"What do we do now?" Rachel asked.

"I don't think there *is* anything to do but wait, is there?" Jacob said.

"But you know how I hate to wait."

"Well, we could always explore."

"But then we turn our backs on the house."

"I have another idea. This might kill a few minutes," Jacob said. "Rain!"

"Yeah," she said, still standing up near the van.

"Are the keys in there?"

Rachel and Jacob approached the back of the van as Rain went up to peer in through the driver's side window.

"They are," she said. "That's not like Bones at all. Leaving the keys to his van."

"Good. I have an idea."

"So what's your big idea," Rachel said.

"Well, I'm thinking the five gallons of gas we have might not be enough to, you know, burn down an entire house... but an *explosion*. That could do some real damage. So, if the house decides to make an appearance, I suggest we pour the gas around the perimeter of the house, take the van up to the hill and run it into the house."

"That might be a better idea."

"And we can just hope it explodes."

"Knowing our luck, it probably won't. What time is it, anyway?"

Jacob looked at his watch. "A quarter after five."

"How much longer does that mean we have to wait."

"It should start getting dark around seven."

"A couple of hours then."

"So we're left to wait... always *waiting* for them."

"Always waiting for them. A little better when you *know* they're coming, though."

"I guess."

"You want to get the van up on the hill?"

"Might as well."

On the other side of the reserve, in the neighborhood of The Oaks, Charlotte Black and Autumn Jackson performed a raid on Charlotte's parents' liquor cabinet before they came home from work. The idea was to find the desired substance and stash it in the woods without being seen so when they retreated into the woods later her parents wouldn't suspect any type of corruption.

Giggling, the two girls found two half-empty bottles of red wine. This was the cheap stuff her parents drank for the occasional special family dinner they had. It wasn't the good stuff they broke out for guests or her father's clients. This stuff wouldn't be missed. Her parents drank enough anyway and Charlotte's continual removal of things from the liquor cabinet probably made them think they had occasional blackouts and staggering gaps in memory.

Charlotte didn't feel too bad about it. She thought it would have been hypocritical for them to complain. Besides, she figured the more she drank, the less likely she was to think about Zack. If she spent all night thinking about Zack then she wouldn't be any fun. Of course, she *would* be thinking about Zack. She planned on telling Autumn everything, just like she had promised. She was tired of carrying the burden herself. She needed to share these certain dilemmas she had come up against. Ultimately, what she would be jockeying for would be Autumn's support. She wanted Autumn to approve of Zack and the circumstances of their almost purely physical relationship. She wanted Autumn to say, "If it feels good then, by all means, carry on." Because Charlotte wasn't so sure something that felt so good could be a healthy thing.

After selecting the wine, the girls carried it out to the edge of the woods, just far enough in so they couldn't be seen. It wasn't entirely legal to build campfires on land that was technically owned by the county. But they were always careful and Charlotte couldn't see the harm in it. No one had managed to burn down the woods yet and the rest of the neighborhood would just think it was someone burning off leaves.

Once there, they hid the wine in a knot at the bottom of an old sycamore, where it would stay cool and out of the dying sunlight. They built the fire. It was a small fire and they were experts in fire building by now. The lighter would not be put to it until after dark.

A ring of stones encircled the dormant fire. They built a pyramid out of small dry sticks and filled the pyramid with dry leaves and newspaper. When that got roaring, they would throw a small log onto it. They didn't really care about the size of the fire. The most important thing was that it burn for as long as they wanted it to burn.

They went about this act with the carefree nonchalance of dozens of Fridays over the past couple of years. They laughed about the stolen wine. They felt empowered by the hidden secrecy of their little fire as they retreated to Charlotte's room to listen to music until dark. Doing so, they moved in the shadows of the town, on the outskirts of Lynchville, not knowing that they should feel so connected to it. Not knowing they moved on the surface of some dark, ancient, and ugly truth.

Twenty-two

Rain did the honor of driving the van up onto the hill. She turned it around so its rear would be the first thing to hit the house, figuring that would give the gas tank a better chance of exploding. They pulled it just far enough up the hill so it could gather some good momentum without curving too much either way and missing the house entirely. Of course all of this was rather suspect. They didn't have any idea of where the house was actually going to be—if there was going to be a house there at all. They had to plan for this. They had to realize the house might just not show up and then they would be just as lost as they were before. A small part of Jacob hoped the Devils had moved on, that they had moved to some other town that wasn't his. But he dismissed that part. He wanted them *here*. He wanted them right in front of him so he could try and knock them back into whatever hell they had come from and if he died trying to do this then at least he would die with the knowledge that he had tried to do something good.

Besides, he knew they were here. He couldn't explain it. It was just some kind of quality hanging in the air around him. It was the way the wind felt on his skin when the breeze picked up. It was the fragrance of the dead leaves in the woods around him and the sweet smell of fire somewhere far out in the town. It was the look of the cold moon, coming up early in the blue sky. It was the cold cackle of a wolf or a wild dog.

They were here. Somewhere. He knew they were.

Twenty-three

Ilya and Ernst sat in the front pew of the Low Church, staring up at the stone slab of the altar. The pews were stone; they looked like they had been chiseled from bedrock, like they had always been there. Maybe they had not always been there, but they had been there for as long as either Ilya or Ernst could remember. This place, the Low Church, was what made Lynchville special. And what made the church special was the thing that thrived in the room behind the altar. They had to think of it as a thing because how else could something be both a person and a place?

The Dark Fire.

Neither a he nor a she, it had to be an it. It was both Heaven and God. Or maybe it was both Hell and Satan. It was the promise. That was how Ernst and Ilya thought of it. It was a place of the spirit. Most of the spirits, it rejected. The Dark Fire wanted seasoned spirits. It wanted trained spirits that had looked upon the world, the world that had rejected it, for hundreds of years.

Take the boy they had fed to the Dark Fire just last night. Immediately rejected. Sent into some kind of nebulous free floating region beyond human sight and mostly out of the reach of human understanding as well.

Ernst stood up from the pew and walked over to one of the walls. The walls were adorned with the dead; they hung there like sconces, in various stages of decay. He stroked the leg of the corpse nearest him, feeling her powdery gray skin beneath his fingertips.

"They're here," he said.

"I know," Ilya replied, continuing to stare up at the altar.

Ernst looked at her, surrounded in the blue light that lit the church, that blue light that came from nowhere.

"I can smell them," he said. "There are three of them."

"Are we going to let them see it?"

"Of course we're going to let them see it. I don't think we can afford not to. It will draw them like moths to a flame." Ernst chuckled at his trite metaphor.

"But not yet."

"No. Not yet. It is not dark yet. We need strength. Do you think they have any idea why we are here?"

"I doubt it. I'm not even sure I know why we are here."

"Because we are entering the Dark Fire."

"It's always been that simple to you, hasn't it?"

"Yes, it has."

"And you think it's going to be that simple. You think we can just discard our old powers into fresh new bodies and it is going to let us in?"

"I think it's time. Think of everything we have done for it. Nights we have starved so we can offer it up a nice juicy human. The years we have sacrificed."

"What if both of us don't make it?"

Ernst came over onto the pew, sitting back down next to Ilya. He placed a hand on her thigh.

"How could that be possible?" he asked.

"I don't know," she said. "It just seems like something it would do... as a joke."

"If you're not there, then I do not want any part of it. Do you want to be there? You seem reluctant."

"Of course I want to be there but there are going to be things about this world I miss."

"Like what?"

"Like the feeling. Like the flesh. I like the flesh. I like *my* flesh. I like *your* flesh. All of our victims, all through the years, I have craved their flesh—the source of all their screams. All that pain."

"You're going to miss the pain."

"Sometimes it seems so sweet. You can't say you don't feel it?"

"No. No, I've felt it. And I would be lying if I said that, at times, I didn't relish it. The pain was always our art, wasn't it? That was what we were good at? Pain and fear."

"And fear is really just some other kind of pain. It is like a mental pain."

"Are you feeling as cruel as I'm feeling?"

"I think so. If this is to be our last night of the flesh we need to make it something spectacular."

"Without getting distracted."

"Of course, without getting distracted."

Ernst moved over to kiss Ilya, feeling her plump lips against his, her cold tongue inside of her mouth. He grabbed her arms, as cold as the stone they sat upon. Still, it stirred him. He longed for it but could not allow himself to become distracted. Not tonight.

"We need to go fetch the boy," Ernst said. "For strength."

Zack had come back from Lynchville High and collapsed onto the couch, knowing he would have at least a couple of hours before Ilya and Ernst needed him again. Now he woke up. It was not yet dark. Meager sunlight poured through the windows and he was pretty sure he heard voices from outside the house. In his brain, he heard Ernst calling him. He needed him to come downstairs. Zack went over to the window to see if he could see the source of the voices but the only thing he could see was dense fog, rolling past the window. He knew that meant the house had become invisible again. If there was no looking at the house then there wasn't any looking out of the house either. It wasn't like a two-way mirror.

He took a deep breath and went to the back of the house, opening the door leading to the narrow staircase. Already, he could feel their lips at his wrists. They would undoubtedly be hungry. They needed his blood. He was getting tired of the routine. He wondered when he was going to get some of *their* blood. When they were going to suck him dry and then bring him back to life.

He knocked on the door at the end of the stairs.

"Enter," Ilya said.

He pushed the heavy door into the room.

They were seated at the large table.

They looked pale, nearly as dead as they really were. Zack wondered what they would do if he was to refuse them. If he was to cut off their supply. Of course, he *knew* what they would do. They would simply find someone else.

He stood at the table and proffered his wrists to them.

"Thank you," they each said, taking a wrist and sinking their teeth in, puncturing the skin, sucking the blood. Sucking gently, careful not to take too much.

Ernst pulled back from the wrist, blood smeared around his lips, his dark eyes going somehow through Zack.

"Tonight is the night," he said. "Tonight is the night you become one of us."

"Thank you," he said.

"Do you think you are ready?"

"I know I am ready."

"It is going to be a difficult night. Are you aware of that?"

"Yes."

"You need to bring us the girl. This one you have been chasing. We need her. We cannot wait another night. Before you go to get her, I think you need to see what all of this is for. I think you need to see the Dark Fire."

"Yes. I would like very much to do that." Zack had read about the Dark Fire in the *Leaves of Six*. He only knew the book said the place was too beautiful to describe.

"Follow me," Ernst said, standing up.

Zack felt a kind of excitement rise up within him. It felt like he had waited so long for this and now that it was actually happening, it seemed like it was happening too fast. From what he had read, he knew what Ernst had proposed to show him. Yet, it was still a complete mystery. It was like reading about Heaven. What was an individual's idea of Heaven and did it change from person to person? Was the Dark Fire some kind of concrete paradise or would it be specifically tailored to him?

He followed Ernst into another room, into the Low Church.

Zack had never been in this room. The stone pews rose from the stone floor. He looked, open-mouthed, at the corpses dangling from the walls and he looked at Ernst's back, how the man slid through all of this casually. Of course he slid through it casually, he had seen it all countless times before.

It all seemed so simple now.

Everything clicked into place for Zack.

He was a replacement. Ernst had specifically sought him out and then tested him to make sure he could perform in Ernst's place. And where was Ernst going? Off to the Dark Fire, of course. Zack felt his excitement rise further. If he was taking Ernst's place, did this also mean he was going to "inherit" Ilya? No, he knew this could not be the case. Although he had not spent a lot of time around Ilya and Ernst, he felt there was something very much like love that passed through them. Sure, it may not be conventional love, but it was as close as they could come. Zack didn't think anything could transplant spending that many years being near one another. They had to either love each other or hate each other and he knew that if one of them hated the other then at least one of them would be dead. But, weren't they both dead? Okay, one of them wouldn't be around.

When Ernst reached the large, elevated stone altar, he turned to Zack and said, "Now, when we go in here, you are not to say a word. Do you understand that?"

Zack nodded his head.

"And we are not going to be in there a very long time. A few seconds at most. And if we do not have a lot of time to talk tonight, you need to remember one thing—do not come in here again. What you are going to see is very powerful and you will not want to leave but if you stay, it will consume you. And the Dark Fire will need to be fed. It needs its sacrifice. That is what keeps it in existence. But when you bring people to it, use the lesser Devils. They are about. You will know who they are. They are the shells. They are the ones without sight and the ones without souls."

"Zombies," Zack said.

"If that's what you want to call them. Are you ready?"

"Yes."

"Very well then. I hope this does not destroy you."

Ernst swung back the door and Zack expected the man to enter the room with him and then remembered the flaw in that thought. If he could come in the room with him, that would negate everything the man had just told him. He was alone. On his own. He walked into a vast room and heard the door shut behind him.

It was more like a cavern.

He stood surrounded by stone, staring at a huge fire on the far wall.

Was this what he had come to see? A fire? It didn't seem that spectacular.

Nevertheless, he stared into the flames, squinting his eyes against them. Suddenly, he lost himself. There was no other way to describe it.

A sensation snaked through his body and he fell to his knees. Not only did he look at the fire, he somehow saw *through* the fire. What he saw on the other side was what he had always wanted to see. He wasn't exactly sure what it was. He didn't think he would be able to stare at it long enough to see exactly what it was and he didn't think he would be able to know that without being in there because it seemed to be so many things at once.

It was a beautiful, full-moon night.

It was a lush woods or a garden, green and sunlit.

There were people there. Every beautiful person he had ever seen in his life was on the other side of that fire and they all looked at him with a kind of longing that seemed terrifying. And he knew that if he could reach through the fire and touch just the air of that place then he would be able to feel the air on his skin and wherever he touched it would be like a million different orgasms.

The door opened behind him and he heard Ernst call his name.

He didn't want to go back but he wasn't so far gone that he had forgotten the warning. Yes. He needed to shut his eyes on it now. He needed to turn his back on it now so that sometime down the road it could all be his.

Unable to shut his eyes, he put a hand over them, stood up and nearly ran back to where he thought the open door was. He smashed into the wall and felt along it with his free hand until he reached the opening door.

Stepping out of it, Ernst shut the door behind him.

Zack removed the hand from his face and looked at Ernst. "Do you think it will be worth it?" he asked.

"I know it will be worth it," Ernst said. And that removed any doubt Zack ever thought he would have. He realized he was crying with the sheer beauty of the vision. It was the first time in his adult life he had ever done that.

"You are touched now," Ernst said. "Tonight you drink and become one of us. And everything you do from there on out is to sustain the fire. And how well you do that will be what helps you gain admittance to the land beyond."

Ernst clapped an arm around his shoulders and led him into the Low Church.

Twenty-four

The threesome lazed on the hillside. Lazed as much as they could, anyway. Their ears were all a little sharper. Their eyes a little shiftier. Their reflexes a little tighter. Jacob had retrieved an old blanket he kept in the back of the car and threw it down over the grass. They all stared at the bowl of the hollow, waiting for something to happen and each of them were probably thinking the same old cliché: "A watched pot never boils."

"It's getting chilly," Rain said, crossing her legs over each other, tugging Rachel's shorts down as far as they would go.

"It'll be getting dark soon," Jacob said.

"Then it will only get colder," Rain said.

"I meant, maybe it will be over soon."

"Yeah... over," Rain said, wondering exactly what that meant.

Rachel sat quietly, Rain on her left and Jacob on her right. She stared up at the sky, as though willing darkness to come or mentally pushing it away. Jacob took the opportunity to look at her. Even though they had been together nearly constantly for over two years he still liked looking at her. The way her dark hair, tinged with just a little red, fell behind her ears, the absolute flawlessness of her skin. If they were not in the middle of all of this, he didn't think he would have been able to keep his hands off her. Another thought crushed him. What if this really *was* the end? Not of the Devils, but of them? What if tonight was the night they died? And what if they could not be together in death? What if all of that were just super- stition and the dreamings of Christianity? What if he never, after tonight, had the chance to look at her again? What if he never had the chance to hold her, to slide inside of her, to feel the heat that seemed to grow and pulse around him?

Rain disturbed him from his musings.

"Shit, guys, did you see that!" she blurted.

"What?" he and Rachel said simultaneously, immediately alert.

"Something... Down there," she pointed toward where they all apparently thought the house should have been.

"I don't see anything," Rachel said.

"Me either," Jacob said.

"I saw *something*," Rain said. "I know I did."

"Well what the hell was it?" Rachel asked.

"I thought it was a man."

"A man?"

"Yeah. But I don't see him now either. It was just a second. I swear I saw him. He took a couple of steps, looked up towards the sky, and then he was gone."

"I guess we could go look around," Jacob said. "Did you just see one person?"

"Yeah, one person. It was a guy."

"Was it Bones?" Rachel asked.

"No, it wasn't Bones. Definitely not Bones."

They all stood up at the same time. Jacob brandished the tire iron out in front of him. "Do you think a tire iron is a cool weapon?" he asked.

"No," Rachel said.

"Why not?"

"I think it's a desperate weapon. It's like what people use when they're not prepared. It's like having to wipe yourself with leaves if you get stuck out in the woods."

"But it'll do the trick, right?"

"That depends on what we're dealing with, I guess."

"For the sake of safety, let's pretend it'll do the trick."

"Okay, it'll do the trick."

"And let's pretend it's a cool weapon."

"Okay, it's a cool weapon," Rachel said.

"The coolest," Rain said.

Jacob led the way down the hill. A nearly palpable sense of dread enclosed him as they reached closer to the bottom, where the foul house should sit. Jacob knew it was them, working whatever power it was they had. The darkness seemed to increase the farther down they went. It grew colder.

"Where do you think this ghost thing would have been going?" Rain asked.

"Well, town is that way," Rachel pointed to her right, toward the woods rising up the smaller hill there. "Through the reserve."

They universally turned in that direction.

"I'm starting to get a really bad feeling," Rachel said.

"Yeah," Jacob said.

"Yeah," Rain said.

"Like the proverbial shit is about to hit the fan," Jacob said.

"Exactly," Rachel said.

"Good thing I have this tire iron," Jacob said, and then added, "The coolest weapon in the world."

They moved slowly, the ground beneath their feet feeling almost marshy. Reaching the edge of the woods, they stood still, peering into the darkness. In the woods, it was already dark, it was already nighttime. Not one of them saw what was in the woods. The two wolves looked at the three humans and growled lowly, nearly inaudibly. Not one of the three of them heard this, but goosebumps pimpled each of them, chills shivering down their spines. And each of them had a flickering moment where they thought maybe they shouldn't be here, maybe here was much much more dangerous than they had at first suspected.

Twenty-five

Bones knew it wasn't all the way dark yet but he didn't think he could stay buried underground any longer. Boredom and restlessness begged him to move. Raising his arms from the damp soil, he cleared the dirt away from his face, standing up, smelling it in his nose. It was odd that he could smell everything so strongly without breathing. He didn't need to breathe now. It was like the scents just seeped in through his pores.

These new found senses amazed him. He knew these woods were full of spirits like him. Some of the spirits inhabited animals. Some of them inhabited trees. Some of them moved freely, only to be seen by certain people, and how many people would see them in the remote areas of the woods anyway? Bones didn't *see* any of them. But he felt them. He felt them deep within the soul inhabiting the body of Daniel Clock. And he *knew* things about them.

It was amazing, the amount he knew now.

Some of these spirits chose to serve the masters he had chosen. The rest were in hiding. Hiding from the masters. Too weak to do their bidding. Bones did not want to be like them. He would have done something to hurt them if he could. But he knew if he grabbed the bird that chirped, off to his left, and strangled it in his hammy fist, then only the bird would be killed, the coward soul left to seek some other shell.

How many had the Devils claimed over all these years? he wondered. The number was obviously very vast. Uncountable.

And Bones was here to help them claim more. He didn't know how he was supposed to do that. Ernst had given him specific instructions before burning him up in the fire but, already, those instructions were becoming confused in Bones' head. He couldn't remember exactly what it was he was supposed to do.

Slowly, trying to fight the rigor mortis setting into the body, he wandered through the woods. Sometimes he found himself without the cover of trees, the remaining sunlight glinting through, washing his skin. Wherever the sun touched, it made him itch, like he was developing some kind of rash.

Through the woods he walked. Not knowing where he was going. Not knowing what he was supposed to do but knowing tonight was a very special night for Ilya and Ernst and he didn't want to let them down. He wanted to be part of their nocturnal network.

He wanted to ensure it ran smoothly. He wanted to show them he was more worthy of their praise than Zack.

Bones thought back to last night when he had spit on Zack lying on the couch. A thrill ran through him. It had felt good to do that. Maybe he would use the powers he had acquired in death to kill Zack. But maybe that would only put Zack closer to where the Devils needed him to be. Things were so confusing. Bones wished it were dark. If it were dark, he knew, his thoughts wouldn't be nearly as jumbled and confused as they were now.

Twenty-six

It seemed a strange combination of light and shadow. Not one of the three saw the wolves at first. Two wolves, charging out of the woods, coming toward them.

Jacob opened his mouth, ready to say something, maybe ready to say, "Run!" But the word never came out. He was to Rachel's left, Rain to her right. The wolves pounced on Rachel and Rain. They were huge, black and snarling, driving the girls down to the ground. Jacob sprang into action as quickly as the wolves were upon them.

One of the wolves held Rachel down, his large paws on her shoulders, ready to take a bite out of her jugular. Jacob stood over top of it, straddling it, and brought the tire iron against the side of its head, trying to snap its neck in a direction away from Rachel. It worked, at least momentarily. Jacob swiveled from atop the wolf, ready to bludgeon the one that had driven Rain down.

It wasn't there.

Rain wasn't there.

Jacob looked toward the woods and saw the wolf dragging Rain's body toward the wooded cover. Part of him wanted to charge after the wolf. Even if Rain was already dead he wanted to run after it and catch it, beat it to death with the tire iron and dance in its blood. But something inside of him told him it wouldn't do any good and Jacob had learned to trust those voices. He had to deal with Rachel's wolf first and then they could go stalking in the woods once that one had been put down.

Rachel's wolf had become his wolf.

As he turned back to her, he heard the snarl and then felt the wolf's teeth bite into his leg with savage ferocity. He screamed. It felt like the dog's teeth went down to the bone. Everything happened so fast and yet there was a great deal of clarity there. Maybe it was like the killer taking a snapshot of the fear in his victim's eyes before he pulls the trigger. Jacob looked down and saw the wolf clamped onto his leg. He saw the gash on the side of the wolf's head where the tire iron had struck it and how the blood ran over the wolf's right eye, turning the white to red. And, almost absurdly, he saw Rachel behind the wolf, taking hold of its tail and pulling because that was the only thing she could do.

Jacob really wished they had brought some other form of weaponry.

Right now, he needed to get the wolf off his leg. He struggled for a good grip on the tire iron, a good angle to hit the dog from.

With everything he had, he brought the iron down across the bridge of the wolf's snout. He felt the teeth rip downward in his leg. The last thing he wanted to do was fall. The last thing he wanted to do was put himself at the same level as this powerful, snarling beast.

Repeatedly, he brought the iron down, feeling the bone in the wolf's snout crack, feeling the wolf's teeth work against bone.

He turned the iron around so he held the arched end in his hand and the beveled end with the little notch on it was pointed toward the wolf, seeking out a soft spot. He angled it to where it impacted on the corner of the wolf's mouth.

This did it. Maybe it severed some vital muscle there or maybe it simply broke the wolf's jaw, but the bite loosened.

Now it turned its attentions to the one pulling its tail. It whipped its lithe body around, gnashing its teeth. Or trying to. It was a ghastly sound. Like loose, bloody gums flapping together. Jacob wanted to laugh. Served the fucker right.

He wasted no chance. With the wolf's back to him, Jacob went after the spine next, beating it with the metal bar, right in the center of its back, hoping to shatter something all-important to the wolf's ambulatory faculties.

Finally the wolf crumbled, lying on the ground and whimpering.

Jacob breathed harshly.

"Seems like it would be cruel not to finish it off, huh?"

He didn't wait for Rachel's response. With his good leg, Jacob turned the body of the wolf over. Its legs dangled just over the torso, probably paralyzed. He stood over the wolf, pointing the sharp edge of the bar where he thought the heart would be. He drove it down, putting all of his weight behind it. The bar entered smoothly and Jacob, losing his balance, nearly fell on top of it. He threw himself to the right at the last minute, landing on the grass beside it, already smelling the blood and death stink coming from it.

Rachel came over to him, inspecting his leg.

"Does it hurt?" she asked.

"It's unbearable," he said, looking up at the darkening sky.

"It looks pretty mangled."

"I would say so."

Rachel rolled up the leg of his pants. She moved her hand over the bloody, tattered skin.

Something had given Rachel this gift. He wondered if they were somehow *meant* to defeat the Devils.

Aside from being with Rachel that had become his one driving purpose in life.

If he wasn't the one, then surely Rachel was. Why else would she have that gift? That beautiful and amazing gift? If they weren't meant to defeat the Devils, then at the very least they were meant to protect others from them.

But they hadn't protected Rain, had they?

Rachel moved her hands over Jacob's wound, her fingers sloshing around the wet fringes of his skin. She brought them together, smoothing the skin like one might smooth a piece of crumpled paper or try to match up the edges of a tear.

He felt the power run through him. A deep itch. Something like an orgasm. Or the beginnings of one. An orgasm that would never come to fruition. It was the skin growing back together. The muscles growing back together. The tendons and nerves doing the same.

It wouldn't be perfect. Rachel wasn't that powerful yet. But it wouldn't continue to bleed and it wouldn't hurt as bad. Jacob knew there would probably always be a scar there and he might end up walking with a slight limp in the long run but, right now, the only thing he cared about was getting through the night.

"What about Rain?" he asked.

"The wolf took her. *They* took her."

"Should we go after her?"

"Of course we should go after her."

"Are we *going* to go after her?"

"What do you think?"

"I think we should."

"We can't spend all night looking for her."

"I know. But we can't abandon her. She came here to help us."

"She got herself further involved with something she never should have been mixed up with in the first place."

"And that's worth being abandoned for?"

"Piss on your conscience, Riley."

"Until dark. And then we come back."

"Until dark. Now get up and let's start looking."

It was that reluctance. That reluctance that assured him Rachel's feeling about this being their purpose was the same as his.

She held out her hand to help him up.

"Thanks, by the way," he said. "That's a hell of a Band-Aid you've got there."

"Well, thank you for getting the fucking thing off me."

"You're quite welcome."

Twenty-seven

An integral part of any teenager's life, especially one in rural Lynch-ville, was driving. After Wake Up Screaming, Charlotte and Autumn drove back to the high school to get Charlotte's car. There, Charlotte had driven back to her house, Autumn to hers. From there, Autumn drove over to Charlotte's house.

Now they sat, side by side, in front of the small but warm fire. Both of them had changed clothes. It being a chilly October evening, both of them had opted for jeans. Charlotte wore a black thermal shirt and Autumn wore a red hoodie over her t-shirt. They had already put away the first half-bottle of wine and were now working on the second. Autumn waited for when Charlotte was going to talk about the mystery boy and then decided she wasn't *going* to unless prodded. Autumn was now just drunk enough to do a little prodding.

"So are you going to tell me what's been bothering you? About this boy."

Charlotte pulled another Camel Light from the box and lit it. This was the only time either of the girls smoked, around the fire. They both agreed it was actually a pretty disgusting habit and they tried to keep it to a minimum.

"He's just weird, I guess," Charlotte said.

What kind of answer was *that?* Autumn wondered.

"How do you mean, he's weird?"

"I don't know. He just doesn't seem like other people, is all."

"Like how?"

"Well, he bites me."

"He *bites* you?"

"Yeah."

"So he's kinky?"

"Maybe. But it's not like he playfully bites. He breaks skin."

"He breaks skin?"

"He makes me bleed."

"He sounds like a psychopath."

"And I like it."

"You *like* it?"

"Yeah. A lot, actually."

"Doesn't it *hurt?*"

"Like hell. But that doesn't stop me from liking it."

"That *is* weird."

"That's not all."

"Okay, tell me."

"You're going to think I'm fucking insane if I tell you."

"Try me."

Now Autumn pulled a cigarette out of her pack. This was getting good. She turned to face Charlotte a little more. That way she could tell if the other girl was telling the truth or making up a story.

"It has to do with the Devils."

Autumn's first instinct was to laugh. Then she remembered her lingering dream from last night, the one that had made her feel icky for the greater part of the morning and decided not to.

"So, what?" Autumn said. "You believe in the Devils now?"

"I've always believed in them. Well, I've always *wanted* to, anyway."

"Why?"

"I don't know. You hear about so many things and then you have to start telling yourself they *are* real. I mean, it would be like too many coincidences if they weren't real, you know?"

"I've heard all of that too but I wouldn't go so far as to say that I *believe* in them. It's geographical. Like Christianity. You hear a lot about that too but I don't know if I would consider myself a believer. And if you're going by sheer numbers then what about Islam and Judaism and Buddhism? A single person can't believe all of them but each group boasts a huge amount of believers.”

“Okay. I didn’t mean to bring religion into this or anything.”

“I’m sorry. Tell me what you started to tell me.”

“All right. Well, this kid, he just like comes out of nowhere, you know. And he doesn’t go to school and he doesn’t talk about his family or anything like that. He says he doesn’t even *live* with family. He says he lives with friends. And he’s always wearing the same clothes and he shows up at really odd times and today I think I saw him disappear.”

“Disappear?”

“Yeah. Okay, well, he came to the school today. He was in the bathroom when I went and we did our thing and then I started to leave and when I looked back he just… wasn’t there.”

“There are so many things wrong with that I don’t even want to go into it. I think you’re just trying to freak me out.”

“Why would I do that? Take this seriously, please. I’ve needed someone to talk to for a while. The worst thing is that, when I’m around him, there’s like this magic. I can’t explain it. It’s like something inside of me just shifts. I start to feel good. I feel like this is the right thing. I mean, it’s an actual *physical* feeling. And then when he goes the only thing I can think about is seeing him again. So, what do you think?”

“What do I think about what?”

“Do you think I should keep seeing him?”

"I think you should keep seeing him until you find out the truth. Everyone has their kinks. Maybe he's not a psychopath although he kind of sounds like one but it doesn't sound like he's done anything completely insane yet. Except for the disappearing. That's just weird."

"You don't think I really saw it, do you?"

"Well, it's kind of hard for me to believe. I'm sorry."

"Yeah, I don't even know if I believe it myself. There's just something about him that feels almost like a figment of my imagination. I wish you could meet him. That would make him more real."

"Well, any time you want to bring him around, I'd be happy to meet him. Do me a favor, okay, and just be careful. You don't really know everything there is to know about this guy and as magical as it all sounds you have to realize there's the potential he might be a dangerous person."

"Yes. I realize that."

"And you're too smart to let him drag you down."

"Thanks, Mom."

Autumn threw her finished cigarette into the fire and took a slug from the wine bottle, warmth sliding down her throat.

A loud popping sound startled her and she dropped the bottle. She and Charlotte both looked toward the sound, toward the perimeter of the woods.

They saw a silhouette against the outdoor lights of Charlotte's backyard.

"Shit," Charlotte muttered. "What's that?"

"I don't know," Autumn said under her breath.

"Hello?" Charlotte blurted, already standing, ready to run.

Autumn tightened her grip on the bottle of wine, ready to use it if she needed to.

The man grunted. Autumn wanted to get closer to him, to see if he was someone they knew. She also wanted to run. She didn't get a very good feeling coming from this man at all. Maybe he was just someone drunk and stumbling through the neighborhood but Autumn didn't think The Oaks really had that many homeless winos and she had a minimal amount of faith in the ever vigilant neighborhood watch program.

"Hey!" she called, a little more forceful this time.

The man grunted again, staggering toward them, coming into the ring of the fire's light.

He wasn't right.

Charlotte and Autumn seemed to observe this at the same time, both of them gasping.

It looked like he was either rotting or had been very badly beaten. Badly beaten and then maybe dragged through the mud.

"This isn't good," Charlotte said.

"No," Autumn agreed.

"Get the fuck away," Charlotte said.

Hoping it would startle him into leaving, Autumn broke the bottle off on a tree, feeling like she was ready to get into a bar fight.

"Hello," the man managed to grunt out, raising his arm up in the air.

And then he burst into flames.

There was an audible *whoosh* as he expanded outward before being drawn back into the flame that had come from the inside of his body.

Charlotte screamed. Autumn jumped, grabbing hold of Charlotte's arm.

The man collapsed into a charred heap on the ground in front of the fire. The girls surrounded him, looking down at him, still wondering what the hell was going on. Still terrified but now for completely different reasons. People did not just burst into flame. It was impossible. It didn't happen.

Then again, people didn't disappear.

"What's going on, Charlotte?"

"I don't know." Charlotte was crying now. This was all too much for her to handle.

"What do we do?"

"What do you think we should do?"

"I don't know."

They looked down at what remained of the body, just a few

crackling embers and, after a few moments, even that was gone. Now there was just a pile of ashes that could have been left over from any fire.

"Do we call someone? The police?" Autumn asked.

"I think that's a bad idea."

"Okay, well then what the fuck are we supposed to do?"

Now Charlotte did not look so much terrified as excited.

"Don't you see?" she said. "This is a mystery. This is something we're supposed to figure out. I think our lives just got a lot more interesting."

"Well, I don't know about you, but I think my life just got a lot scarier."

"Certain things make sense now."

"Oh, shit. Like what?"

"Come on. I have an idea."

"Where are we going?"

"Have you ever heard of the Sad House?"

"Of course I've heard of the Sad House. But I've never seen the Sad House. *No one* has ever seen the Sad House. And they've never seen it because it's just a stupid made-up myth like the Devils and everything else in this town that's supposed to be scary. Christ, if all this shit were true, who in their right mind would live here?"

"I'm going to the Sad House. Are you going to come with me?"

"I don't see what that has to do with any of this."

"Maybe it doesn't have anything to do with this but I want to see Zack. I want to ask him a few things and I think I know where to find him now."

"Great. So, let me get this straight. Not only does he disappear but he lives in a house that doesn't really exist? And you just came to this conclusion after seeing some guy... fucking *spontaneously combust* right in front of us?"

Charlotte cocked her head, as if thinking about this and said, "Yeah, I guess... if you want to put it that way. Coming with me?"

"Do I have any choice?"

"Yes. You do. You have a choice. You can go home if you want to and leave me to face all the awful creatures of the night alone," Charlotte pouted. "Me, your bestest-estest friend."

"You know I really hate you."

"How else are you going to make the exploding man make any sense?"

"I don't think any of this is going to make any more sense in the morning."

"But we have to go just to find out, don't we?"

"Whatever you say. I'm listening to you now, remember?"

"That's a good choice."

Autumn half-expected Charlotte to go through the back yard and head out to the street. She was surprised when she began going back toward the woods until she remembered the Sad House was supposed to be on the other side of the reserve, out on Barker Road, and it made just as much sense to go through the woods as it would have to circle all the way through town.

The shock of what they had just seen still lingered within them and yet it was almost outside of them. Maybe that was what shock was. Some numbing sensation to keep them distanced from what really happened. To keep it from sinking in. And that, in the end, was why Autumn followed Charlotte. She was hoping to see something that would make everything make sense. She was hoping to see something that proved the burning man didn't exist or maybe just to prove the burning man was another hallucination on a night of hallucinations. Or maybe she even secretly hoped to see sights even worse than the burning man, just to drive that initial image out of her head. She had woken up this morning dreaming about wolves and now she was with her best friend, on the way to a most likely nonexistent haunted house after hearing her boyfriend might be a Devil. It was a strange day and she didn't think it showed any signs of letting up.

Twenty-eight

Bones guided the body of Daniel Clock out of the reserve and back into his fancy neighborhood. It had one of those expensive signs at the entrance. An elaborate brass carving between two pillars of brick. "The Oaks," it said. There he stumbled across the back yards, hoping he wouldn't be seen until he came to the people who were supposed to see him. He heard Ernst (*or was it Ilya, or was it both of them*) whispering in his brain. They would tell him what to do once he reached those who were supposed to see him.

It was just two teenage girls sitting around a campfire, filling the night with banal chatter and Bones couldn't see what Ilya or Ernst would possibly want with them but it wasn't his job to question. He was only there to serve the master. If he served the master correctly then he could claim his rightful spot. He was still wondering what that spot would be. He didn't know what they wanted him to do but it seemed like they wanted him to get rid of the body he was in.

It was a test.

It had to be.

Bones didn't know how he was going to go about it. At first, he tried to just exit the body, imagine his spirit somewhere else, but this didn't work.

Then he imagined destroying the body. He imagined it burning from the inside and the body swelled out, catching on fire he did not feel. And then he was outside of the body. Above the body. Looking down at it. Watching it burn.

Once outside the body, he heard the masters' commands even more clearly. They were calling him back to them and they wanted him to enter his own body. They had it laid out and prepared for him, washed in the mysterious fire and hopefully stronger than before.

Bones soared above the twilight trees of the reserve, going back to the small valley.

Twenty-nine

By the time Zack reached the woods from the house, he was no longer invisible. He didn't know if the three people who had seen *something* leave the house, saw him become more substantial again or not. Grateful for the coverage of the woods, he raced along a path, hoping the three wouldn't see him and start after him. He doubted he would be able to outrun them.

When he heard the wolves behind him, crawling across the ground and stalking toward the edge of the woods he had just left, he knew he was safe for now. Ilya and Ernst had called the wolves. They had called them to protect him and that made him feel something like one of them.

He stopped running and slowed down, catching his breath and regaining his composure.

He had never really seen Ilya and Ernst in action. Had never seen their powers on anyone other than him and that other creep, Bones. He wanted to watch the wolves. Zack stopped and turned so he could look out at the wolves, careful to stay behind a large tree. He stared at the haunches of the black wolves, watching them spring into action. They went for both of the girls and for a second Zack seized up, hoping the boy would stay and try to fend them off rather than making a dash into the woods after him. Zack knew the boy had played the Devils' game before and he wasn't exactly sure how he would react. One of the wolves went after the girl on the left, grabbing her around the wrist and coming back into the woods.

Coming toward him.

He started to run away before stopping.

The wolf brought the girl to rest about five feet in front of him.

Was she dead?

He approached them. The girl looked up, saw him, and screamed. The wolf looked at him, looked *into* him, as though expecting some kind of order.

Zack knelt down beside the wolf.

"Take her deeper into the woods," he said. "But leave her alive. Don't hurt her any more."

He stroked the back of the wolf, running his hands along the coarse greasy hair.

The girl's eyes were livid, insane, darting around in their sockets.

"You have to help me!" she screamed. "You have to!"

"You are not mine to help," Zack said, turning his back on her, disappearing deeper into the woods.

Thirty

Ilya followed Ernst up the narrow stairway leading from the lower level, the Low Church. His hand trailed out behind him and she clutched it delicately. Outside, the sun fell rapidly and they both knew what they were going to do. Her throat grew thick with the thought of it, as it did every night.

Together, they entered the ground floor of the house that could not be seen from the outside. The only thing that could be seen from the sagging windows was the milky white fog. They crossed the rooms until they reached the staircase at the back of the house. There, they ascended that staircase as well, going to the bedroom on the top floor.

This room was the same as it was two-hundred years ago. Maybe a bit more aged. The wallpaper was peeling in places. The bed sagged in its old wood frame. But the setup of the room was the same. And the feeling was the same. Ilya felt the same giddiness she had when Ernst had first taken her virginity in this room so very long ago, when they were both alive, when they were both human.

It amazed her. The human body amazed her. Even though hers had not been technically alive in so many years, it still yearned for all those things that had made her feel most alive before she had experienced her unnatural death.

A breeze blew in through the windows, bringing the sadness of late summer with it. The breeze always hinted of late summer. Even in the winter, it carried that scent, that dying heat. Ernst laid her down on the bed and her head was alive with the scent of old wood made fragrant by the humidity and the clean linen of the bed clothes.

"This might be the last time we do this here," Ernst said.

"Tomorrow we might not even need to use our bodies," she said. "Can you imagine what that will be like?"

He leaned over the bed and kissed her. It was a deep, loving kiss, his tongue sliding in her mouth. Together, they generated their own kind of warmth. He untied the string holding her black dress up above her breasts, sliding it down, exposing her fully. Then he re moved his clothes and climbed in the bed with her.

Time became irrelevant as they moved against each other. They made heat out of coldness. They put moisture where there wasn't any. No area of their bodies went unexplored. This was how it had always been. And while there had been nights filled with frivolities involving other men and women, those were just amusements, some exercise of the flesh that ended in death. But those were the nights and this was twilight, this was sunset, and that had always been their time. That was the time Ilya knew she had Ernst. And not just that she had him against her, filling her, but the time she knew she had his mind and something as close to love as he could come. As most people grew more tired, they grew stronger as the day birthed the night. Through everything, she often thought this was the most important time for her, Ernst holding her, inside of her. This was the time that meant everything and she didn't really care if it took place in this house or if it took place beyond the Dark Fire, it meant the same thing. It meant that, wherever she went, she would have this other soul to look out for her and protect her.

Each of them climaxed as the sun sank below the horizon.

Ilya lay against Ernst, in the soft spot of his shoulder, smelling the same man she had smelled all these years. He absently played with her hair and stared at the ceiling.

"We shouldn't be doing this," he said.

"Doing what? We've done this every night."

"No. Not that. We shouldn't be simply lying here, enjoying ourselves. There is too much that needs to be done."

"We can't prepare any more than we already have."

"You know there are more people out there, don't you? People who want us gone."

"One of them is the girl. I can sense that. My replacement. Rachel."

"And here she is, wanting to kill you."

"Is that irony?"

"Not sure. You think Zack's a good one?"

"I think so."

"You know he has someone else in mind, don't you?"

"Yes. But I think he'll warm to our choice."

Ernst took in a deep breath. "She is beautiful."

"Which one?"

"All of them. Except that shit that fucked everything up last time."

"I thought we had him on the ropes."

"Thought he was going crazy, didn't he? Voices. Depression. Sacrifices right there on the television. If I had another week, his brain would be jelly."

"We were focused on other things."

"We'll be able to handle him. Getting the girl will be the important thing. Getting Zack away from the other girl will be something else. What's her name?"

"The blood on Zack's tongue says 'Charlotte.'"

"Think she's dangerous?"

"Could be. But I also think she's in love. We both know what that will do."

"Yes," Ernst said. "Yes we do."

"Tonight, we will be drank to death."

"Drained completely."

"Maybe the boy... what's his name?"

"Jacob."

"Maybe he'll come in handy when Zack tries to make Rachel drink your blood."

"Perhaps."

"Maybe Charlotte was meant to be the replacement."

"No," Ernst said. "We cannot trick the Dark Fire. It was very clear about that. It has to be Zack and Rachel. We can't lose her again. She's the challenge. Not everyone comes to us as easy as Zack. Everyone else has to die. They can't know anything about what goes on here."

Outside, the milky fog lifted, replaced with the purple of the sky. Already, even as the sound of the insects was dying off, the singing of the dead began. A sad lament that sank into the bones. Both Ilya and Ernst knew that if they looked outside, they would be able to see the dead, emerging from the ground, emerging from trees, emerging from animals—thin spirits, blue-white, nearly transparent, that almost no one else would be able to see. If needed, he knew, he could draw them to him. He could bring them to do his bidding. Those that wanted to help him would come and those that did not would stay away. Those that did not want to help him were the dead who had not yet seized upon this unique power he had to offer them—the power of a parasite. It was really only common sense. If a dead person wants to feel more alive, they must feed from the living. To be dead was to be beyond morality, beyond good and evil.

He drew Ilya closer to him, bracing himself for the night ahead and waiting for the end because he, of all people, knew that every end heralded some wild and mysterious beginning.

Thirty-one

While Jacob and Rachel were not gathered around the house to see it emerge, it did. More than emerge, it became a substantial thing, carved out of the air. Like watching a Polaroid develop from the slate gray background, the images became more colorful and clearer. It took only a matter of minutes once the sun disappeared from the sky. Once, where there was nothing, there now stood a house, looming over the wild grass of the valley.

"Fuck! Fuck! Fuck!" Jacob shouted. "She's fucking nowhere. Just... gone. I don't even... what the hell are we doing here, anyway?"

They had reached a clearing in the woods. Darkness loomed above the canopy of the trees. Already, they had looked for Rain longer than they had agreed upon.

Jacob continued. "Why does everything have to be so fucked up?

You know, everything was going along okay until last night when everything was just shot to hell. Blown to pieces. We need to go back. Why don't we just go back home? Why can't we just go back home?"

Rachel placed a hand on his arm. "Let me take you back about twenty-four hours, Jacob. I was sleeping peacefully when somebody came through my closet to kidnap me with every intention of bringing me here because someone that lives here told him to do it. You were at your house when you saw something on the TV that caused you to smash it into little pieces and the last time we were at your 'home' there was a gutted dog on the floor and a rather ominous slogan written in blood on the wall. Of course, now that I think about what was written there, it seems to be more prophecy than slogan. Do you still wonder why we can't go home?"

"No. As usual, you have placed things into a very cheery perspective."

"Glad I could be of service."

"We need to go back to the van. We need to see if that fucking house is there."

"I thought you were the one who didn't want to leave her."

"Do we have any fucking choice? I mean, really, do we have any *fucking choice* when it comes to any of this?"

"If she was meant to be found then we would have found her."

"What's that supposed to mean?"

"Look, there's no sense in us standing here and arguing. We can either continue to look for Rain or we can go back to the house. It's up to you."

"I don't want it to be up to me. Then whatever happens becomes my fault."

"Oh, you want it to be *my* fault?"

"Have I ever blamed you for any of this?"

"You just did."

"What the hell do you mean?"

"Just that, if it wasn't for me, you would have never come face to face with this."

"If it wasn't for you, I'd be dead."

"And if it wasn't for you, I'd be one of them."

They looked at each other, reaching that silent understanding that had become inevitable.

"None of that matters now, anyway," he said.

"Don't you realize what we did last time? We did something very important. We stopped them from whatever it was they were trying to do. I did it and you did it. And that made them scared. Scared of me and scared of you. They came for me just as much as they came for you. So stop wallowing in your self-loathing and face the facts that we are in this together. That I couldn't walk away from it, could never have walked away from it, no matter how much I might have wanted to. And I don't know about you but I haven't been the same person since the last time we dealt with these things."

Jacob stopped. His last bit of argument was gone. He guessed there were a lot of things they hadn't talked about over the past couple of years. Now was not the time to drag all of that out in the open but it was there, left in the back of his mind for him to meditate on.

He had never told her why he hated to leave his apartment or how, if he stared too long into a person's eyes, he saw things. It overwhelmed him. Even people he had always thought were good were capable of some of the worst things imaginable. And he didn't know if these things were true or if he saw these things as a result of the Devils trying to somehow trick him. Like maybe they wanted him to see the evil in people so when they came back for him he would be easier to take, easier to convert. And she had never really told him everything either. Even though he knew it was there. He saw it every time he looked into her eyes. He saw it. He saw her giving her first blowjob to a neighbor boy when she was thirteen. He saw her contemplating a bottle of her mother's pills. But none of this had made him hate her. It only made him love her more. It made him fear for her. It made him want to keep her close to him so that nothing could ever happen to her again, so she would never have to look at a bottle of pills and think swallowing them would be better than waking up to the humiliation of another day.

He drew her close to him and hooked her hair behind her ear, bending down and giving her a slow kiss.

She pulled away from him, wanting more, desperately wanting there to be nothing more to do than stand there in the middle of the woods and kiss forever.

"So we're leaving Rain to fend for herself?" he asked.

"Come on. No one dies in Lynchville. You know that. Sure, maybe a big bad wolf came along and ate her but we'll probably see her walking down the block tomorrow. Or at least tomorrow night. I hear the dead are rather fond of the night."

"I just feel so..."

"Mean? Cruel? Heartless?"

"Yeah. Something like that."

"If we were to continue looking for her, you do realize we would just be looking for a corpse, right? I mean, there isn't a chance in hell she's still alive."

"Yeah. I'll tell myself that."

"And this is what she would have wanted."

"No. She would have wanted to live. That's what she would have wanted."

"Well, at least if we do this, then she can have a proper death with a heaven and a god and all of that stuff rather than coming back as a werewolf or a zombie or a vampire or whatever the fuck these things are."

"A heaven and a god and all that stuff? Are you delusional?"

"No. Just hopeful."

"Okay. Now is not the time to talk religion, I guess."

They left the clearing, going back toward the hollow, Jacob wondering what part religion played in all of this. He had always thought of himself as an agnostic. He could see how a person who had a firm religion would be adamant about stopping the Devils, why the legends abounded in quite the way they did around Lynchville, spread, as they were, by its mostly Christian citizenship who thought the concept of earthly life after death was unholy. Jacob didn't really know what he thought about holiness. Personally, he found the concept of life after death appealing. He didn't really have any desire to leave the earth. Heaven was a gamble, he had always assumed. He wasn't so ready to leave the world behind and head off to a promised land that might not be all it was promised to be. The thing that bothered him about the Devils was the evil they seemed to bring with them. But maybe he couldn't think of them as being evil. Maybe they were just doing what they had to do. Like what he told Rain about them being parasites. Maybe he was closer to the truth than he thought.

Did they have religion? he wondered. And, if so, what kind of promises did that religion contain? Most of the Christianity he had been exposed to had centered around death—you lead the "cleanest" life possible in hopes that you will be accepted by God upon death so your soul can gain admittance to Heaven. But what would the religion of the dead be like?

He hoped he would have time to think about this later. Shifting the tire iron to his left hand, he grabbed Rachel's hand with his right.

"Do you think it's going to be there?" he asked her.

"The house?"

"Yeah."

"I don't know. I guess we'll know when we get there."

"Good answer."

They walked through the woods that now seemed very dark, each of them wondering exactly how far into the woods they had wandered, when they reached the edge and stared down into the hollow and the house that had miraculously appeared there while they were away.

"Holy shit," Jacob said.

"That's right," Rachel said. "I'm so happy we have something to burn."

"I say we run for the van."

"You okay to run?"

"I think so."

"Go," Rachel said and took off running toward the van.

He now realized things were happening faster than he wanted

them to. He had wanted to douse the perimeter of the house in gasoline and then back the van into it so that, hopefully, the van exploded and the fire spread around the house but now that the house was actually there, he found that he wasn't in the greatest of hurries to get very close to it.

But he knew he had to. They couldn't come all this way to do an even more half-ass job than they already were.

Their quick sprint to the van left them both panting, out of breath.

"We need to make sure it isn't going to turn off the path," he said.

He opened the driver's side door of the van and crept inside. The claustrophobic interior of the vehicle, coupled with the fact that he knew this was where Rachel was held captive, greatly disturbed Jacob. He wished he would have seen Bones. He wished he could have been there to help Rachel. He didn't think Bones would still be alive if that were the case. Jacob would have done whatever he could have to destroy him. Being able to destroy the guy's van was only a small consolation.

Between the two seats, he found a length of white rope that looked like the kind used for clotheslines. This was probably what they had tied Rachel up with. He created a tight knot around the bottom of the steering wheel, in the middle. He took the other end of the rope and wrapped it around one of the mechanisms below the seat. He thought it was probably the lever that was used to slide the seat backward and forward. Tightening the slack, he wrapped the rope between the steering wheel and this device. Hopefully, this would keep the wheel from turning during the van's descent. It was already on a hill so Jacob didn't think he would need anything to hold the accelerator down like he had seen done in movies so many times. All he would have to do was put the van in neutral and hope it gained enough speed before it smacked into the house.

"Can you get the gas can?"

Rachel, who had been silently observing him, nodded her head and started for the Saab.

By the time he got the rope as tight as he wanted it, she had returned with the gas can.

"Okay, great," he said. "Now, here's what we're going to do. I'm going to run down there and do a quick lap of the house with the gas can. Then I'm going to try and catch the gas on fire. When you see that it has caught fire you need to put this puppy into neutral and let it go. Is that simple enough?"

"You're going down to the house?"

"I have to. I think it's important that it burn as quickly as possible."

"'Kay," she mumbled.

"I love you," he said, leaning into her, putting his hand under her chin and angling her face toward his for a kiss.

"I love you too. Be careful. If you see anything strange come back up here. Okay?"

"I will. But I think we've already seen some pretty strange things so I'm not exactly sure what you're classifying as strange these days."

"You know what I mean."

"Yes. If I sense danger, I will tuck my tail between my legs and come running back to you."

"Good."

"Let's get this done."

He took the gas can from her and started at a light trot down toward the house, dread creeping into his bones. He just wanted this to all be over.

Approaching the house, he looked in the windows.

He didn't see how it was possible anything unsavory could be going on in there. It just looked empty and abandoned. With the pale moonlight shining down on it, it was a little creepy looking, but it didn't seem to be dangerous.

He flipped open the air hole at the back of the can, took the cap off the spout and started a steady stream. It came out with just enough force so he was able to douse the actual boards of the house rather than the ground around it. Hopefully, this would ensure the structure itself actually caught fire and if the van exploded upon impact, that would be even better. Especially if those things were inside. He didn't know if it would kill them or not but it would at least have to give them one hell of a shock.

He quickly scampered to his right, encircling the house with the gasoline.

The house wasn't especially large and it took maybe a minute at most to get back around to the front of it. He decided to use the remainder of the gasoline on the porch. He bounded up the steps, emptying the can in front of the door. This would make sure the exit was blocked too. That was an idea he liked. Trapping those fuckers in there with nowhere to run.

He pulled his lighter out of his pocket and turned toward the hill to see if he could see Rachel. The night was relatively clear and the moon afforded a good amount of light. He could see all the way up to the road. Rachel's pale face wavered in the darkness beside the black splotch of the van.

He struck the lighter and reached down, touching it to the damp gasoline, knowing this wasn't the best idea in the world. He heard it sizzle and swoosh.

From the top of the hill, Rachel put the van into neutral, backing away from it as it began its descent.

He lingered on the porch for just a moment, making sure the gas had caught.

Adrenaline rushed through Rachel. It seemed like Jacob stood on the porch too long. What if he got hit by the van?

He probably hadn't stood there that long. The van wasn't even halfway down the hill yet.

Then she saw the door to the house open quickly, cutting through the fire, and a strange-looking something that wasn't wearing much clothes grabbed Jacob and pulled him into the house, slamming the door behind him.

Rachel's mouth dropped open. The van slammed into the house and everything else went according to the plan. It exploded on impact, partly due to the nearly rusted-through gas tank. And the house, so much old wood, burned at an alarming rate.

Alone, Rachel ran down the hill toward the house, half-thinking she could go in and pull Jacob back, but by the time she was anywhere close to the house, it was already completely engulfed in flames. Slowly, she backed away from the intense heat, wondering what she was going to do next.

Thirty-two

Rain lay in the darkness of the woods. The smell of molding, decayed leaves surrounded her. She smelled blood. In her nose. Coming from her arm. The wolf no longer had her by the wrist but it was close. She was afraid to move too much. She was afraid to angle herself so she could get a better view of it. She did not want to alarm it. She wanted to make it think she was going to be down for a while and, for all she knew, she probably *would* be down for a while.

It suddenly occurred to her that she might die out here in the woods. Alone. Stranded out in the backwoods of some rural town. She wanted her parents. She wanted to go back home to California. If she was going to die, she didn't want it to be like this. The only reason she had left with Bones in the first place was to escape the pervasive banality of her suburban life which, in and of itself, was a kind of death to her. She didn't think she would now be staring it face to face.

If she could manage to stand up, if she stayed conscious that much longer, she wasn't sure she would be able to make a run for it. She *knew* she wouldn't be able to outrun the wolf. It would be on her in a matter of seconds and then it would probably make her pay for trying to escape. She knew it wasn't just a mindless wolf skulking around the perimeter of her body. If it had been a real wolf then it probably wouldn't have attacked her in the first place and if it did it wouldn't have just dragged her out here to the woods to sit and wait. It certainly wouldn't have taken orders from that other guy. She had never seen him before but wondered if it was the Zack kid she'd heard Bones mention. It almost had to be.

This wasn't as bad as it was going to get. Something else was going to happen. The wolf acted like it waited for something. Like it was guarding her.

Jacob and Rachel were her only real hopes for escape. Deep down, she knew that. She only hoped they would come looking for her. Sadly, she realized this was probably not the case. They were not here for her. They were here for themselves. They wanted something out of that house. For all Rain knew, Rachel and Jacob were the truly evil people. That was entirely possible. The whole thing between Rachel and Bones could have been a concoction. Bones could have been testing her faith toward him and Jacob and

Rachel could have led her into this trap. After all, she didn't see Rachel get hurt and Rain's wolf seemed in an awfully big hurry to get her away from them.

No.

She knew none of that was true. Things were as they had been. She knew Jacob and Rachel were good as soon as she met them. Just like she knew, deep down, that Bones had been bad news. She was partly to blame for this. Not only was it stupid to come with Bones in the first place it was wrong to just sit by and watch as he embarked on atrocity after atrocity.

Her arm was really mangled. She could hardly move it. The blood pouring from it had dampened the ground beneath her. Her grasp on consciousness was no longer that strong. It seemed to waver in and out with each breath she took.

Thirty-three

From somewhere high above the woods, Bones could see every-thing. It was like he could see through the night and he could even see through the leaves hanging from the trees.

The house was burning. That was the first thing to catch his at-tention. That must have been why he was called back. Maybe Ilya and Ernst needed him although he hadn't received any distressful feelings coming from them. Rain was in the woods, somewhere behind the house, not that far from the perimeter of the valley. There was a large black wolf circling around her.

Bones knew he would have to go to her before going to the house. If Ilya and Ernst were in trouble, they could let Zack help them out of it, he thought ruefully. He had some business of his own to take care of. He didn't really know if he would see Rain alone. He figured the other girl and her boyfriend had probably taken her somewhere out of town so the little bitch could flee back to her rich mommy and daddy. He couldn't pass up the chance to stress his dissatisfaction with her. He couldn't risk her getting away from all of this and telling the police or somebody about all the things he had done. Not that he really thought she would do that. Not that it would really matter if she did. She would come off looking just as guilty as he would. But, even if she tried to cover everything up, it would leave too many questions unanswered. Eventually, maybe, the right people would try answering those questions.

He brought himself toward the wolf, this vehicle of animation. The spirit that had occupied the wolf gladly left. Bones never realized there were all of these spirits everywhere. Most of them did not partake of the joys of actual flesh and blood like he planned on doing. The only time most of them did this was when Ilya or Ernst commanded them to do it. Like they had undoubtedly ordered this spirit into the wolf, ordering it to do the things it did to Rain.

Immediately upon entering the body of the wolf, Bones felt that hypersensitive rush of living flesh pass through him again.

He enjoyed using this new magic. He sniffed around Rain until she looked at him. Then he backed away.

It was time for some more magic.

He willed himself to take his old form. He realized he would end up looking just like he imagined in his head so he performed some minor alterations while still remaining, essentially, the same person.

His hair was a little fuller. The acne scars were gone. He had maybe just a little more muscle mass than he had before.

While he took this shape, he looked at Rain, studying her, not just making sure she didn't run but relishing the look of shocked horror wiping itself across her face. She probably thought she would never have to look at him again either. He was about to show her exactly how wrong she was. Exactly how wrong she had ever been to leave him.

Thirty-four

Unconsciousness threatened to grab Rain and take her under until the wolf pressed its wet nose vigorously against her arm, startling her. She looked at the wolf, watched it slowly back away from her, and consciousness suddenly flooded back to her.

The wolf was changing.

It stood up on its hind legs and Rain thought crazily that it was like watching a werewolf in reverse. For some reason, she knew the end result would be more terrible than the wolf itself.

The change was quite rapid, the wolf's fur not falling off but just disappearing completely. It was becoming a man. She watched the wolf's skin stretch and then bulge with muscles. She watched as clothes were painted onto the naked body, gaining substance, and then she looked at the man's face and her breath caught up in the back of her throat.

"Bones?" she said. She had to ask because even though he looked a lot like Bones, he looked a lot different than the Bones she remembered. It was almost like this person could have been Bones' more attractive older brother.

"That's right," he said.

"How did you do that?"

"Because I've seen the other side. They finally let me in. I told you it would happen only you decided to run out before it could."

"You're sick, Bones. You were sick. The things you were doing were wrong."

"They've already poisoned you."

She struggled to stand up. She did not want this confrontation with someone who had always been stronger than her, who had always been able to overpower her. She just wanted to get away.

Nausea threatened to double her over once she was able to stand upright in front of Bones, two feet away.

"Nobody poisoned me, Bones. I saw you that one night, you know? That night you did those things to that dead girl."

"I had to see what it was like."

"No you didn't. There are some things people can live without knowing."

"No there aren't. We have to experience everything we can."

"I'm getting the fuck out of here."

"Like hell you are."

"Stop me."

She took off walking through the woods because a walk was the only thing she could muster. She felt too broken to run.

"Come back here, Rain."

"I'm finished listening to you, Bones."

"No you're not."

Suddenly he was behind her, grabbing her arm, as though unaware it had been mauled. He grabbed her head and tried to kiss her. She pulled away from him, the thought of those lips touching her made the nausea grow even worse.

"You're not going to get out of this alive," he said. "You are mine and you will always be mine. You and any other bitch I want now."

"Just let me go, Bones. I promise if you let me go I won't tell the police anything about what you did."

"I don't need to worry about police anymore. Can't you see that, Rain? Can't you see how I've changed? I'm dead but I've never felt this alive."

"Fuck off."

Bones reached out and smacked her, lightning quick. His knuckles felt like stones cracking into the side of her face. She went back down onto the ground.

"The only question I have to ask myself now is if I should fuck you when you're alive or when you're dead."

He fell on top of her.

"Bones. Stop."

His hands were beneath her shirt, pawing at her small breasts, his hips grinding against her.

"I don't have to stop. There isn't a thing you can do about it."

She wanted to scream but was afraid that if she did then the sound of her own shrill voice would send her back into unconsciousness and then Bones would be free to do anything he wanted to without her even being able to put up a fight.

She wondered what was more important to her—keeping Bones from raping her or her life. In one sense, she thought if he raped her she could almost just think of it as him fucking her like he had countless times in the past and God knew that sometimes when Bones fucked her, even when she had let him, it was something similar to rape. But if he killed her then he killed her and that was it. Of course, there was a good chance if she let him fuck her, he would end up killing her anyway.

"Can this wait?" she asked.

"I don't think it can," he said. He worked at getting her shorts down her legs. She didn't wear any underwear. She hadn't minded putting on Rachel's clothes but she drew the line at someone else's underwear.

He put his hands around her neck, squeezing.

"I can take you to them," she spat, seeing it as being maybe her one chance at survival.

"Who?"

"Jacob and Rachel."

She could tell that Bones thought about this. About how good he would look to those mysterious strangers if he could redeem himself by getting not just the girl they had come for but the boy as well.

"You're lying," he said, unfastening his own pants.

"They're at the house. I can take you to them."

"You just told me where they were. Why do I need *you* to take me to them?"

"But they're hiding."

"I can sniff them out myself. I can see things now I couldn't see before. I saw you laying down here from all the way up in the sky. Did you know I can fly now?"

Rain didn't like the sound of his voice. Panic filled her. He hadn't bought anything she said and there was a part of her that wondered if she would really lead him to Jacob and Rachel if he let her go. She thought maybe she might, if it meant keeping herself alive. And she really hated knowing that about herself.

"Jesus, Bones, just let me go."

"Can't do that."

He rolled her over on the ground and she could feel his cock in between her buttocks. She was crying now. Uncontrollably. She saw all of her life up until this point and wondered when things had grown so dangerous and sad. She felt pain as he pushed himself into her, wrapping a large hand around her chin before yanking her head back toward him and snapping her neck.

Rain saw a bright light, heard the pop of her neck, and then everything was silent.

So this is death, she thought.

She felt her spirit rise up out of her body. She could not bear to look down. She could not bear to witness the things that Bones did to her dead body.

Finally, she felt free. She thought about Jacob and Rachel, wondered if there was any way she could help them and then she realized she wanted to be done with all of it. Rising higher and higher above the woods, rising until she could see the house burning and the whole of Lynchville below her, Rain looked to the West, toward home, and started off in that direction.

Thirty-five

Fuck.

The hands clutching Jacob's arms were unmercifully strong.

As soon as he was in the house, thrown back into the main room, he heard the van hit. The plan had worked amazingly well, he thought as he heard the van explode, except for the one tiny little hitch of him being in the house. He was definitely not supposed to be in the house. And, worst of all, now he was separated from Rachel. She was somewhere out there and he was in here.

He wondered which was worse.

The person holding him threw him to the ground and Jacob looked up to see him.

If it was a him. Whatever it was, it was an abomination. It was naked save a dirty loincloth that had ridden to one side, exposing the thing's hideously malformed genitals.

So it was most assuredly a him, Jacob thought. The genitalia weren't the only things wrong. This guy looked like a human being who had been put together all wrong and he briefly wondered how he could have been overpowered by someone who looked so feeble.

Jacob struggled to his knees, trying to stand up.

"Just get the fuck away," he said.

The man scampered across the room toward him and Jacob looked into his lopsided eyes. What he saw staggered him, nearly dropping him to the floor.

Looking into the man's eyes, he saw every atrocity that had been performed on him. He saw a different man, one who was very good-looking in a dark sort of way, observing this. He felt the bones breaking. Heard the skin ripping. Heard the screams and the constant pleas to stop.

Part of Jacob took pity on this man.

The man grabbed him by the neck and pulled him up. Jacob remembered he still had the tire iron in his hand although he must have dropped the gas can somewhere while being jerked in. He didn't know if any of it mattered or not. He didn't know if he would be able to get out of the house even if he bashed this guy's head in.

Already, the heat was intense.

The walls of the house flamed around him, chunks of it dropping away.

The manthing pulled Jacob up and pushed him onto the couch in the corner of the room. He hit the couch and then bounded back, swinging the tire iron at the manthing. It connected solidly with his head and, while it tore out a chunk of skin, it didn't seem to faze him. Jacob figured he must have been quite accustomed to pain at this point.

The man continued to approach him, grabbing the wrist containing the tire iron. He began lurching toward the back of the house.

Jacob thought maybe he could try reasoning with him.

The house was filling up with smoke. He couldn't even see to the back of it. Sweat streamed down his skin and his lungs burned.

"No, look, we have to get out of here."

The man grunted, continuing to drag Jacob. Jacob took a bare-handed swing at the back of the man's head. The skull felt soft beneath the thin greasy hair and, again, this did not stop the man.

They reached the back of the house and the man took Jacob to a door. With a grotesquely long arm, the man reached out and opened the door. Stairs led down into darkness. Jacob became dead weight, trying to push back against the man.

"This whole place is burning!" he shouted.

The man grunted and thrust Jacob toward the steps with strength Jacob found nearly impossible. He lost his footing and tumbled most of the way down, sacrificing the tire iron in order to wrap his arms around his head. The last thing he needed was to let this night pass him by while he lay at the foot of the stairs with a concussion.

He half-expected the man to be behind him, pushing him to some greater depths but realized the man had stayed on the surface.

He had stayed on the main floor so he would be burned alive when the interior of the house finally caught fire. That man would rather be burned alive than to go another day being the way he was. The way he was *made*, Jacob reminded himself. He could almost understand. Hell, he wanted to cry for the guy. But there wasn't any time for that. Not now. Right now the only thing he could really think about was either making sure he was safe from the flames and the smoke or trying to find some way to get out so he could get back to Rachel. Anything could be happening to her out there. She was the one these people had come for in the first place. He hadn't been there to protect her at her house and he wasn't there to protect her now. Some boyfriend he was turning out to be.

Of course, he knew, if there were any protection to be had, then she could most probably do a perfectly adequate job of protecting herself. He may be physically stronger but, in many ways, she was a lot tougher than he was.

He stood at the bottom of the steps and wondered if he should charge back up the stairs and try to find his way out of the burning house or if he should go through the door in front of him and see if he could penetrate any further into the mystery that had plagued him the past two years.

He climbed up a few steps and grabbed the tire iron. He sat down and tried to collect his thoughts.

Upstairs, he heard the manthing screaming as the flames scoured his skin from the bone.

Jacob decided to open the door.

Not an insanely strong person, he struggled with the heavy wood. Once opened, a strange blue light met him and he was suddenly struck with the question of how far this place went down. Jacob had the feeling it wasn't just this simple little room but many rooms, possibly going farther and farther into the earth. Only he knew it wasn't really going farther and farther into the earth. Like the house, this place appeared and disappeared at will. He knew he could have stood in that spot where the house was and started digging and not found anything except dirt and rocks beneath his shovel.

Sitting at the table were two people. A man and a woman. A couple.

Jacob's heart leapt when he saw them. Like he and Rachel had suspected, they were dealing with completely different people.

The couple stared at him, their eyes boring through him and Jacob stared back at them, going back and forth between each set of eyes.

"Jacob Riley," the man said.

Jacob looked at him, trying to pick something from his eyes, and got nothing. This staggered Jacob. Most of the time, he had to look away from people's eyes because even a casual glimpse would tell him more than he needed to know. This was not the case with this man. Jacob saw nothing. Regardless of how much he willed himself to travel into that secret place that carried all of those memories, he came away with nothing.

"Yes," Jacob said. "I'm afraid I don't know you."

"You are correct. You've never seen me before."

"Then why are you doing this to me?"

"Doing what to you? As I recall, you are the one who came here. So maybe I should ask you the same question. Why are you doing this to *us*?"

"You know why I'm doing this to you. You tried to hurt Rachel. You're responsible for death after death. The disappearance of kids."

The man continued to stare at him, as if weighing what Jacob told him.

"Yes," he said finally. "I guess we are. And you're here to... what? Stop us?"

Jacob realized how stupid he must look, standing there, in what was most probably their home, holding a tire iron and threatening them even though the man could probably have conjured a hundred ways to kill him on the spot at this very second. Part of him wanted to simply excuse himself and back out of the room but he had come this far and he wasn't about to turn back. Instead, he decided to say nothing.

The man continued. "Because if you *have* come to stop us, I think you will be sadly disappointed. There isn't anything to stop. You have the wrong idea about us. I've heard about you. I've heard about how you saved our precious Rachel. It was a setback. That's all. We need her. We will have her. She is part of the plan."

"And exactly what do you have planned?"

Ernst stood up from the table, smoothed down the front of his jacket, slowly scooting the straightbacked chair across the floor until it was flush with the table. Ilya remained seated in her chair to his left, her simpering eyes continuing to burn into Jacob.

"Preparation," he said.

"Preparation for what?"

"I don't really need to tell you that, do I? Why should I stand here and justify myself to you?"

Jacob didn't have an answer for that.

"Let's just say that it is time for Ilya and I to move on."

"What do you mean by 'move on'? Going to another town. Tormenting some other people?"

"Oh, we've already done all of that already. I don't see any point in continuing with that. Let me ask you a question, Mr. Riley... Do you believe a person can be *chosen* for something?"

Jacob thought about this. He realized he had been holding the tire iron at the ready, brandishing it in front of him. Thinking about this man's question (and it bothered him that he still didn't know his name), he lowered the tire iron somewhat.

Did he think a person could be chosen? Philosophically, he wasn't so sure about that. He didn't think he did. Whenever he heard about someone being chosen it automatically made him think of Hitler and cult leaders, wackos who fulfilled the sick instructions their minds received, claiming it came from some higher power. There were times when he thought he and Rachel had been chosen although he could never really figure out what it was they had been chosen for. All of this Devils business seemed rather pointless and without any kind of definite end.

"No," he said finally. "I don't believe in anyone being chosen to do anything. I think we do things to the best of our ability and the rest is up to fate."

"Fate?"

"Yes."

"So you believe in fate but you don't believe in someone being chosen?"

"Maybe I said that wrong. Maybe I said 'fate' when I should have said 'chance.'"

"Ah, 'chance,' that's better. That's a little more realistic, isn't it?" The man opened his eyes as he spoke, moving closer to Jacob. He leaned into his ear and whispered, "If you do not believe in fate then what the hell are you doing here?"

Jacob felt the man's demeanor change but, before he could prime the tire iron for striking, the man's huge hand was around his forearm, completely overpowering him. Ilya guffawed from the table.

The man was behind Jacob now, holding him around the biceps, pulling his arms back. He spoke into Jacob's ear again.

"My how you should curse chance, Mr. Riley. Of all the places it could have taken you tonight, it has brought you here. And let me assure you this is the worst place you could ever want to come to. You've heard of the Low Church, haven't you? The Dark Fire? Where we Devils get all of our sick energy?" The man didn't give him time to answer. "No matter. I'm going to show it to you now. If you're lucky, I will kill you when it is all over. But you aren't afraid of a little death are you?"

The man began pushing Jacob toward the back of this room where there was another door on the right.

Jacob felt defeated and lost and, at that moment, he felt very very afraid of death.

Thirty-six

Rachel backed away from the burning house, amazed at how quickly it went up. The smoke furled toward the purple moonlight-filled sky and she felt a deep sinking inside of herself.

Was Jacob dead?

The seriousness of what they were doing finally hit her. She had to realize it was entirely possible that Jacob *was* dead. That she was all alone now. If Jacob was really gone, she wondered what her part in this was. Coming here, they were so much a part of each other it was like they were a team. Coming here in the company of Jacob made it seem like it made sense, it felt like, together, they could accomplish something. Standing out here in the dark, alone, watching the burning house, Rachel thought it felt more like suicide. And that didn't make any sense at all. Part of her wanted to get in Jacob's car and drive back home, curl up in her bed, and wait for the nightmare to end. If Jacob was dead, she didn't really know if she wanted to continue living. If Jacob was dead, then part of her was already dead along with him. She could wait for the Devils to come and get her and if they did come for her then it wouldn't really matter. She wouldn't go with them but she wouldn't have anything to lose. She would fight them to the death.

She knew she couldn't think like that. If she thought like that then it jeopardized everything. This wasn't just about her and Jacob. After what had happened the first time, she grew to believe all of the stories she had heard about the Devils; all the atrocities, all of their false promises. Before that, she had seen the destruction wrought by them without realizing what it was she was seeing.

The students in her classes. All of the ones who had mysteriously moved or died tragically. Those, she now knew, were not accidents, they were not chance happenings. And if they were chance happenings the only chance involved in it was the students' meeting with the Devils. She desperately wanted to stop that. She wanted to stop that and she wanted to be able to live out her remaining years without the constant fear of the Devils. At least the other residents of Lynchville had the comfort of telling themselves the Devils were just a legend, that they weren't real. But Rachel knew the truth and it was the truth that provided her with all of those grim waking nightmares.

She continued walking until she reached the top of the hill. She opened the door to Jacob's car. His cigarettes lay on the console between the front seats, under the emergency brake handle. She reached in and pulled one from the pack, pushing in the car lighter, staring absently into the night while it heated up. Once heated, it clicked out, causing her to jump. Touching the lighter to the tip of the cigarette, she inhaled deeply. Tired, she sat down in the driver's seat.

What a sad night it had been so far. Rain was probably dead. Jacob was probably dead and she felt a hopeless lack of accomplishment.

What had they come here to do, anyway?

Did they really think they were going to march up to some bad people and stop them from doing whatever it was they were doing? And who were the bad people anyway? How many of them were there?

These were all questions Rachel thought they should have asked themselves before coming. They would have probably figured out they shouldn't have come at all. If Lynchville had existed for a couple hundred years under the shadow of the Devils, it would survive for a couple hundred more.

The first time, they had acted in defense and had managed to get away from two guys who had been completely transformed. Had, in fact, managed to successfully destroy them. This time, she didn't really know what it was. But they had wanted her. The Devils had wanted her and she couldn't really figure out why unless it was to destroy her completely and she didn't really know why they would want to do that. It wasn't like she was any kind of threat to them. She just wanted to forget about them. That was why she buried herself in school and work and Jacob. So she didn't have to think about them.

Unless she contained something that frightened them. Unless she was, in some way, every bit as powerful as they were.

Tonight was the first night she had used the healing on any human other than herself. She wasn't even really sure it would work. She had always thought it could have been her imagination more than anything. The only things she had ever made go away were a few cuts she had received from kitchen accidents and general clumsiness. And then there was the cat… Jesus, that felt so long ago. It seemed like a dream or a prelude to a nightmare.

But why would the Devils be afraid of her powers to heal? There wasn't anything destructive in that. What was she going to do? Heal them to death?

She thought about that. It almost made her laugh. But then she thought maybe it wasn't a joke. What if they *were* afraid of being healed?

Or what if she could heal all the people they had hurt and destroyed? Is that what they were afraid of?

But she did have a destructive power. One she tried never to think about. Even experimenting with it terrified her. It was that ability to reach into a person's mind, to make them see and do things. She was afraid, if she used that ability too much, she would lose control of it, do it subconsciously. Hell, she could be the reason for Jacob thinking he was going insane. It would come as no great surprise to her that the person she spent the most time around was also the most terrified, depressed, and suicidal individual she knew.

Now she wished she had experimented with that ability even more. She wished she had found a way to strengthen it and train it. Maybe she could have stopped the wolves from carrying Rain off. Maybe she could have commanded Jacob to turn around and come back to her as soon as she saw what was happening.

She had a hard time imagining the Devils being afraid of anything. She thought that she and Jacob were more of an inconvenience. If that was the case, then they already had Jacob out of the way and she guessed they would come after her next. That was the next logical step. And it made her even more afraid to be sitting in the car with absolutely no way to physically defend herself if something tried to attack her.

What if the wolves came back?

What if it was something else, something worse?

She exhaled the smoke from the last drag of her cigarette and tossed it out into the dewy grass. She watched it, nearly hypnotized, until the last of its fire winked out.

She had to find something. She had to find something or she had to get the fuck out of there.

It was all so maddening. Here she sat in the middle of the woods, in the middle of nowhere, land spread out everywhere before her, and she had never felt so claustrophobic in her life. She felt trapped. Like she was being forced to stay there until something came after her. If she ran, that would be too much like abandoning Jacob although, looking at the house as it burned, pieces of it collapsing, Rachel didn't see how Jacob could possibly be alive.

There had to be something, she thought. Maybe in the trunk.

She pressed the little button in the door until she heard the distant click of the trunk unlocking. Rising from the seat, she realized exactly how tired she was, how much she would like to just crawl into the backseat and take a little nap. But she couldn't. There wouldn't be any rest for her until this was all over and she knew that. She walked around to the back of the trunk and raised the lid. The light didn't work. Figures. She searched the trunk's dark confines.

For a relatively messy person, Jacob had a remarkably clean trunk. That didn't really surprise her. She didn't even know why he owned a car. He never drove, unless it was to come and pick her up so they could go someplace. When by himself, she was pretty sure the only place he went was the gas station on the corner to buy beer and cigarettes.

Her hand found something cold, a can of some kind, and she brought it out of the trunk, trying to figure out what it was.

It was a can of Quick Fix Tire Sealant, some substance you put into your tire when it had a slow leak. Rachel went back to the driver's seat, sat down and flipped on the map lights.

She had never wanted something to be dangerously flammable more in her life.

Reading the big, boldfaced warning on the side of the can she found that, indeed, this product *was* highly flammable. That was even better than plain old flammable, she thought.

Now she would be in luck if the only lighter besides the car's wasn't in Jacob's pocket. She flipped open the console between the seats.

And couldn't believe her luck.

It was like, when the world ended, Jacob wanted to make sure he had plenty of lighters. There had to be at least a dozen of them in there. All different colors and sizes and brands. She picked out an orange Bic because orange was the color of fire.

She held the lighter in her left hand, far in front of her face, shaking the can of tire sealant in her right. Then she flicked the lighter, holding the nozzle of the can about an inch away from it. She pressed the tab at the top of the can quickly, she didn't want to waste any of it, hoping the can did not explode in her face. The sight of the stream of fire shooting out from the can made her nearly giddy.

Now she had a weapon of sorts, a mini-flamethrower.

She sat in the car, staring at the burning house and waiting for all of the bad things to come. Sitting there, she found she almost *wanted* the bad things to come. That would have to be better than sitting here and waiting for something to happen.

The house had burned incredibly quickly. With one final, inward collapse, it became a pile of flaming rubble. She thought about going down to check it out, to see if anything was stirring. She remembered the screams she had heard coming from the house and silently wished they were not Jacob's but knew they almost had to have been.

But what about the man who had dragged him into the house? Had he gone up in flames too? What if the people Rain told them about *were* in there? Would they burn themselves up to destroy Jacob?

The answer to all of those questions, she knew, was "no." It wasn't really like they were under some sort of attack. They had no reason to be martyrs because no one really knew about them. No, Rachel was certain that if Jacob was dead then they were still alive. They might not necessarily be in the house, but they were someplace. Lurking. Waiting to do whatever it was they had come here to do if they hadn't done that already.

Given that she was still safe, she didn't figure they had.

Watching the flames flicker over the spot where the house used to stand, an incredible wave of fatigue washed over her. It was more than just the casual sleepiness and general tiredness she had felt moments earlier. It was like when she had the flu or something, when there was absolutely no way she could hold her head up. She thought she wanted to stand up and move around so this feeling could not claim her but she couldn't manage to stand up. She could hardly think about anything except closing her eyes and putting her head down on the steering wheel, the feeling was so intense. Or whatever the opposite of intense was. Surely being sleepy couldn't classify as intense, could it?

And, of course, she knew exactly what this was. This was their way of fighting back. If they could simply knock her unconscious then she wouldn't be able to threaten them anymore. If she would just go to sleep until it was all over or until something heinous was upon her... something that could finish her off.

Yes.

That was exactly what they wanted.

That was exactly what they wanted her to do.

She had to stand up. She had to get out of this seat that was so very very comfortable and smelled so much like Jacob. She had to stand up and move toward the fire. Had to go down and make sure there was nothing there. But she couldn't move her head from the soothing coolness of the steering wheel.

What did it matter if she got up? She didn't *want* to get up. She just wanted to put her head down for a minute. There wasn't any harm in putting her head down for a minute. If she could just shut her eyes and rest for a second then when she opened them she would be ready to think about what she was going to do, she would be able think a little more clearly. But only after she put her head down on the steering wheel. Yes, just like that, the lighter and the can of tire sealant slowly slipping out of her hands. She shut her eyes and gave up her grip on consciousness, the night left to rage on without her.

Thirty-seven

Following Charlotte into the woods, Autumn had the strangest feeling. She didn't have any idea what they were doing. Didn't really have any idea what they had just seen yet she had never really felt so magical or alive before in her life. It was like witnessing that man explode before their eyes set her free from her old life and now she could begin anew.

The feeling scared her. She thought it must be what career soldiers or serial killers felt.

The girls laughed as they ran deeper into the woods, deeper into areas they had never been to before—dark, mysterious areas.

The smell of smoke filled the air. Autumn didn't think this could be the lingering smoke from their campfire. Surely they were out of its range by now. And, besides, this smoke smelled different. It smelled like incense—heady and intoxicating.

Autumn felt like her head was spiraling around her body. She felt drunker than she had a few minutes before. Nearly giddy. Wine coursing through her veins, pumping through her heart, swelling into her head.

"Charlotte," she laughed as they ran along, their breaths spuming out to make vaporous ghosts in the night air. "Where the hell are we going?"

"The Sad House," Charlotte said. "I told you that."

"Ah, yes, I forgot!" she said and they both blurted out in fresh laughter.

Autumn felt the wild energy coming from Charlotte and she didn't think it was just coming from the girl in front of her. The whole woods seemed to be alive. There weren't animals scurrying around them or the usual insects chirping in the trees. She thought it was probably getting too late in the year for that. No, it was something else. It was like the very wood of the trees themselves vibrated with a force she didn't entirely understand. She didn't know if she wanted to understand it. If she understood it then it would lose a bit of its magic.

They were on a clear cut trail and this offered a little solace but Autumn realized it was a solace she didn't want. It was a solace she didn't need. She saw it now as merely a manmade mark on nature, to show that humans had cut out a path through something not meant to have paths.

Catching up with Charlotte, she caught the girl's thin elbow in her hand and tugged her off the path, into the thicker woods.

"What are you doing?" Charlotte laughed.

"We'll never find what we're looking for on a stupid path." Autumn didn't know why she had said that but it made perfect, indescribable sense to her.

Now the girls ran nearly side by side, the dead leaves crunching under their feet and coming off the lower trees as they brushed past them. It suddenly occurred to Autumn that everything around them, everything in the woods, was dying for the year. Which made it even stranger and more intoxicating that they felt so alive.

Charlotte, just slightly ahead of Autumn, came to an abrupt stop and Autumn nearly ran her over.

Then she saw why Charlotte had stopped.

Someone else was in the woods with them. It was a man or a boy, standing less than ten feet in front of them, next to a tree. He came closer and Autumn caught a glimpse of weird light coming from his eyes. She had a feeling she knew who it was.

She nudged Charlotte on the arm. "Is that..."

"Zack," she said into the night.

The boy came forward.

"Charlotte," he said. "I was hoping I'd run into you."

"Well, it looks like you did. You know, if you wanted to run into me there are ways to arrange that. Like telephones. They've always worked for me."

Autumn huffed out a breath of resignation. It was like all of her excitable feelings rushed out of her. She didn't want it to end with her watching Charlotte and her boyfriend have a fight in the middle of what was promising to be one of the most exciting nights of her life.

"Now is not the time for joking." Zack approached her, cradled her chin in his hand. "Tonight is a very important night."

Autumn felt some of the excitement rush back into her. Finally, someone else realized the gravity of this night.

"You've brought a friend," he said, looking at Autumn.

She felt her heart leap in her chest as she met his eyes. It wasn't attraction, exactly. It was something else. Like a transference of power. It wasn't hard to figure out why Charlotte had fallen so hard for him. And it only took her a second to figure that out. She imagined him biting her, doing some of the things to her that Charlotte had described and she knew she wouldn't have any problems with that at all. Yes, she thought. He could bite me until I bleed and I wouldn't mind.

"This is Autumn," Charlotte said.

Zack stuck out his hand and she tentatively held out her own.

"Autumn," he said. "It's very nice to meet you. Autumn, my favorite season."

Autumn would have thought that sounded lame coming from any other mouth. Instead she mumbled, "Thank you," and stepped back from him, retreating behind Charlotte.

"We were on our way to see the Sad House," Charlotte said. "Do you want to come with us?"

"I was thinking about taking you there myself," he said. "There are some people I want you to meet."

For some reason, him saying that sent shivers down Autumn's spine. For just a second, the little spell he had over her was broken. She didn't want to go to the Sad House anymore. She didn't want Charlotte to go to the Sad House and she certainly didn't want them to meet anyone this guy wanted them to meet. In the second the spell was broken, Autumn thought she saw through him and saw someone who was very evil. Or someone who was driven by something that was very evil.

She wanted to laugh at herself for using that word, "evil." It was a word she normally only used to describe certain teachers and warmongering politicians. Maybe a few sadistic neighborhood kids from her childhood. But now using it to describe another person who was within arm's reach seemed absurd.

He was a human just like they were and Autumn did not think humans were, by and large, evil. Not individually.

"Are these the people you live with?" Charlotte asked.

"Yes. They are."

"Do you live in the Sad House? Have you *been* living in the Sad House?"

He paused for a moment, leading the way. "Yes," he said finally. "I live in the Sad House."

"I knew there was something strange about you. You're one of them, aren't you?"

Autumn still couldn't believe any of this. It was like she was mixed up with all of the legends surrounding Lynchville and here was Charlotte speaking casually about it as though it was possible for all of this stuff to exist. But maybe the boy had previously challenged Charlotte's realities in a way her own had never been tested. The most unreal thing she had ever seen was a man spontaneously combusting in Charlotte's backyard, oh, about a half an hour ago.

"I'm afraid it's not that black and white."

"No?" Charlotte asked.

"No. No, it's not. See, I only aspired to be one of them. Tonight is the night I become one of them. Fully. And you could become one too. With me."

They stopped walking abruptly. The boy turned to Charlotte and held a hand up in front of her face. Moonlight glinted off the blood that wrapped around the fingers. Autumn wondered how he had cut it. She stood relatively close to them but had drawn back a little.

"Would you like that?" Zack asked.

Charlotte bent toward his hand, almost greedily, and began sucking at the blood.

Once again, Autumn broke through the spell. She couldn't believe how she had just stood here and watched this. She couldn't believe how she had let Charlotte get involved in all this. She ran up to Zack and tried to pull his arm away from Charlotte.

"Stop it!" she said, knowing how powerless that sounded.

She avoided looking at Zack as she tried to pry his arm from Charlotte.

"Get the fuck away from her!" she screamed.

Autumn looked at Charlotte, trying to find some reason inside of the other girl. Trying to trigger something that would make her pull away and put an end to this madness.

But she couldn't see anything. Charlotte was already lost to Zack. Her eyes looked glazed as she continued to suckle at Zack's hand.

"It needs sacrifices," Zack whispered to Charlotte. "It needs people to feed its flames."

It didn't take Autumn long to figure out what they meant. She let go of Zack's arm, resigning them both to whatever sick fantasy it was they wanted to play. She tried to dart off but Charlotte's arm was out, clutching her, raking her nails down her arm and laying the skin open.

"Oh God no!" she cried. "Charlotte, this is Autumn! This is your best fucking friend!"

But the two of them overpowered Autumn, driving her down to the ground before lifting her up, each of them grabbing a different arm.

"The Sad House waits," Zack said.

"Show me," Charlotte said. "Please... show me."

Autumn wanted to tighten her muscles and allow herself to go no farther. But she couldn't. She felt like she had no control over her body whatsoever.

She felt betrayed.

Betrayed and doomed. How could Charlotte turn on her so quickly? Then she told herself it wasn't entirely Charlotte's decision. She remembered how she had felt, if only for a second, upon looking into Zack's eyes and couldn't exactly fault Charlotte for doing the things she was doing. After all, she had done much more with this boy than simply look into his eyes.

She couldn't even manage a scream. She kept her head down as the two others led her along, her feet dragging the ground.

"I don't even know if the Sad House will be there anymore," Zack said.

"Why?" Charlotte asked.

"Because when I left it was burning to the ground."

"Why?"

"Enemies," Zack said matter-of-factly.

Autumn wondered how much farther she was going to be dragged. She wondered what fate would hold for her when they finally reached the house. She couldn't think of anything positive that could come of this. She had fallen into one of the horror stories she was so fond of only, in this one, there wasn't a definite ending. She didn't know how long it was going to go on. She didn't know which characters would be alive at the end of the book.

Then they stopped. She raised her head.

They were on a wooded hillside, overlooking a small hollow. At the bottom of the valley lay a vast pile of smoking rubble. Part of her wanted to cheer. This was Zack's house and someone had burned it down. It made her feel like she had someone on her side.

"It's gone," Zack said sorrowfully.

"What do we do now?" Charlotte asked.

"I don't know."

Autumn continued to look at the rubble and then she saw something she knew she didn't really want to see.

The house came back.

It was odd, unlike anything she had ever seen and she would have found it wonderfully magic if it were any other house. It simply built itself up, as though carving itself out of the night air. It thickened and grew more substantial. It didn't take long and Autumn wondered if she was dreaming all of this. She had had a fucked up nightmare last night. Was it possible she had gone home after the Wake Up Screaming and fallen asleep on her bed with all of those thoughts of Charlotte and the Devils still fresh in her brain?

As much as she wanted to believe that, she knew all of this was really happening right there in front of her and by the time she could process that thought, the house had come back.

"It calls to us," Zack said. "We have to go in now."

They continued to drag Autumn. She finally found the strength to fight back and, since it came so suddenly, it caught them off guard. Their holds loosened and Autumn turned immediately back toward the woods and ran as hard as she could. But Charlotte was behind her. Autumn heard her harsh breath rasp against the air and the other girl launched herself toward Autumn, dragging her down.

"Please, Charlotte," she tried again. "I'm your friend. You can't let him hurt me."

"Oh, nobody's going to hurt you," Charlotte whispered into her ear. "I've heard what Zack has said. I've heard what he has been told. Death is not painful at all. Death is the most beautiful thing you can ever experience and you will be able to roam this earth as a completely different person. One without laws or rules."

"It's all a lie," Autumn said out of self-preservation.

Charlotte pulled her hair back, lifting her head off the ground, before slamming it back down.

"Zack does not lie. *They* do not lie."

"You'll see," Autumn spat out through her bloody mouth.

And then Zack and Charlotte had hold of each of her arms again and they dragged her down to the Sad House.

Thirty-eight

Being shoved through the door was like being shoved into an atrocity. The room on the other side of the door looked kind of like a church but it was a church bent on destruction and carnage. The pews were from some kind of stone that seemed to rise from the very earth itself. There was a raised stage area but instead of a pulpit there was a large stone slab that looked like a sarcophagus. Lining the walls were the corpses of some of the Devils' victims. They hung like lanterns or lamps on the wall, their bodies in various states of decay, twisted, black mouths opened, radiating a death stink.

Jacob recognized a couple of the faces. They were people from town. They were his neighbors. They were the normal people he had always wanted to be.

"Do you like the artwork?" Ernst asked him.

"Fuck you," Jacob said.

"So unimaginative," Ernst mocked.

"You know you're not going to get away with this, don't you?"

"Stop threatening me. You have nothing. There is not any way we can*not* get away with this. This is what we have lived our lives after death for. Who do you think is going to stop us, really? Your girlyfriend? Well, let me give you an update as to her condition. As of this moment she has just drifted off in the car and, soon, she is going to receive a visit from a very charming young man."

"Bones," Jacob hissed.

"Whoever," Ernst said. "He's on quite a rampage. He's already put away the other girl you came with. He's coming in a lot handier than I thought he would. For a halfwit."

"You're lying."

"You know I'm not."

And, the worst part was that Jacob knew this man was right. He had no reason to lie.

"So there is no one who can help you. There is no one who is going to stop Ilya and I from tasting the Dark Fire. You've heard that name, haven't you?"

"No. Guess you guys aren't as popular as you thought."

"Beyond the Dark Fire is like Heaven and God all in one. It appears as fire but a whole world burns within it."

Jacob guffawed. He couldn't help it. At that moment, Ernst reminded him of a Baptist minister.

"Very well. Let me tell you what it is we intend to do. I want to make sure you are not going to run away first."

The couple led him up to the stone slab. The man pushed Jacob down on it but Jacob wouldn't simply lie down. He waited for the man to loosen his grip and then he was back on his feet, taking a wild swing at him. His fist glanced off Ernst's cheek, leaving absolutely no damage whatsoever.

Jacob dashed for the door.

With his hand on the cool handle, he felt a shimmer of excitement run through his body but, no matter how hard he pulled, the door would not open and his excitement completely dissipated.

Ernst laughed from the other side of the church, walking slowly toward Jacob.

Jacob knew he was going to have to stand and fight. He had no choice. But he didn't know what he was supposed to fight with. The tire iron was long gone.

He charged at Ernst. Ernst stepped out of the way, grabbed Jacob's arm, and threw him into one of the stone pews. Jacob hit the pew with his shoulder and heard a sickening pop.

"Fuck!" he screamed in pain.

Jacob scrabbled to his feet, convinced he was going to go after the woman, thinking this might be the man's weak spot. He charged at her and launched himself, wanting to take her down completely, but Ernst was there, snatching him from the air as though he weighed absolutely nothing.

This time, Ernst wasted no time in placing him on the slab, holding him down by pressing a huge hand on his chest.

From beneath his back, Jacob could feel the stone quivering. It felt alive, malleable. Sections of the stone snaked up from either side of his waist until they met in the middle of his stomach. There they fused together.

"There," Ernst said. "That should keep you from moving around a whole lot."

"Tell me why you're doing this," Jacob said. He realized he was practically begging. If he was going to die, he didn't want to die without knowing the answer to the mystery. He didn't want to die thinking people like the Devils existed solely to destroy the human race like reckless gods playing a game.

"I deserve that much," Jacob said.

"Well," he began. "If you're referring to your present situation, that would be because Mr. Latch seems to have disposed of himself and we need someone to fill in in that capacity. Are you aware of what happened to Mr. Latch?"

Jacob thought about what he saw in the deformed man's eyes. The horrors he saw there, more extreme than anything he could imagine.

"That's not what I'm talking about. You know that."

"I see. You're talking about a more all-encompassing kind of thing. Well, I guess if you think we owe that to you, then we are somewhat obliged to answer. After all, this is an evening of conclusions. I don't see why the end to your sanity is any less conclusive than the end Ilya and I have planned for ourselves.

"But I think we need to get to work as time is running a little bit thin so I guess we will just have to converse as we go along. Try not to scream too loud. You'll disrupt my thought processes."

Jacob looked at Ilya, who seemed to be reaching under the stone altar. She came up holding a large horseshoe-shaped metal device. It reminded Jacob of a pair of bent scissors, the tips flattened down.

"It's really pretty simple," Ernst said. He held Jacob's left arm down. Jacob struggled to move it but the man's strength was just too great. Ilya placed the tip of the scissor-things on his elbow and began depressing them. Jacob drew in a wince with the first sign of pain.

"There are all kinds of what you would call Devils. Some of them have been around far longer than others. The oldest of those are no longer human. They are more like pure energy."

The scissor things tightened on his elbow. Jacob heard a pop and then a crunch. He cried out at the pain, shooting all through his arm. Ernst held his forearm and twisted it in a clockwise fashion, the shattered bones grating together as he did this. Sweat drenched

Jacob's head, the pain only increasing.

"These old ones are kind of like our gods, here to usher us through the Dark Fire. But they need human forms to hide within. More than that, they need souls to hide within so that, wherever there is a god, there is a body of flesh with two souls in it."

Methodically, Ernst popped each of Jacob's fingers in that hand, breaking them at the middle knuckle. That pain was nothing compared to his arm, it felt lost in the throbbing redness.

"The gods are very careful about who they choose to hide themselves in. Many many years ago, they came to Ilya and I. It was more than two-hundred years ago, in fact, and it happened right here in Lynchville."

Together, Ilya and Ernst crossed over to his other arm.

"Please stop this. Don't turn me into that. I don't know what you want. I don't know what I can give you but please don't turn me into that man upstairs."

"I think we should remove his tongue," Ernst said. "That way he can listen to our story, because it has to be told, and he won't be able to tell it to anyone. Oh, sure, he could try and write it down but I don't know what good his fingers will be." Ernst chuckled.

"Jesus, stop this. Just let me go and I'll do whatever it is to stay away from you."

"Aww, where's the brave Jacob we used to know? You came here to stop us and now the only thing you want to do is to escape without hideous deformity."

He grabbed Jacob's jaw with his huge, strong hand, prying the teeth apart. Ilya inserted the device into his mouth, clamping it around his tongue. Jacob tried to scream a few things but the pathetic sound of his trapped voice made him too sad to continue. She pulled the tongue out, touching it to his chin.

Ernst held a hand before him, his fingernails long and razor sharp. He drew the nail over the back of Jacob's tongue. Jacob tasted blood, felt it fill his throat. He wanted to spit it out but could not. At least it hurt less than his arm.

Jacob didn't know how long the torture continued. It was spliced with Ernst's tale from the past. Jacob was not blessed with unconsciousness, was not allowed to feel its painless black depths, so he listened to Ernst murmur on.

It happened one summer when they were fifteen. Ernst was the son of the only Lynchville minister, also the founder of the town, Sparrow Lynch. He didn't name a specific religion he was minister of. Ilya was the daughter of the church's treasurer. That was how they met each other. Of course, given the miniscule size of Lynchville, they were bound to meet each other eventually. But, upon meeting, they fell instantly in love. Consequently, falling in love with each other, they had somehow fallen out of love with the church. Ernst had always had his doubts about the powers of the church but he thought this might have stemmed from his hatred of his father more than anything. And Ilya, Ilya would follow Ernst wherever he went.

That was when they found this house. And the man who lived in the house, before it was abandoned. Ernst did not give the name of this man. Ernst described some of the things the man was able to do. Predict deaths in the town. Summon fire from the sky. Disappear. Change his shape. Speak inside of the mind without moving his lips. See one's past, see one's future. Ilya and Ernst were enchanted.

The main reason they continued to go to this house, however, was because the man was often away, and he didn't care how they used it. So Ilya and Ernst copulated constantly. That was what teenagers did, especially when there wasn't anything else to do.

Ilya ended up pregnant and that was when Ernst first became aware that people in the town were talking. They knew about the man in the abandoned house. General consensus believed he was the Devil, a tortured soul who was hellbent on torturing everyone else's soul. But the talk grew stranger than that. Ilya had kept her pregnancy a secret until she began to show. The rumors said the baby was most likely the Devil's. They were too naive to believe Ilya and Ernst, two children of upstanding church leaders, were capable of performing these ungodly acts.

The man in the house sensed Ilya and Ernst's unease. He began to regale them with legends of a place beyond the Dark Fire. Then one day, he offered to show it to them, if only for a second. He told them it was beneath this very house. They followed him down there, figuring it couldn't do any harm. From the way the Devil talked about it, they were not sure if this world beyond the Dark Fire was a place or a person or both. He showed it to them. It was only a few seconds they stared into the roaring flame, but they saw enough to last them several lifetimes. They saw enough to devote those lifetimes to gaining admittance to the Dark Fire's paradise.

On the surface, things were getting worse. The townsfolk had banded together. Headed by a Dr. Millicent, they were determined to end Ilya's pregnancy. Although they did manage to forcibly re-move the fetus, it did not end there. Ilya and Ernst were not pre-pared to let it end there. They fought back with extreme ferocity, having had their unborn child pried away from them and murdered before their very eyes. Now they were intent on doing some mur-dering of their own.

The townsfolk retreated out of the house, convincing themselves that the Devil, the evil man in the vacant house, had taken control of their souls. Gathering around the house that night, not caring if Ilya and Ernst were inside sleeping, they burned it to the ground and cursed the ashes it became.

As it turned out, Ilya and Ernst *were* in the house. Yet, somehow, they had changed. They were dead but not dead. And they had powers they did not have before. They had powers they thought the Devil had revealed to them only as some kind of hoax. But now they knew all of that to be real. And they realized this was part of their journey beyond the Dark Fire. The Devil had told them certain things, mostly what they were telling Jacob now, and they knew these gods must be inside of them, empowering them and giving them the ability to empower others, or remove that power when it was necessary.

That was a violent year in Lynchville. There would always be disappearances, but never as many as in that year when, by next summer, there were only seven members left in the community.

And now, Ilya and Ernst felt as though they had served the gods well. They thought maybe it was time for the gods to move onto someone else and for themselves to move into the awesomely powerful land beyond the Dark Fire.

Maybe that was it, Jacob thought, even though he was not really capable of rational thought at this point. Or maybe it was all lies. He didn't care. He was as good as dead, he knew. Once a large stone had been smashed onto his pelvis to shatter it in half, he stopped feeling the pain. He could only see out of one eye and the only thing he wanted to do was close it and slip away but he knew he would not be able to do that.

Thirty-nine

Rachel opened her eyes and couldn't believe what she saw.

The house was back. She was certain she had seen the house burn down until it was little more than a pile of rubble but there it was in front of her and she had a terrifying thought that it looked better, *stronger* than it had before.

Her heart jumped when she realized she shouldn't have been looking at all. She had fallen asleep behind the wheel of Jacob's car. Why was she out here, on the grass, looking at the house? Why wasn't she in there, trying to help him?

In a rapid flood, the present exploded through her. She was being dragged toward the house. Someone's hands were around her ankles. She was very confused.

"Jacob?" she said.

"I ain't Jacob," a voice, frighteningly familiar, called back to her.

She saw broad shoulders under the moonlight. With every bit of energy she had left, she tightened her leg muscles and clawed her fingers into the ground, trying to bring the descent down the hill to a halt. She knew who it was dragging her. It was Bones. In Rachel's world, she figured people only really got one chance to kill her and then it was time for her to fight back.

She remembered her tools, the can of tire sealant and the lighter that were, hopefully, still up by the car. Now it was just a matter of reaching them.

She plunged her legs to the ground, trying to turn over onto her stomach so she could stand up and bolt.

Bones did let go of her ankles, but only for a second. She scampered momentarily along the grass, trying to stand up, before he hurled his crushing weight down on her.

"No you don't, bitch," he whispered harshly in her ear.

"Fucking watch me," she said, driving a sharp elbow back into his ribs.

He grunted with the blow, retaliating by taking a fisted swipe at the back of her head. It felt like a rock shattered her skull, knocking her forehead into the mercifully soft ground. She was too focused to let the pain stop her. The only thing she wanted to do was get to the car. Once she got to the car, once she reached what she needed to reach, she would worry about finishing this guy off for good.

He seemed surprised when she brought her head back up and

began her scrabble anew. She knew if she could just manage to break away from him, she could manage to get to the car.

Bones grabbed the back of her shorts, dragging her up. She let him do this and when she felt her feet leave the ground, she brought her foot back, ramming it up between his legs.

"Fuck!" he shouted, still holding onto her. "You can't hurt me!"

Maybe he was right, but that didn't mean she couldn't try. She just didn't know how she was going to do it.

She surprised him by planting her feet on the ground and running toward the house. He had his weight leaning the opposite direction and this toppled him over. She took a couple of steps, just enough to allow her to turn around and go charging up toward the car. He was right behind her. He seemed bigger than she remembered.

She charged up the hill as fast as she could.

Within feet of the car, Bones caught up with her. She made one more desperate lunge for the car. Bones simultaneously reached his hands out for her, unable to get a grip, and this only served to propel her into the car.

The door was still open. She cracked her head on the roof of the car and collapsed on the soft cushion of the driver's seat. Blood began a rapid rivulet down her forehead but she saw the can in the floorboard and grabbed for it. Bones had her by the left ankle, yanking her out of the car. On the way out, she saw the lighter lying in that no-man's-land between the seat and the door. She flicked her hand out and grabbed it.

Once outside the car, she flopped to her right and banged her shoulder on the inside of the door.

She wasted no time. She knew Bones would be leering over her any moment now. She tried to hide the spray can as much as possible in her right hand. She let him get right down over top of her, until she could feel his hot breath and smell its death stink.

Quickly, she held the can just inches away from his face, flicked the lighter, hoping like hell it ignited on the first try, and depressed the tab on the tire sealant. A thick blue-orange flame shot out, spewing into Bones' face. His hair caught fire instantly and Rachel thought she saw a look of genuine surprise on his face.

This stuff was like napalm. Drops of it dripped, burning, onto her lower stomach where it felt like it melted into her skin.

He leapt off her.

He backed up a couple of steps and she followed, igniting another flame, showering his body with the burning fluid.

Bones screamed as his clothes burst into flames.

Finally able to think for just a second, Rachel found herself entranced as Bones burned. Something wasn't right. She had learned to never ignore intuition. Something told her that Bones was already dead. There was just too much of a difference between this Bones and the one who had kidnapped her. It was impossible, she knew, for a boy to bulk up this much overnight. And then it hit her. He *was* dead, of course. He was one of them now. Which meant that when his body burned, his soul would be free to go wherever it wanted to go and why would it want to go anywhere when there was a perfectly good girl standing there in front of it? A girl who could easily get into that house and go places Bones had only dreamed about going.

Rachel sprayed him once more with the fluid. He moved toward her this time, rather than backing away, like he wanted to hug her with this fire that consumed him.

Rachel sidestepped until she was behind him. The burning was at least confusing him, distracting him. She thought he was burning entirely too fast and then... *and then he would be loose.* The thought of him inside of her, spiritually or physically, made her want to vomit.

What was the thought she had earlier? she wondered. Something about healing them to death. She almost laughed at herself. There wasn't any healing for something as far gone as Bones and she didn't really think she wanted to heal him anyway.

So she thought about her power, about how she had made the blood move back into Jacob's body, his skin solder back together, and then she thought about this power *in reverse.* Surely those who can heal can destroy just as adequately. It was just that, usually, the power to destroy was not in her. It was not something she let herself think about an awful lot.

But now she did. She focused on it. Feeling that screaming blue magical power roll through her.

She wanted to destroy Bones. And not just his body that burned before her very eyes, now nothing more than a dancing black skeleton. No, she wanted his soul. She wanted to destroy it and make sure it could never escape.

In her mind, knowing that was where Bones would end up going, she created a kind of horrorshow. A kind of hell, waiting for his arrival.

His bones crumbled and she felt him come screaming into her. She turned back toward the house with a smirk, casually brushing the blood from her forehead as though it were so many stray hairs.

Forty

The soul must consume itself. That was the realization Bones came to that night. Whether it is through dreams or nightmares, the soul must consume itself. There is not a third party who can extinguish that vital essence of life. That night, Bones' soul did just that. He saw things he never wanted to see. And he realized his soul had no place else to go.

He entered the girl thinking he had beaten her. Wouldn't it have been something, for her to have burned him up, thinking she had won some small victory, only to realize he was in her head, destroying her from the inside? But as soon as he entered her he knew something was wrong. There was blackness. And a door stood in front of him.

On closer inspection, it looked like the door was made of hundreds of bird skulls. There was an intense odor coming from the door. It was worse than death. It was the stink of his soul rotting. He knew that without consciously grasping it. It was an all-pervasive stink and seemed to induce a physical reaction in him only there was no longer a physical part of him to act. He opened the door because there was not any place else to go.

The door opened into a room filled with murky light. The stink, if that was possible, was even greater in the room. Once across the threshold, the door slammed behind him. He saw things he never wanted to see. Beneath his feet, maggots squirmed across the floor. The whole floor was white-gray with them and he could feel them squirming up his legs, getting thickly caught in his leg hair. He wanted to retch but he couldn't. It was like all the nausea just got caught in the back of his throat.

The room didn't make any sense. There were tables nailed to the ceiling and chairs nailed to the wall. There were bones strewn across the floor, maggots squirming over them. Thin spiderwebs brushed his face, something that had always caused chills to shoot over his spine and panic to scream through his veins. He tried to brush them away but his arms wouldn't work. Fat spiders with skinny legs danced down his back.

In the center of the room he saw his father raping Rain, holding the severed head of his mother in his right hand.

He knew this was not happening but he also knew it *was* happening because there was not any going back. He tried to turn his eyes away from the atrocities in front of him but every time he turned his head it kept whirling back to the same disgusting image.

The walls around him were black and glistening, breathing and oozing. Bulging. A hundred different shapes stretched out of them, rending the wall outward until it popped like a bubble of tar and Bones recognized the decayed corpses that emerged from it.

They were his victims. All come to join him in this final dance of insanity.

Bones' soul could have lived. He knew that. If he was willing to spend eternity in this room, he could have stayed until that horrible girl died.

But he didn't want that. He *couldn't* want that. And even though there was something inside of him saying this was it, this was his price for wanting to live in an eternal state of life, he chose to close the eye of his soul, blacking everything around him.

And that was the end of Bones—soul and all.

Forty-one

His vision stained red, Jacob wondered how it was still possible he was conscious. There was not a single part of him that had not been somehow broken or mutilated.

"Now I think it's time we destroy his brain," Ernst said.

Jacob thought he would be beyond horror but he cringed at this thought. He didn't know how they intended to do it. Would they stick something in his ear? Would they open up his skull and re-move just enough gray matter to be brain damaging?

"The Dark Fire," he heard Ilya mutter.

"Yes. The Dark Fire. We'll take him in there and once he sees it he will not be able to think about anything else. Like a junky always going through withdrawal."

Ilya reached down and put her hand upon the stone belt holding Jacob fastened to the altar. It vanished beneath her touch and Ilya and Ernst were on either side of him, carrying him through yet another door.

"Zack will be here shortly," Ernst said. "And then it will be over."

Once through the door, Jacob heard a deep rumbling and knew this was the same fire he had seen in the video or whatever he had been shown last night. Then he remembered that the fire was never actually seen. It was implied. He hadn't actually laid eyes on it. Last night seemed so very far away. He could barely hold his eyes open but the fire was impossible to miss.

They dragged him across the stone floor and let him collapse in front of the fire.

"We're not finished with you," Ernst said, running a long fingernail beneath his chin. "We'll be back later. Or someone will be back later. We have better things to do than deal with weak little meddlers like you."

Jacob heard their footsteps retreat into the distance. He lay there on the floor, staring into the fire. It didn't take him long to realize this wasn't an ordinary fire. There were things behind the flames. There was a whole other world behind the flames and, suddenly, things made a lot of sense to Jacob. In a way, it was like Ilya and Ernst weren't even responsible for all of this. It was whatever lay beyond the fire that had soiled them. It was that place or that person beyond the flame they longed for.

Jacob wanted to laugh. This was the reason for all the disappearances. This was the reason for all the legends and all the terror. In a way, it was like an entire religion spread before him. It was a religion that both intrigued and terrified him.

He felt the Dark Fire, or whatever lay beyond the Dark Fire, working on his brain.

There was a green depth beyond the flame, lush grasses and thick trees, a perfect blue sky, people too beautiful to imagine and he had the distinct feeling that if he were to cross over he could have any of those people he wanted, or all of them. But he didn't want them. He didn't want the Dark Fire, he didn't want Heaven or Hell. The only thing he wanted was Rachel.

He could not die like this. He could not *become* what the man and the woman had set out to make him become.

Yet, he had no choice but to lie there. There wasn't any way possible he could move and that was the most disturbing thing he had encountered, coming this far only to be rendered utterly powerless. Somehow, he managed to draw a little closer to the fire. He didn't know how he did it. His bones were gone, shattered and broken. It felt like he did it by wriggling his skin and moving like a snake. There were people behind the flame. Surely, someone could help him. Surely there had to be something.

Within a foot of the fire, Jacob stopped, knowing it would not burn him if he continued. But it would kill him and, by killing him, it would make him its servant.

He looked up into the towering wall of flame. A multitude of people looked back at him, their faces sallow and forlorn. They all looked relatively young. Jacob made eye contact with a frail looking boy toward the front.

Their eyes locked and energy shot through Jacob.

Completely unlike looking into the empty eyes of the man, Jacob saw everything within this boy. He saw how he had been lying in his bed, afraid of everything, when Ernst had entered and dragged him away.

He let his eyes trail to other members of the pack. Jacob saw more of the same. And behind every set of eyes, Jacob could sense something else.

Anger.

Raw and hurting, intense as everything he had ever felt. Their stares could not put Jacob back together again but, maybe, he would be able to reach out in some way toward them. He strained his mind to think as clearly as possible.

Forty-two

Autumn screamed hysterically as Zack and Charlotte dragged her through the door. Ilya and Ernst sat on that strange blue couch, staring toward them. The sight of them sent fresh waves of panic though Autumn. Ernst stood up and came toward them. Autumn quivered at the sight of him. He did not look like the type of person who had ever had wholesome intentions. She was surprised when he reached out to touch Charlotte instead.

"You brought her," he said, running a finger down her cheek. "Are you ready to begin?"

"Yes," Zack said.

"The other one is on her way."

"The other one?" Zack asked.

"Yes. You didn't think you got to *choose* who you crossed over with, did you?"

Zack looked down at the floor.

"First we need to gather our strength." He turned to Autumn. "Two for the price of one."

"Yes," Zack said once again.

"What?" Charlotte said. "What's going on, Zack?"

Close to Ernst, Autumn saw he was covered in blood, it glistened on the surface of his black garb, ran in streaks down his cheeks.

She wouldn't have time to think anything else.

He reached out one large hand and slashed her jugular with his sharp fingernails. Blood shot out of her neck, covering him. Zack and Charlotte let her fall to the floor. Ernst was on top of her, sucking hungrily at her neck. Ilya sauntered across the floor, kneeling down and following suit. Charlotte and Zack stood watching them as they drained Autumn, the color leaving her face, the life leaving her body, absorbed into Ilya and Ernst.

Zack wanted to drop and join them but he knew this was not his place. Not yet. Not until the ceremony. After the ceremony, the blood would be his. His and Charlotte's.

But Charlotte tried to get away. She didn't understand. Zack gripped her arm.

"You'll be okay," he said.

"I wanna go," she said.

Ernst sprang up from the floor, renewed and powerful, taking Charlotte down.

"No!" Zack shouted.

Ernst continued to sit on Charlotte, who was now screaming. He looked at Zack. "You knew she wasn't the one. You've wasted your time with her."

"Just... let her go then," Zack said.

"Let her go," Ernst laughed.

He turned to look at Charlotte. "Do you want us to let you go?"

"Yes," she said.

Amazingly, he stood up from her.

"Well," he said. "There you go."

She stood up, straightened her shirt, looked around the room, trying not to see Autumn at the mouth of Ilya. Slowly, she walked toward the front door.

"Do you really want her to go?" Ernst said. "If she was dead, she could be your plaything. Your slave. As it stands, you may never see her again."

"Charlotte?" Zack said.

And she turned. Perhaps because she thought he had changed his mind and was going to come with her.

He crossed to where she waited.

"One last kiss," he said.

"I need to go, Zack," she said. "This is all... unreal."

He bent toward her and she held up her hands noncommittally. He brushed them away, leaned in, and tore out her throat with his teeth.

Behind him, Ernst clapped and guffawed.

Forty-three

Still a good distance from the house, Rachel had seen three people wander across the field. A boy and a girl dragged another girl who was screaming hysterically. Rachel had stopped for fear of being seen. Waiting, she thought back to last night and it was almost like looking at the same scene only all of the characters had different faces. She wanted to run up to them right there and stop this, stop whatever horror was about to happen to the girl but she was afraid she would be outmatched and she couldn't risk that prospect this late in the game. So, feeling helpless, she watched them drag the girl into the house and continued to wait.

She crept closer to the house, more cautiously now she knew there was somebody inside of it. Were the people she saw dragging the girl the same ones who had brainwashed Bones?

No, she thought. They couldn't be.

Whoever governed that house was afraid to leave. Either they were afraid to leave or they were unable to leave. Maybe they were weak. Maybe their power didn't extend far beyond the house. Rachel thought she could stand outside the house and think about this for the rest of the night if she wanted to. Or she could crouch out there in fear for the rest of the night, not allowing herself to go in.

There were only two things that would propel her forward. Two thoughts. The first was that, somewhere in there, there was a chance Jacob was still alive. If the house had remained crumbled after burning down, she wouldn't have had that thought. Hell, she might have abandoned everything altogether and gone running home. But the fact that the house built itself back up only meant she now had someplace to go. Once again, she had a goal. Her second reason for not merely sitting outside of the house was the fact she *knew* she had been there before. She had sensed its power. That night two years ago when she had stood on the porch. Had that really been the beginning of all this? No, it hadn't. Only for her. For her and Jacob, that had been the definitive beginning and she wanted to make tonight the definitive ending.

Still, Rachel found herself terrified at what she might find inside. Would it be worse than last time? *Could* it be worse than last time? Those creatures who had wanted to do things to her?

She waited for only a few moments, taking in the stillness of the night around her. It may be the last time she saw it, she told herself. She breathed in the fragrant fall air, thought about how much she had always loved the night, and vowed she would come out through the door or she would die trying to kill the things that had terrified her and Jacob and countless others.

Forty-four

The two stood up slowly from Autumn's corpse, now even more covered in blood than they had been. Zack drank greedily of Charlotte's neck and sex. His pants around his buttocks, he buried himself in her dying heat, his tongue lapping at the gaping wound in her neck, not caring that Ernst and Ilya were free to look on.

"Upstairs," Ernst said.

"Upstairs?" Ilya asked.

"Yes," he said. "That is where it has to take place. Follow us."

Ernst moved slowly toward the couch, reaching under the cushion and grabbing the *Leaves of Six*.

Ernst stood over Zack.

"Finished?" he said.

Zack continued to suck and hump away.

Ernst swatted the back of his head with the book.

Zack stood up from the corpse, buttoning himself and wiping the blood from his chin.

"Follow," Ernst said.

Zack followed them up the stairs to the bedroom.

"Shouldn't the ceremony be performed near the Dark Fire?" Ilya asked.

"Soon," Ernst said. "The Dark Fire will be all around us."

"Just tell me what I have to do," Zack said.

"It's quite simple really. Ilya and I are going to lie here on the bed and you are going to drink us until there is nothing left. You are to start with Ilya. The other will arrive in a few minutes and you may need my help to subdue her. Together, you will drink. Then our bodies are to go into the flames of the Dark Fire and all will be complete. You will have what you want and we will have what we deserve."

Ilya and Ernst lay down on the bed, placing the book between them. Zack didn't really understand what the purpose of the book was. He could sense their anticipation and he was in a hurry to get this over with himself.

Ernst said, "You already have the powers of a Devil, although they may need a little refinement. What you will be getting when you drink our blood is immortality. It is up to you how you choose to use that although, let me warn, you there will be great demands placed on your sanity and your morality. Demands that you have never known before. You will become a house for one of the Old Gods."

"I'm ready," he said.

"It's best if you drink from the neck," Ernst said, running his finger down Ilya's ivory skin.

"Yes," Zack said, kneeling down beside the bed, placing his mouth on Ilya's neck.

He sunk his teeth into Ilya's flesh. His eyes rolled back as her blood, centuries old, flooded into his mouth. His tongue came alive. It was like drinking aged wine.

The house trembled, rumbling from deep down.

"This isn't supposed to happen," Ilya said.

"We need to finish this quickly," Ernst said. "Drink. Drink."

Forty-five

Rachel felt as though she had gone on autopilot. She had no idea what awaited her and she didn't really care. She opened the front door onto the sight of the two corpses. She nearly slipped in a puddle of foul smelling blood. It looked like one of the girls had been violated as well, her pants around her ankles, her underwear shoved to the side. Rachel looked away. She didn't want to see that. Knowing these two had been vibrant teenage girls only ten minutes ago made her want to burn these people out even more.

The house quivered around her. She didn't like the way it felt but she didn't really pay it any notice. She didn't like the way a lot of things felt. She resigned herself to the fact that she didn't really have a choice in any of those matters.

She knew if there was something in here it would have to be down in the lower sections of the house. Whoever stayed in this house had to have a place to hide during the fire. But she was not in a hurry to go down there. She figured it was best to make sure the upper floors of the house were empty before walking into the very heart of the beast.

Moving slowly toward the back of the house, she saw the staircase ascending to the second floor. Hearing voices coming from up there she closed her eyes, straining to listen, desperately hoping one of the voices was Jacob's. Try as she might, she couldn't figure out if any of the voices were him or not.

Brandishing the can and the lighter in front of her, she slowly walked up the stairs. Once on the landing she turned to her right and gently pushed open the bedroom door. She didn't know what it was she witnessed upon opening the door but she knew she didn't have time to figure it out.

A man and woman lay on the bed. The boy she had seen earlier crouched on the far side of the bed, his mouth clamped to a striking blond woman's neck. Something that looked like a book lay in the middle.

Rachel rapidly approached the bed and began spraying the can. She didn't need to wait for an explanation. These people had to be the Devils. If they weren't, she was willing to live with that mistake. The only person in this house she was concerned about was Jacob. Nothing else mattered. And if it turned out that Jacob was dead then she would find some way to destroy this house. She wouldn't care how much time and energy it took.

The shooting flames brought the threesome out of their collective stupor.

The boy removed his mouth from the woman's neck and looked at Rachel, confusion in his eyes.

The bed caught fire and began burning quickly.

The man stood up slowly in the bed.

"Take her!" he shouted.

Zack lunged across the room at her. Rachel backed up and shot fire at him. It caught on his clothes and he stood there as if deciding to pursue her or put out the flame.

Rachel turned to run. Jacob was not in this room and that was who she had come for. She darted down the stairs, wondering if all of the people upstairs were going to follow her.

Ilya and Ernst followed Rachel out of the room. Ilya was also weak, paler than usual.

"Ernst? What's happening, Ernst?" she stammered.

Zack stood at the foot of the burning bed, flapping his arms and screaming, "Help me! Dear God, I'm burning!"

But the room was now empty, save for him. He was all alone. Feeling betrayed. If they had just followed his plan then everything would have worked out fine. He wasn't going to give them the satisfaction. He would see their plan never came to fruition. They couldn't use him if there wasn't anything there. What did it matter whose bodies the old gods inhabited? He had his heart set on Charlotte. Something had drawn them together. But Ilya and Ernst hadn't even listened to him. Not only did they not even consider his plan, they'd made him use Charlotte as meat. Not even worthy of being consumed by the Dark Fire. And Zack, caught up in the violence of the moment, had taken her blood, had taken her sex, as if that could somehow bring her back to life. It hadn't. And now he was alone and confused and mad as hell.

They wouldn't expect him to do this. He found something sweet about that revenge. Maybe he was still feeling some lingering madness but he liked that thought. He was the sure thing. He knew that's what Ilya and Ernst thought.

A sure thing.

Fuck them.

If life was this painful, why would he want to continue living after death?

His skin burned.

The bed burned before him, its flames licking the ceiling. The book still lay in the middle of the bed. Zack hoped it would burn too.

Spreading his arms, he collapsed into the bed, throwing his body on the book, merging with the flame and tasting darkness.

Following the rumble that now threatened to topple the whole house, Rachel found the door to the lower level. She pulled it open and darted down the slippery steps, nearly losing her footing. At the bottom of the steps was another door. She pushed this open and entered a room that looked like some kind of spartan dining room, adorned only with a large table.

This room contained two doors. The rumbling seemed to come from her right and she was convinced she also heard screams coming from that direction. She darted through the room and opened that door.

This door opened onto something that looked like the interior of a church. There was a large altar at the far side of the room, blood covering its smooth gray surface. At the back of the room was another door. She ran to meet the door, pushing it open to see the raging Dark Fire and, in front of the flames, a crumpled form.

God, she hoped it wasn't Jacob.

She ran to the person on the floor, not even realizing the fire didn't seem to generate any heat. She put a hand on his shoulder and he turned his face toward her. Whatever it was, she thought, it had once been Jacob. The sight of him removed the life from her body. She collapsed onto the floor and screamed, tears pouring from her eyes.

She wasn't even aware of Ilya and Ernst entering the room behind her.

Forty-six

Stranger things happened when Ilya and Ernst entered the room.

The Dark Fire pulsed with even stronger life, emitting a white light that was nearly blinding.

Rachel crouched next to Jacob, holding him, rubbing him, saying over and over, "Oh, Jacob, what have we done?"

Ernst stormed across the room, Rachel snapped away from her ministrations, staring up at the intimidating man.

There was nowhere to run. Nowhere to hide. She was lost. All was lost.

Ernst grabbed her from behind her neck, pulling her up, pulling her close to him and whatever power she thought she had left. He raised his other hand, prepared to swipe it across her neck.

And stopped.

He looked behind her, his eyes growing wide.

It pleased Rachel to see that look in his eyes. She thought, maybe, it was fear.

His hold loosened.

Rachel turned toward the fire, following his gaze. She was prepared to charge into the fire. She would do that before letting him and his bitch get to her.

Tongueless, near death, Jacob moaned from the ground.

Rachel's eyes adjusted to the light of the fire and yet another wave of disbelief grabbed her, pulling her into the undertow.

People emerged from the fire. They looked like ghosts. They had the coloring of ghosts but these people were more substantial. They stepped from the fire, ethereal, and gained definition the farther they walked from it.

Sometime during the proceedings, Ilya had moved next to Ernst, leaning on him.

"We have to get out of here," she said.

"No!" Ernst shouted.

"Yes," Ilya returned. "This is the end. We have to run."

"I've waited lives for this!" Ernst screamed, shoving Rachel out of the way as though she stood between him and his grand prize.

The people surrounded Ilya and Ernst, a multitude of hands taking them down to the floor. The ghost things, the other Devils, fell upon them, each of them squirming for a piece, squirming for a taste, stealing the flesh and drinking the last bit of life from Ilya and

Ernst.

Rachel moved closer to Jacob, feeling his warmth against her body, happy he was still alive.

The group of people surrounding Ilya and Ernst laughed as they suckled and Rachel didn't think she had ever heard a sweeter sound than that.

"It'll be okay," she whispered to Jacob, taking his bloodied head into her lap.

The ghost people were now tearing Ilya and Ernst apart. Rachel could hear the sickening rending of flesh as they did this. She couldn't bear to watch until the screaming had stopped. When she was left with the roar of the fire and the somewhat contented moans of the dead, she turned, watching as they carried the remains back into the flames.

After the last of the Devils had filed back into the Dark Fire, a bright light filled the lower chamber of the house. It was a cleansing burst of fire. A hungry burst of fire, devouring the house around them, taking it back into whatever dimension it had come from, leaving Jacob and Rachel to sit in the hollow, trying to piece together what had just happened to them.

Rachel spread Jacob out on the ground and moved her hands over him. She knew she wouldn't be able to undo the damage in a single night but, given time, just about anything could heal. For now, she only hoped to make him well enough to walk back up to his car. She was way too tired to carry him and she just wanted to go home.

Surrounding the house, the other Devils, in all their various forms, watched…

The house was no longer burning. But something was different. The predatory Devils, the ones who took the shape of wolves and dogs, gave pause. They no longer felt protected. There was a time when they would make sure no harm could come to the two powerful figures that lived in that house. But that time had passed. Now they knew they were being watched by the good Devils. The ghosts, the ones who inhabited the trees.

They didn't know what to make of this.

And so they watched.

And they waited.

Conclusion

Several months later, Jacob lay on the bed in the guest room of Rachel's parents' house. They had both agreed they would not take him to the hospital. She thought her parents would go insane at the sight of Jacob, demand a doctor be involved. That was when Rachel had broken down and told them everything. The legend of the Devils was powerful in Lynchville. Just the mention of it made them stop questioning her.

Rachel had nursed Jacob back to health with her hands. It was a long tedious process, running her hands all over him, all over his broken places. He did not heal all at once. The damage was extensive. He was still not up and moving more than a couple of steps at a time.

Rachel thought they needed to put the incident behind them. At least for a while. She knew Jacob knew far more about the situation than she did. She waited to restore his tongue. She didn't want to know what happened to him for the moment.

Eventually, she couldn't put it off any longer.

He begged her. Scrawling on a little notepad beside his bed, he begged her to give him the gift of speech once more.

One miraculous and oddly twisted afternoon, Rachel clenched her mouth over his. This was the first instant they had shared any erotic contact since that night. Her tongue explored his mouth, at first so empty. Gradually, she felt the tongue come back to life, growing, taking shape and awkwardly moving against hers.

His speech was clumsy at first. He didn't like the way it made him sound so he practiced only while alone. After nearly a week, while Rachel sat bedside and massaged his knee, he said, "So, we did it again, didn't we?"

"I'm not exactly sure what we did but, yeah, we did something."

"Do you think that's the end?"

"Honestly?"

"No, lie to me. That should be the basis of every relationship, I think."

"Oh, I see, he's got his tongue and his sarcasm back."

"Fuck you. Yes, honestly."

"No, I don't think it's over. Is that what you want to hear?"

"No, not really."

"What the hell happened back there? I felt like I walked in on something I knew nothing about."

"Oh, well, they decided to fill me in on it as they went about rendering my body. I think we stopped them from some kind of heaven they called the Dark Fire."

"How did we do that?"

"Their bodies were vessels for some kind of god. Each of them contained one of these gods. They said the gods needed some form of human vessel and they had served that role too long. The boy you saw, he was to be one of the new vessels." Jacob took a deep swallow, looking almost like he wished he didn't have his tongue back. "You were to be the other one."

"Jesus," she said. "So what happened to the gods?"

"I think the others carried them back to the Dark Fire. There was a ritual they were trying to perform but they weren't able to carry it out. The gods could still be out there, looking for bodies to inhabit." He paused, looking out the window. Rachel couldn't tell if it was a look of longing or a look of fright. "They could be in me or you."

"For now, let me pretend you didn't say that. I haven't sacrificed anyone yet, so I prefer to think I'm evil god free."

"I don't know if that's such a good idea."

"What else are we supposed to do?"

"I'd like to leave."

"So when are we planning to get the hell out of this town?"

"How 'bout as soon as my legs will carry me?"

"Sounds great."

"You know, if we get married first, we can call it a honeymoon."

"That sounds even better."

She leaned over the bed and kissed him on the forehead, trying not to smell the fear leaking from his pores. She held his hand while they sat quietly, looking at the early summer sunlight through the windows and thinking about the beautiful fire that burned beneath the Sad House.

Wayne Hixon lives in Illinois where he has no phone and no television. *Vampires in Devil Town* is his first novel. You can email him at wayne66hixon@yahoo.com.

* 9 7 8 0 9 8 2 6 2 8 1 3 3 *